"Come on, Livy. I can count. And I know you."

"You *knew* me."

"Fine, I knew you. There was only me for you."

"Too bad that didn't work the other way around."

Garrett's lips tightened. "I never touched another woman in Savannah."

"No, not another woman. For you the mistress was life.... Adventure, excitement, travel—something new, someone different.... Anywhere but here...anything but love."

"That's not true." He looked at the ceiling, then back at her. "Arguing isn't going to get us anywhere. I want to see my son. I want to know him. I want him to know me."

"No."

"You can't deny me my son."

"He's *my* son. And I can do anything I please."

His eyes narrowed. "Then so can I."

He kissed her hard—desperately seeking, heedlessly searching. He smelled like sultry nights and sin in the rain. How could she still want him? But she tore her mouth from his and slapped him with all she had. "You're not going to see Max."

"Fine, Counselor. I'll see you in court."

Livy liked that line a whole lot better when *she* said it.

Dear Reader,

A few years ago I visited Savannah, Georgia, and fell in love. The city is both the most beautiful and the most haunted place I have ever known.

When it came time to work on an idea for my next Superromance novel, I knew I had to go back to Savannah, if only in my mind.

The moment I sat down at the computer, eight-year-old Max Frasier walked onto the page. The inspiration for him must have come from the little boy who lives at my house, who also has an imagination that just won't quit. We call him "no fear boy" and hope with every new year that this one will be E.R. free. Like Max, while physically fearless, he can imagine some pretty fearsome things.

For Max, anything is possible—especially in Savannah, where the trees whisper, the river mumbles and ghosts have been known to walk.

Wherever Max goes, trouble follows. Luckily for Max, there are a lot of people who look out for him. His Gramma Rosie, a ghost-walk tour guide, his mother, Livy, a lawyer in a town that has little use for them, and his new friend Garrett, a horror writer who turns out to be a whole lot more than Max ever dreamed possible.

I hope you enjoy this journey to Savannah and your time spent with Max, his friends and family.

For future releases and news of contests, check out my Web site at www.lorihandeland.com.

Lori Handeland

Leave It to Max
Lori Handeland

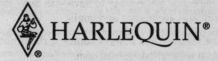

HARLEQUIN®

TORONTO • NEW YORK • LONDON
AMSTERDAM • PARIS • SYDNEY • HAMBURG
STOCKHOLM • ATHENS • TOKYO • MILAN • MADRID
PRAGUE • WARSAW • BUDAPEST • AUCKLAND

3 3113 02033 0801

ISBN 0-373-71004-6

LEAVE IT TO MAX

This edition published by arrangement with Harlequin Books S.A.

® and TM are trademarks of the publisher. Trademarks indicated with
® are registered in the United States Patent and Trademark Office, the
Canadian Trade Marks Office and in other countries.

Visit us at www.eHarlequin.com

Printed in U.S.A.

For Chery, Debra, Gail, Linda C.,
Linda J. and Pam—
my wonderful online friends
whose daily e-mails of sympathy,
support and encouragement have kept me writing

"Savannah is more than a city,
it's a state of mind."
—Arthur Gordon

CHAPTER ONE

NIGHT DESCENDED upon Savannah like the wings of a great black bat. Cool air wafted along the ancient city streets. Dawn would not tint the river for hours upon hours.

Max Frasier should not be out at night. He was only eight and his mom would have a hissy fit. But when his best and only friend, Sammy Sontag, pulled him aside after school and whispered, "There's a vampire livin' in the old Alexander place. Wanna go see?" he'd agreed before he'd remembered that vampires only appear at night.

By then he could not back out. As it was, a lot of kids thought him a wussy already, on account of he was little, skinny and scared of a lot.

Max didn't much like the dark. He'd always been spooked by closets and basements and such. He couldn't even go in the bathroom without opening the shower curtain, as well as every door and drawer in the place. Drove his mom nuts, but he couldn't stop.

Who knew what lay in wait within those shadowy compartments? The one time he didn't look would be the last time he needed to.

Those were the rules of his world. Under the bed

lived awful things. In closets lurked monsters un-
imaginable. And in the dark? Anything could happen.

"Come *on!*" Sammy urged. "It's almost time."

Max inched up next to his friend. "For what?"

They skulked behind some low bushes, just like the
bad guys always did in his dreams. Max had a lot of
dreams—sometimes even when he was asleep. He
shivered as cool fingers drifted along his neck. But
when he turned around, no one was there. No one
ever was.

His Gramma Rosie, though she refused to answer
if he used the word *Gramma,* said Max was sensitive.
Max figured that was a nice, adult way to say wussy.
Still, Rosie always understood when he was afraid.
His mom just looked concerned—as if *she'd* done
something wrong. Moms were like that, Rosie said,
especially moms like his.

"You'll see for what," Sammy answered. "As
soon as the sun goes all the way down, a light will
go on upstairs, and he'll come outside."

"Just 'cause he likes to come out in the dark don't
make him a vampire," Max pointed out.

"Guess not. But no one's ever seen him during the
day. *Ever.* He has all sorts of stuff delivered. At night.
No one knows his name. He hasn't come over to meet
the neighbors, like a gentleman should."

"Still doesn't make him undead."

"What about the coffin?"

Max gulped. "Wh-what c-coffin?"

Sammy slid him a sly look. "The one the movers
took in the house. I was watchin' and I saw every-

thing—furniture, coffin. No people but the movin'
guys. 'Cause it was daytime, see?''

Max saw. The other weird thing about Max was
that even though he was scared of things that went
bump in the night, he was also fascinated by them.
He liked nothin' better than a good scary story or a
creepy old movie. Which made no sense—but what
did in this world?

His grampa had died jumping out of an airplane.
Max had no idea why you'd want to jump out of a
perfectly good plane. It had been a bad idea for
Grampa, anyway.

His gramma was a fruitcake, or so most of Savannah said because Rosie liked to stand up for people
and animals that had no one else to stand up for them.
It didn't matter to her if snails were slimy or fish had
cold blood or ghosts often disappeared before sayin'
thank-you. To Rosie what was right was right, what
was wrong stunk, and she knew the difference better
than anyone.

But Savannah was used to odd characters. Like Viola and Violet, the elderly twin sisters who kept a
trained goose in their backyard—something that
drove Rosie crazy and had started a running feud between her and the sisters. Or the man who continued
to walk a dog years after it had died, and the lady
who wore clothes dating from the War of Northern
Aggression so the ghosts in her parlor wouldn't know
that they were dead. With all those characters, and
then some, wandering Savannah, the folks who called
Rosie a ''fruitcake'' did so with a fond smile.

They never said ''lawyer'' that way, even though

his mom insisted she was the kind of lawyer who helped people. Savannah had never taken much to lawyers. In the oldest, olden days lawyers hadn't even been allowed in the Colony of Georgia.

The thing that made the least sense of all to Max was how his dad had died before Max was born, and Mom still seemed awful mad about it—so mad she never mentioned his name but once. Heck, Max wouldn't even know his dad was named James unless he'd asked a hundred thousand times.

Maybe she was mad because Dad had died before they could get married, which explained why Max, his mom and his gramma all had the same last name. Though, no one else seemed to care, so why should she?

"There," Sammy said, and Max jumped.

A light came on upstairs. The Alexander place was a monstrous house built on one of the outer squares of old Savannah. The place had been empty for a long time—no one had been able to afford the high price. Until now.

"You know vampires live forever, so they have lots of time to make money," Sammy whispered. "He probably has houses like this all over the world."

"What for?"

"So he can run to another safe place when the mob comes to stake him."

Max couldn't imagine the laid-back folk of Savannah getting riled about much of anything—least of all a vampire. They were kind of a live-and-let-live—or maybe die—sort of crowd. But then, you never knew.

Look what had happened to Count Dracula in every single movie.

The front door of the mansion creaked open. Max shivered at the sound, straight from one of those movies he'd just been thinking on. Then someone appeared on the porch.

At first all Max could see was a tall outline. Then the street lamps flared to life, and the man flinched, putting his hand up to shade his eyes. When he dropped his arm, the silver glare slanted across the porch. Max and Sammy caught their breath.

His dark hair brushed the shoulders of his black shirt, and his skin glowed pale beneath the wash of shimmering light from the street. The guy looked like Frank Langella, before he got a crew cut and started playing really bad guys.

The man breathed deeply, as if he couldn't get enough of the fresh river air, then stretched his arms upward, leaned his head back and gave a hissing groan. Max gasped.

The sound wasn't loud, but the man stiffened, stilled, then slowly dropped his arms, turned his head and looked right at their bush. Right at them.

Max and Sammy ran.

GARRETT STARK WATCHED the kids disappear into the night. Up until now, only the brown-haired one had been hanging around. Tonight he'd brought along a towhead for company.

Garrett smothered a smile as the boy stumbled, fell, then righted himself and ran on. The towhead appeared to have mighty big feet. Garrett remembered having a whole lot of scraped knees for a whole lot of years. At least until he'd grown into his feet.

Would the two be back tomorrow with friends? What was so darn fascinating about him?

These days he didn't even interest himself.

They couldn't know who he was. He'd had his agent rent this place for him. He never connected a phone, preferring a cell phone because he moved about so much. Even if the kids had heard his name, weren't they a bit young to know the work of Garrett Stark, bestselling horror novelist?

Or at least he had been a bestselling novelist up to his last book—which just might be his *last* book the way things looked.

Today had begun well enough. He'd rolled out of bed with the sun, watched the wake-up news while he ran on the treadmill, a necessary but horrific evil in his opinion—both the news and the treadmill— then taken his coffee into the office, answered his e-mail and begun to write.

As with every other day for the past nine months, things had gone downhill from there. By lunch he had one page. So in punishment, he skipped lunch. He wasn't hungry anyway. He ought to recommend panic sauce to Jenny Craig International.

By early evening, he had two pages. However, when he read them over he decided the two could be combined into one, and he was back to where he'd started at lunch. What could be a suitable punishment for that?

At the insistent buzz of his cell phone, he glanced at the caller ID, which revealed cruel and unusual punishment. A call from his agent, Andrew—never Andy, never Drew—Lawton. As if anyone would address someone of Lawton's demeanor as Andy.

Lawton might resemble a proper English earl, but his negotiation skills were pure New York City, where he'd lived all his life. Andrew worked fast, talked fast; hell, he even walked fast.

"I expected a rough draft by now." Andrew never bothered with such trivialities as "Hello."

"Me, too," Garrett mumbled.

"Come back?"

"You'll be the first to know when I've got one."

"You're right, because I'm coming down there to get it."

Garrett blinked, then gaped at the phone, but Andrew was already rattling off his arrival time—tomorrow. Agents didn't *do* things like that in the usual course of publishing. Or at least, most agents of most writers.

But Garrett's agent had once been his editor. Andrew had yanked Garrett's tome from the proverbial slush pile and taken them both from eating canned tuna to smoked salmon, if not imported caviar.

Andrew had always loved a good deal just a bit more than he loved a good book, so a few years back he'd left editing and become an agent. His caviar dreams were still just that, but he had high hopes, which explained why he felt he had to come to Savannah to protect his future.

Garrett cursed.

"It doesn't matter what you say, I'm coming."

"I know. It's one of your charms."

"That's me. Charming Andrew."

Garrett snorted. One thing Andrew was *not* was charming. That was why Garrett liked him so much. But no matter how much Garrett liked him, no matter how well they worked together on the business end, regardless of the fact that Andrew was the only true friend he had, the quickest way to smother any breath of creativity would be for Andrew to arrive in town. The man had an imagination deficit.

"If you start hanging around, I'll never finish." Garrett wasn't required to admit that he hadn't even started. While he should be in the middle of the book, the only thing he seemed to be in the middle of was a panic attack.

Silence from the other end of the line made Garrett frown. Another thing Andrew was *not* was quiet. Had he hurt the man's feelings? Impossible. Andrew had few feelings to hurt. Another reason Garrett liked him.

"You'd tell me if anything was seriously wrong, wouldn't you?" his agent asked in an uncharacteristically sympathetic tone.

"Seriously wrong?"

"Like if you were dying of brain cancer or congestive heart failure."

"My, aren't we cheery."

"You've got me worried, Garrett. You're just not yourself."

Garrett wasn't sure *who* he was anymore. That was why he'd come back here.

"This book is important," Andrew continued.

"It's your chance to be more than a paperback writer."

"I *like* being a paperback writer."

"But don't you want to move up? Be bigger, better, more?"

God, Andrew was such an...agent.

"I always thought I did."

As usual, Andrew took Garrett's indecision and made it a decision he wanted to hear. "Great. Glad to hear it. This is the opportunity we've been waiting for. Your first hardcover." He said the three words the way a patriarch might say, *Your firstborn son.* "But with the size of the advance...the book has to be *special*, Garrett."

He resisted the urge to snarl. He hated that word. It didn't mean dink—especially when applied to a book. One man's special was another man's crap.

"Special. Right," Garrett agreed.

"So what's the idea?"

Special crap.

Garrett's laugh ended up sounding just a bit crazed. He snapped his lips shut, but not before Andrew heard. The man might be oblivious about some things, but he worked with authors every day. Andrew knew trouble when he heard it.

"I might be able to catch a red-eye."

"I'm fine." *Or as fine as I can be as I watch the chance of a lifetime go up in flames.* Garrett cleared his throat and put some steel into his voice. "I'm not kidding, Andrew. If you come down here, you're fired."

Incredibly, Andrew laughed. Technically, Lawton

worked for him. But Garrett had never had the guts to point that out.

"Okay." Andrew managed to stop laughing for a minute. "I'll stay put. For now."

After Andrew hung up, Garrett went inside, made himself a drink and returned to the porch. Since coming back to Savannah, he'd made having an after-work libation a habit. At this rate he'd be doing an Edgar Allan Poe imitation before long. Why was it that so many brilliant, famous writers were also drunken psychotics? Made a man consider a change of vocation.

What person in his right mind would sit in an office as the sun shone bright and stare at a computer screen, never showing his face in the light of day because he was too occupied with the people who lived within that little gray box? Like one of those creatures of the night, Garrett only turned off his computer and ventured outside after dark.

You went where the Muse took you, or where she said you must go. If you didn't, she might go silent. She might just run away and never come back. Garrett had never thought his Muse, voice, gift—whatever— would get testy on him.

He toasted the rising moon. "Another day, another piece of crap. Very special crap." Garrett drank, but the burn of alcohol in the depth of his empty stomach did not jump-start his Muse. How had Poe managed?

What, Garrett wondered, had brought on this un-characteristic detour to the bottle? The fact that he could no longer write? Or the fear that he'd never been able to in the first place?

The last time, Savannah had been magic for him, and when he'd left he'd written his first book in a whirlwind of creativity that had earned him money, accolades and stellar reviews.

He had already been here a week, and his Muse was as quiet as the house he'd rented, far from the madding crowd on River Street, from the gaily painted trolleys that chugged around and around the historic district, from the red-brick museums and the nighttime ghost walks and the white marble monuments—from everything that made Savannah, Savannah.

He'd never before had a problem with inspiration. Fresh vistas, an illusion of freedom, the reality of solitude—all fueled his creativity. He rented a new house for every new book, kept his personal belongings to a minimum and his emotional entanglements even lighter. He was living the life he'd dreamed of all those years ago and loving it—or he had been, until nine months ago.

"When everything went to hell."

The sound of his own voice, unnaturally loud in the darkness, made Garrett place the tumbler of whiskey, still half finished, upon the porch railing with a *thump*. He suspected Poe had done a lot of talking to himself, too.

Perhaps a brisk walk through this fair city would clear his head. Certainly couldn't hurt.

Fall in Savannah was a thing of beauty. The air, as warm as a midwestern summer night, smelled of the sea and the South. To a boy raised on the tang of red-dirt Missouri, the scent of Savannah could make you weep for more. Everything here moved slower, lasted longer, dug deeper. That was why he'd run all those years ago.

Garrett turned in to the Colonial Park Cemetery, final resting place of several Georgia governors and one Button Gwinnett, signer of the Declaration of Independence—though many disputed that the body in Button's grave was actually Button. In Savannah, things like that happened all the time. Sometimes upon exhumation and DNA testing it was discovered not only that the famous body in the grave was not famous, but that it was actually several bodies tossed in just for rascally DNA fun.

How could a writer of horror not thrive in a place like this?

Yeah, tell it to the Muse.

In each city where he'd lived, Garrett became familiar with the cemeteries. For some reason they soothed him, and he often walked at dusk, dawn or any time in between through the peaceful resting places, dreaming, plotting, planning.

A shuffle to his rear made Garrett stiffen, then slow. He angled his head and caught sight of a tiny shadow flitting between the moon-pale headstones. His friend had come back—but which one? Someone's mommy was awfully lenient in the wandering-child department.

But tonight Garrett didn't mind the company. He continued to meander through the cemetery, shadow in tow, reading the names on the stones and making up stories to go with them, like a creative writing exercise. Not that he'd ever taken creative writing, but he'd heard about it.

Looped about one stone was a rosary; along another some garlic; a third sported a necklace of unknown origin, perhaps voodoo by the appearance of the feathers. Over two centuries of cultural, ethnic and religious diversity at its finest.

Garrett looked but did not touch. He respected offerings to the other side. Whatever worked. If he thought it would help him get an idea, he'd make a few offerings himself.

As he continued to walk, alone, yet not alone, Garrett heard the teasing lilt of his Muse, and as he wandered out of the cemetery and along the dark city streets, he no longer thought about his shadow companion, but instead considered the strains of a story tumbling about in his busy brain.

The *thump* followed by the muffled cry did not register in his tossing, turning sea of turmoil until much later—and by then the damage was done.

"HELLO, MS. FRASIER," the duty nurse chirped as Olivia Frasier skidded into the brightly lit foyer of her local emergency room. "Third door on the left."

Livy nodded, not bothering to answer. Her heart blocked her throat, anyway—just as it did each time she was called to this place.

Everyone knew them here. As soon as Max had walked in, alone, the duty nurse had called Livy. Livy had to wonder if her number was on their speed dial by now.

Max had done it this time. He'd broken something.

And not a vase or a plate or a cup. This time he'd broken a bone. Livy was livid. Where had he been in the dark?

Being a lawyer, Livy knew all about horrible things. Having lost Max's father before Max was born, she had been terrified ever since that she'd lose Max, too. Her mother said she was overprotective. Of course, Mama was eccentric—a bohemian, a hippie, a free spirit, a nut—it all depended on who you were talking to at the time.

Mama thought Max should be allowed to roam the streets freely and return at will. "You can't keep the child in a glass case, sugar, no matter how much you might want to," she said.

Glass case? Very funny. Max would break that in no time flat.

Livy slammed her palm against the door to room number three. Max sat atop the exam table—small and wan and scared. He damn straight ought to be.

His hair had bleached in the summer sun and the bright lights made it shine white. Livy had never been able to figure out where the amazing blond hair had come from. Her own was light brown, nothing special at all. His father's hair had been black as the wings of a raven. The only hints of the man in Max was the deep, dark shade of his eyes—and a wandering soul.

The doctor—Smith, she recalled—gave Livy a smile meant to comfort. Such niceties never worked on her, so he got down to business.

"There is a fracture. Almost didn't see it because of the growth plates at this age, but that's what we've got a radiologist for. Max will be fine. Nothing a shiny new cast and some Tylenol won't cure.''

She growled at his happy face, and the good Dr. Smith wisely left the room. ''Spill it,'' Livy snapped.

Max didn't look at her. Instead, he stared at the ice bag on his forearm, then swallowed. To Livy that gulp meant guilty.

''I was hangin' with Sammy.''

''Where?''

''Out near his house.''

''When you say 'hanging,' what does that mean?'' She had visions of him swinging upside down on gnarly tree limbs, ripping open arteries in his thigh, landing on his head, falling into a coma—

''I don't know. Doin' stuff.''

''What kind of *stuff?*'' Livy sounded as if she were in court, but she couldn't help herself. Questions were her business. Panic was her life.

''Kid stuff. Guy stuff. Stuff. You know?''

Livy hadn't a clue, and she was starting to get a headache. ''Well, next time you feel the need to do 'guy stuff,' could you be done by dark?''

''Maybe.''

Grinding your teeth really didn't help a headache, Livy discovered. She sat next to Max on the exam table. ''So how did this happen?''

''I tripped.''

''Really? I'd never have guessed. Where were you when you tripped?''

Max flicked a dark glance at her from beneath his overgrown bangs. No matter how many times she took him to the barber, his hair was always long. No matter how many times she cut his nails, they always resembled a supermodel's.

Livy resisted the urge to brush the bangs gently from his face. Resisted, because if she lost the anger, she'd start to cry. Call her sensitive, but when she got a call from the emergency room as she was frantically dialing anyone who'd ever known her son and asking where he was in the dark of the night... Well, that kind of stuff preyed on a mother's mind.

"I cut through the cemetery. And I fell."

"Aw, Max. I told you about cemeteries. How they're dark, and there're all those stones hidden in the grass, just waiting for boys to fall over them. See what happened?"

"It's funny, Mom, but every time you tell me what's going to happen, it always does."

Livy winced. Max was an accident-prone, self-fulfilling prophesy. "Yeah, call me psychic. Wait." She put her hand to her head. "Wait. I'm getting another flash of the future." She dropped her hand. "You're grounded, buddy."

"But, Mom—"

"Grounded. Two weeks." Hooking an arm around his thin shoulders, she pulled him close. The sweet scent of his hair soothed her panic. He was here and he was whole—albeit cracked. All things considered, they'd gotten off lucky.

Again.

CHAPTER TWO

MAX WAS NO DUMMY. He knew better than to ask his mom about vampires. The first time she'd caught him watching a black-and-white horror movie, she'd come home the next day with a stack of books about Hollywood makeup and special effects. She'd explained movies and how they weren't real—just like all the other fun things, such as Santa and the Easter bunny and the fairy lady who collected teeth. Although Max thought that last one was nearly as scary as a mummy chasin' you through a cave.

Max always listened when his mom got to explainin' because it made her feel better—and she worried a lot. But there was more to this world than what you could see. Especially in a place like Savannah, where the trees whispered, the river laughed and ghosts walked.

He made up for the loss of Santa by believing in darker things than that merry old elf. In Max's world bad stuff happened a lot—usually when he was trying like mad to keep it from sliding downhill and falling on top of him.

So after his mom brought him home and tucked him in, Max snuck from his room and went directly to his expert on all things weird.

"Rosie? Can a vampire really live forever?"

She flicked her long tail of black hair past her shoulder, then peered at him over the rim of her reading glasses. Rosie's hair was pretty, even with the strip of white at her temple that looked just like Lily Munster's.

Mom always said any woman over forty should cut her hair. To which Rosie would reply, "You can cut my hair off my cold, dead carcass."

Sometimes Rosie was pretty funny.

She put aside her book, *Jonathan Livingston Seagull,* then patted the bed, inviting Max to join her. Rosie was like that. When Max had a question, she put everything aside and waited to hear it. "What brought up vampires?"

He shrugged, not wanting to admit that he thought they had one in Savannah. Until he was sure, he wasn't tellin' any grown-ups, not even Rosie.

Max took his time joining her on the quilt she'd sewn from Mom's old dresses and Max's baby clothes. Some days they took the quilt outside, and while they sat in the sun, Rosie would tell him stories about the places his mom had visited while wearing each dress, or the cute things Max had done when wearing every little outfit.

Rosie pulled Max close to her side. She patted his cast, murmured, "Nice," and that was all she said about that. With his mom, he'd probably never hear the end of it.

Max snuggled up to Rosie and took a great big sniff. She always smelled like cookies, even when she hadn't made any. And her arms were strong, even though the side he rested against was softer than soft. But best of all, her lap was always empty and her ears were always open to a little boy who needed someone to talk to. Max figured Rosie was the best gramma in the entire universe, even if she didn't let him call her that.

"Max?" she prompted.

He tried to think of the best way to lie without really lyin'. His mom, being a lawyer and all, was big on the truth.

"I was just reading." True enough, he was always reading. "And the books said vampires live forever, and they can heal anything—cuts and bullet holes and all sorts of gory stuff."

"Well, I think they have a hard time healing a stake through the heart, or decapitation, or a silver bullet."

"That's a werewolf."

"Really?"

Max turned his head so she could see his face, then nodded.

"All right. Forget that last one. But basically, yes, I think vampires are on the indestructible list. Know any?"

"Nope." He spoke too fast, 'cause Rosie's eyes narrowed. She might be an easygoing fruitcake, but she wasn't dumb.

"Max, your mother might worry too much, but that's because she sees a lot of bad things happen. There's a whole lot of crazy goin' on out there, and it could splash over onto us. If somebody's bothering you, sugar, you should tell me."

"Nobody's bothering me." Since that was true, he had no trouble making Rosie believe him.

"And this vampire thing?"

"I thought I'd write a story."

"Oh!" Her face became one big smile. She loved his stories, always praising his imagination and creativity long and loud.

"That's wonderful, Max. And you'll draw pictures, too? You always do them so well."

He shrugged, at once embarrassed and thrilled. "I better get back to bed. You know—"

"—how Mom is," she finished.

A quick kiss, a loving pat, and Max left Rosie with Jonathan Seagull and returned to his bed. He had a hard time falling asleep because his arm ached, so it seemed as if he'd only been out a second when his mom crept into his room.

Usually Max slept hard and didn't wake up for much. But with his arm feelin' funny, sleep wasn't staying with him tonight. Even though he was awake, he kept his eyes closed and stayed real still, because if his mom was creepin', she didn't want him to wake up.

She'd told him once that she came into his room and watched him sleep whenever she was sad or scared. That must be after he did somethin' bad. Max figured breakin' a bone was the baddest thing of all.

She stood next to his bed and stared at him, which was kind of creepy, except this was his mom. Moms always did weird things and called them love.

"Ah, baby," she whispered, and Max heard the tears in her voice. She touched his cheek, and he liked that. Moms also touched you just right when you needed it the most.

Max drifted in a hazy place between asleep and awake. His mom was near and the dark was nearly gone. Lying here like this was almost as good as when she let him sleep in her bed, which didn't happen much anymore 'cause he kicked like a mean old mule.

"I keep seeing you hitting your head in that graveyard and not your arm. Max, you break my heart."

Max felt bad. He never tried to get hurt. Bad stuff just happened to him. The worst stuff of all was the sad in Mom's eyes when she mopped up the blood, or bandaged the cut, or put ice on the bruises and bumps. And when she drove him home from the E.R.? Tears pressed behind Max's closed eyelids. The sad in Mom's eyes spread all over the place.

"I keep seeing my dad, then yours. Silly. They're both gone. Maybe it's just the season." She took a deep breath, then let all the air rush back out. "Maybe."

For a few minutes she stayed quiet, as if remembering, and Max considered holding her hand, letting her know he was awake, until she spoke again.

"This was close tonight. God, I'm scared. Please don't take Max from me. Not another one. Not again. Please. Please!"

The wobble in his mom's voice told Max what he had to do. He'd been playin' around too long.

When she went back to her room, he waited for several quiet minutes, remembering all he'd seen in the cemetery. The dark man with the pale face had glided through the mist with such ease that his body seemed to disappear from here and appear over there with immortal speed. He would stop at certain head-stones, peer at the names, but never ever touch the garlic or the crucifix-laden rosaries.

Max might be scared, but his mom was scareder, and he knew just how to make her happy again—how to make her happy forever. So he got out of bed, dressed and slipped from the house.

Max had a date with a vampire.

GARRETT SLEPT for a few hours after his walk in the graveyard. He'd hoped his subconscious would grow the seed of the idea he'd first heard in the cemetery. But when he awoke there was nothing left of it.

So he gave in to the urge he'd had since coming back to Savannah and walked to the streets where he'd lived all those years ago. He even wandered by the house that held the room he'd rented way back then.

Nothing brought inspiration, so he returned home, ran through his wake-up routine and started pounding coffee. Then he stared at his solitary page from yesterday and decided it was crap, too.

From the looks of this morning, today would be another hellish day.

Garrett's head went up at a surreptitious scrape from the rear of the house. That had sounded like the back door closing, very quietly.

Just as quietly, Garrett put down his coffee mug and crept toward the kitchen. A shuffle, reminiscent of last night's follower, drifted from the dining room, where he'd stored the latest gag gift from his laugh-riot agent.

Garrett and Andrew had a running competition for who could give the most ridiculous and annoying present. Andrew's latest looked to be a hands-down winner because of its size and unwillingness to be off-loaded on any local chapter of Goodwill.

A horrendous *creak* erupted, and Garrett took the last few feet to the entryway in a fancy two-step. He was just in time to see his towheaded little buddy peering into the wooden coffin—Andrew's gift—that Garrett had been using as a dining room accent.

"I'm not in there."

The kid jumped a foot, and barely missed losing a finger as the coffin lid slammed shut. He spun about, huge dark eyes wide in a tiny, pale face. The cast on his arm brought a shadow memory to the forefront of Garrett's mind.

A thump. A cry. Then nothing. Damn. He'd been off in his own little world last night.

"Did you fall in the cemetery?" he asked.

If possible, the kid's face went a lighter shade of gray. Garrett, unused to childlike histrionics and how to avert them, kept right on asking questions in the hope that sooner or later an answer would tumble out. "Why are you in my house?"

The boy's lips tightened, and Garrett figured he wasn't going to get an answer, but he did. "Back door was open."

"Which is an invitation to come right on in?" The child shrugged. What was it about the boy that was so familiar? Garrett had only seen him from a distance yesterday. "What's your name, kid?"

"Max."

Max. Now, that was helpful. "Well, Max, what do you want?"

The child gulped, straightened his spine and walked toward Garrett. The expression on his face was that of a man fated to die but unable to stop it. Why would a kid look like that?

Max stopped directly in front of Garrett and stared bravely into his face. "I want to be like you."

"You know who I am?" Garrett blurted.

He took great pains to keep his face out of the media. He refused to have his picture on the jacket of a book. He did not do interviews or signings. His need for isolation in order to write made such measures necessary.

"Yes, sir, I know who you are. But I won't tell anyone. Not if you make me like you."

Where *were* this kid's parents? Why was he out chasing Garrett through a cemetery after dark, breaking his arm, sneaking into Garrett's house before dawn and reading Garrett's books? They were not for children.

"It takes years and years of practice to be like me."

Max's shoulders slumped. "Really? I thought you could just, you know, do it now, and I'd be like you right away."

"Do what?"

"Whatever it is vampires do."

Garrett was left gaping like the suicidal goldfish

he'd owned once that had flipped out of its bowl and onto the carpet. "You think I'm a vampire?"

"I've been watchin' you. I know how it works. I wanna be undead. That way, whenever I get hurt, I'll heal. And no matter what trouble I get into, I'll never die."

Garrett was too intrigued to set the kid straight right away. He'd always been fascinated with people and motivations. Call it his job. "And why do you want those things?"

"So my mom won't cry anymore."

The answer, delivered with innocent sweetness, gave Garrett a lump in his throat. He coughed to clear the lump, but it didn't want to go. "Your mom cries a lot?"

"Not when I'm lookin'. On account of she doesn't want me to feel bad. I can't help it if I fall down a lot." He held up his cast for emphasis. "She's real scared that I'm gonna fall bad and die. My grampa fell and died. And my dad—well, he just died—I'm not sure how."

Garrett couldn't keep his eyes off Max. He was starting to hear that idea again—coming out of this kid's mouth. He'd never written a book that had a child in it. Kids believed all sorts of crazy things. When you were young, the line between reality and fantasy was thin to nonexistent, and for Garrett that line had never thickened much at all.

"So can you make me undead?" Max pressed. "I kind of need to know right now. My mom's gonna find out I'm not in bed, and then she just might kill me."

"You know what, Max, I think I'd better go meet your mom."

"But—but—" Max glanced toward the window, where the steamy light of dawn spread. "The sun's comin' up. You can't go outside."

"Wanna bet?" Garrett walked through the kitchen and stepped into the morning light. Max flinched, as if he expected Garrett to self-combust.

Garrett laughed. "I can go out." He stepped inside. "I can go in." He jumped back out. "I can go out."

The boy's eyes widened. "You must be a master," he breathed.

"That's what some of my reviews say."

"Huh?"

"Never mind. Where did you get the idea that I was a vampire?"

"You only go out at night."

"Because I work all day. Sometimes at night, too." Garrett made a face. "Though not much lately."

"Well, when you were walkin' in the cemetery, you looked real close but you never touched the rosaries or the garlic on the gravestones."

"And I never will. Those things are special and private." Max still didn't look convinced. Garrett wasn't quite sure what to do. "I swear I'm not a vampire. I'm a horror writer."

"You mean you have to go to summer school and practice?"

For a minute Garrett stared at Max, confused. Then the light dawned. "Not a *horrible* writer, a *horror* writer. I write books about vampires. All day long. I'm not one of them."

"Aw, damn. I mean darn." He glanced at the coffin. "Then what's that for?"

"The fireplace, it looks like. Let me take you home before your mom calls the cops."

Max sighed. "I know all the cops. Nearly as good as I know the nurses and the doctors at the E.R."

Garrett just stared at the kid. He was so perfect it was almost as if Garrett had invented him. "You really thought I was a vampire?"

"Well..." Max appeared sheepish. "I kind of know there's no such thing, but then again...I was hopin' there was."

"I know how that is. Lead on, Max."

"'Kay." Max slipped his hand into Garrett's, as trusting as—well—a child. And a funny tumble started in the pit of Garrett's stomach, which he attributed to too little sleep and too much coffee. All the way back to his house, Max chattered—about vampires and someone named Rosie, cemeteries and Sammy, zombies, voodoo and lawyers. As Max chattered, Garrett's idea rumbled.

They reached Max's house. Surrounded by a gated garden and constructed of Savannah gray bricks, it was located on a quiet, residential square. Garrett stopped dead on the walk. He knew this place.

The door slammed open, and a woman rushed out. Garrett knew her, too.

He dropped Max's hand like a red-hot poker.

LIVY HAD ONLY discovered Max was missing a moment before Rosie called upstairs, "Here comes that boy with a new friend."

Snatching her robe, she shoved her arms into the trailing sleeves as she ran barefoot down the stairs, then burst out the front door.

And froze at the sight of Max's new pal. How could a dream come true if you were having a nightmare?

But this wasn't a dream, or any nightmare. The pavement was night-cold against Livy's feet; the new sun warmed her hair. She was awake, and she was more frightened than she'd ever been in her life.

Her son smiled with angelic innocence as he chatted with the devil. Yesterday and today converged in one man's face. J. J. Garrett had returned, and she wasn't anywhere near ready.

Their eyes met. J.J. dropped her son's hand as if he'd accidentally picked up a dead snake.

No, that wasn't right.

He dropped *their* son's hand.

Livy's lie loomed big enough to burst, and rain truth down upon them all.

CHAPTER THREE

THE INSTANT Max cried, "Mom!" Garrett knew.

No, that wasn't true. He'd felt déjà vu as soon as he'd seen the house where Max lived. His busy brain was already counting backward. And when Livy ran out, all the pieces clicked home.

Garrett suddenly understood why Max seemed so familiar. He looked exactly as Garrett had at that age—blond hair, scarred-up knees, dark dreamy eyes.

The strangest similarity was Max's belief in the unbelievable, his physical fearlessness in the face of fearsome imaginings. Garrett, or rather James, Jr., had always lived life full-speed ahead, regardless of the knocks that were certain to come his way.

Thankfully, Max did not notice the two adults frozen, staring on the walk. He hurried to Livy and threw his arms around her waist.

She ran her hand over his hair, gentle and sure, a caress she'd given him a thousand times before.

And that made Garrett mad.

He opened his mouth, though he had no idea what he meant to say, and Livy went white. He thought she might pass out right on the sidewalk, so he snapped his mouth shut and took a step forward.

She glared at him before glancing down at Max.

"Where have you been? I was just about to call the police."

"Again?"

"Yes, again." She took his arm and marched him toward the house. "And again and again and again, until you learn to be where you're supposed to be, when you're supposed to be there. Take a bath and get ready for school."

Max tugged free of his mother and stepped nearer to Garrett. "But, Mom, I brought home—"

"Garrett Stark," he interrupted.

Livy's deep blue eyes widened. "You cha—" She broke off, tilted her head. "The horror writer?"

"Yes. Although your son seems to think I'm a vampire."

"What?" She frowned at Max. "Baby, we talked about all that. Santa, the Easter Bunny, mummies and vampires—none of those things is real."

She'd told his son there was no Santa Claus? Who was this woman? Certainly not the Livy he'd once adored with all his foolish, young heart.

Max hung his head, nodded, then gave Garrett an imploring, sideways glance.

"What makes you so sure?" Garrett demanded. Max's slow, warm smile was worth the icy stare he received from Livy.

"Excuse me?"

"What makes you so sure that none of those things is real?"

"Come now, Mr. Stark, even *you* know there's a line between fantasy and reality." The sneer in her words did not appear on her face, but Garrett remembered every nuance of that voice. He'd listened to the mellow southern tones often enough in the dark— both in fantasy and reality.

"Even me?" he repeated. She loathed him, and he couldn't figure out why. From where Garrett stood, *he* was the injured party. "I'll tell you what I know. If you believe in something strongly enough, it becomes real to you. And what *is* real, anyway?"

She gave him a withering glare, as if he were too dumb to live. "What you can see and feel and touch. Right here, right now. Belief has nothing to do with it. And I'll thank you to keep your rich fantasy life to yourself. Do not entice my son into dreaming impossible dreams."

She sounded so angry, so certain there was no magic to be had in this world, again so different from the Livy he remembered, Garrett wasn't sure what to say. As if there was anything *to* say in this situation.

"Max, take a bath like I told you."

"What about the cast?" Garrett wondered aloud.

"They're waterproof these days," she said absently, before turning back to Max. "Rosie's already making breakfast, so hurry and get ready."

"'Kay. Bye, Mr. Stark."

Garrett swallowed the lump in his throat as Max disappeared. His own son had called him "mister." Garrett was getting madder by the minute.

"What's going on here, Livy?"

"Shh!" She put her finger to her lips. "We'll have to discuss this later. I need to get Max off to school and be in court by nine."

"Are you in trouble?"

"No, but my client is."

"Y-you're an attorney." He couldn't stop the horror from seeping into his voice. To him, attorneys were all like his father—and the way Livy was acting, James, Sr. would just love her.

"You sound like my mother." Her words weren't a compliment, either.

Garrett stepped closer, caught a whiff of her scent. She smelled exactly the same—like river dreams and night hopes—navy blue, cool spice. His head spun as the memories came hard, fast, furious—from both the best and the worst time of his life.

She looked the same, too. Hair the shade of ocean sand and eyes like midnight on the water. He'd always loved her eyes, so dark, yet blue. Garrett had been captivated by the way they loomed large in her fine-boned face. In times past she'd been tall and slim, on the verge of gangly. She was slimmer still these days, he noted from the cinched waist of her robe.

Then he noted other changes—the shadows beneath her eyes; the lines above her lips; the cut of her hair, shorter and more austere than the long and easy braid she'd once favored. The strands of gray in that hair—few, but apparent—made him wonder how hard her life had been since he'd left Savannah.

Garrett lowered his voice. "How did this happen? Why didn't you tell me?"

"You know very well how it happened, J.J."

"I'm Garrett now."

"And that's why I didn't tell you."

"What?"

"Never mind. Call me later, and we'll set up a meeting."

"Forget later. What time does Max go to school?"

"Seven-thirty."

"Fine, I'll be back at 7:35 and we'll meet then."

"I don't have time."

"Make time. I'm not waiting all day to talk about this. It's now or at 7:35."

Her narrow glare appeared out of place on a woman who'd once glared rarely. How could the eyes he'd imagined so often they'd become a part of him, a comfort in times of trouble, now seem the eyes of a stranger?

Livy must have sensed his determination because she made an impatient sound and threw up her hands. "Don't be late. I need to be in court at nine."

She turned her back on him as if he were nothing to her. As a child he'd heard the same words, been faced with a similar back...

Daddy, play ball with me.

I can't, Junior. I need to be in court at nine.

Garrett shook his head to make the voices go away. But Livy's words still hung in the air. How had the high-spirited, generous, life-loving girl turned into this mouthy, angry, sharp-eyed...lawyer?

"What happened to you?" he murmured.

She stopped with her hand on the doorknob. "*You* happened to me," she said, then disappeared inside.

LIVY CLOSED THE DOOR and leaned her head against the cool, wood panel. She felt as if she'd been crying for hours. Her face was hot. Her eyes burned. Her throat ached with the tears she would not release.

How dared he come back here and ingratiate himself with her son?

Her son! Not his. J.J.—make that Garrett—had run away and never looked back. He had not wanted her love. He did not deserve the wonder of Max.

"Oh, God, what am I going to do?" she whispered.

"Do about what?"

At the sound of her mother's voice, Livy let out a squeak of alarm and jumped away from the door. Rosie came out of the kitchen wearing her usual attire—brightly colored, flowing skirt that ended just above an ankle tattoo of a hummingbird, and a T-shirt imprinted with one of her slogans: *I Can Only Please One Person A Day. Today Is Not Your Day. Tomorrow Doesn't Look Any Better.*

Livy wanted one of those shirts. Unfortunately, no one in her world would take it seriously. In her world, she was supposed to please everyone all the time.

"Max," Livy blurted. "I don't know what to do about Max."

"I told you he'd turn up eventually." Rosie wiped her hands on a dish towel, then tossed it over her shoulder with a nonchalant movement typical of Rosie.

Five nights a week Rosie led tourists about the city as she told legendary stories of the specters that resided amid the architecture of the oldest planned city in America. She was one of the best guides in Savannah. Maybe because she believed in the ghosts.

Livy put her hand to her forehead and rubbed at the ache there.

"You're going to make yourself sick, sugar."

"I already am."

"That child's a wandering soul. Can't help himself. And you can't change him, no matter how many times you try."

A wandering soul. She'd heard that before. She'd hoped to never hear it again.

A childhood full of different towns, different faces, no friends had given Livy a permanent case of roots—or, as her mother said, root rot. Not that she hadn't loved the adventures while she was having them. But once her father had died the fun had gone out of a whole lot of things.

When Livy had come to Savannah she hadn't fit in because she hadn't known how. Livy didn't want that for Max. She wanted him to have a home, to have friends, to belong. Unfortunately, Max seemed to have more trouble with fitting in than she had—and he'd lived here all his life.

"There's so much that could happen to a child alone, even around here."

"Why do you always think about all the bad things?"

"Someone has to."

"Do they? Why's that?"

"If you saw what I saw, if you heard what I heard every day, you'd be afraid, too."

Rosie shook her head and went into the usual litany. "To think any child of mine, any child of your

father's, would become a perpetrator of the establish-
ment.''

"I'm a lawyer, Mama.''

"Look what those lawyers did for O.J. If I were
you I wouldn't be bragging.''

"I practice family law. I'm helping wives and hus-
bands and children.'' Livy threw up her hands. "Why
am I explaining this to you? You know what I do.
Live with it.''

"Your father would spin in his grave.''

"If Daddy was spinning as much as you say, he'd
be out of his grave by now and walking the streets.''

"He is, sugar. He is.''

"Aw, Mama. Please.''

Livy's father had been a gifted carpenter with a
thirst for experience. He'd taken his wife and child
along on his magical mystery tour of the country,
picking up jobs at will and grabbing every adventure
he could.

A skydiving, motorcycle-jumping, snowmobile-
racing maniac, he was also big and bluff, hearty and
happy...the most alive man Livy had ever known—
until he died.

She trudged up the stairs to check on Max. He
might be eight and able to bathe himself, but given
his proclivity for accidents... Agile adults slipped in
the tub, whacked their heads and died every day. She
didn't plan to let her son drown while she was arguing
with her mother. Again.

Gentle splashing drifted from the bathroom. Livy
let out the breath she hadn't known she held. As long
as Max was splashing gently, he wasn't drowning.

According to Rosie, Max was accident-prone because Livy always expected him to hurt himself. Just another pearl of guilt on her already full mother worry beads.

Lies, guilt, secrets, recriminations. Hope your day is happy.

Maybe Livy should try her hand at T-shirt slogans. That would be a job to make her mother proud.

She peeked into the bathroom, and in the mirror saw her son fill a plastic cup, then let the water trickle over his head like a waterfall.

He appeared so thin and pale, sitting naked in the white porcelain tub. Love pulsed at the base of her throat and made her eyes burn again. Max was everything to her. Sometimes Livy felt so much for him it was frightening. She would not let anyone hurt him—certainly not his father.

"How's it going in there?" she called.

He glanced up, caught sight of her in the mirror and ducked beneath the edge of the tub. "Mom! I'm nakie."

"Nothing I haven't seen before."

"Mom!" This accompanied by his latest expression, a rolling of the eyes. She could see him already as a teenager, and it wasn't pretty.

"Have you washed?"

"Yes."

"Feet? Hair? Everything in between?"

"Uh-huh."

"With soap?"

"Soap?" he asked, as if the concept was a new one.

"You aren't washed." Livy resisted rolling her own eyes. "Do you want help?"

"No! I can do it."

The shyness was as new as the sarcasm. His independence he'd had from cradle—or maybe from conception. Sometimes she wondered if he pushed her away all the harder because she held him too close. But she just couldn't stop herself.

Livy winced as the shadow memory of her father falling, falling, falling toward the earth pressed behind her eyelids. She would never forget the day he'd decided to skydive in a high wind. She didn't understand how her mother had.

Once Daddy died, Rosie had brought Livy home to live with her own mother, a woman who had a hard time remembering *her* name, let alone her granddaughter's. Rosie had visited once in a while, never staying longer than a week, being gone sometimes as much as six months. At seventeen, Livy became the responsible person of the house. At first she had no idea how, but as the years went by, she learned the lesson well. Perhaps too well.

Every time she tried to loosen up, as her mother said she should, Livy would see that body rocketing toward the earth, view another picture of a child abused or lost, remember again the man she loved leaving her forever. Then she'd clutch Max closer and hold him tighter than ever before.

Final splashing noises and the swirling belch of the drain broke into Livy's reverie. She peeked again and found Max drying himself off. His cast appeared fine, dry and all in one piece. Modern medicine was amazing. Lucky for Max.

"I'll check on breakfast," she said. "Get dressed and come down."

"'Kay."

Livy took the back steps to the kitchen. Her mother had already skipped off to parts unknown, which solved Livy's problem of getting rid of her before J.J. returned. Rosie wasn't the kind of grandma who hung about watching television and knitting socks. Unfortunately, each time Rosie disappeared without a word, Livy ended up bailing her out of jail.

Rosie liked to organize peaceful protests for every lost cause she could find. Goblins, hawks or cobblestones, Indian burial grounds, geese or tumble-down pirate's cave—it didn't matter. If there was a person, place or thing that needed defending, Rosie would be there—first.

On the high side, her causes kept her busy. On the downside, one woman's peace was a police officer's nightmare. The law enforcement community had discovered the only way to shut up Rosie was to lock up Rosie.

At any rate, Livy had gained a friend out of her mother's proclivity for arrest. Detective Gabriel Klein—Gabe to his friends, Klein to his co-workers—was someone in between to Livy. New in Savannah, yet native to Georgia, he had been of help to her with a few long-term, criminal cases.

His usual fare as a detective was serious infractions, and not Rosie's type of nonsense, which was usually left to the officers on patrol. But because he and Livy were friendly, Klein looked out for Rosie whenever she turned up in jail. He'd also started to look out for Livy and Max, even though she hadn't asked him to. From what she'd heard around Savannah, Klein liked to look after people. It was what he did best.

Max thundered down the steps. How one child could sound like ten on the steps Livy had never figured out, but Max managed.

He sat at the table, and she placed a plate of waffles in front of him. "Thanks, Mom."

"Thank Rosie."

"Thanks, Rosie," he called.

"She's not here."

"That's okay. She said she can hear me even if she's not around."

Livy's lips tightened. "Max, you know sometimes Gramma says things that aren't exactly so."

"Don't call her Gramma."

"Like that. She *is* a gramma. Not calling her one doesn't make it not so."

He shrugged. "I don't mind callin' her Rosie. I love her."

Max and Rosie had taken one look at each other and fallen instantly in love. No matter how much her mother annoyed Livy, she could never split up her and Max. Never.

Livy left Max shoveling his breakfast as if protecting it from ravenous wolves. The boy ate like a truck driver, yet resembled an escapee from Andersonville Prison.

She ran upstairs and into the bathroom, where she

hung up his towel, then shut every drawer and door that Max had opened.

Rosie understood this odd habit and it never irritated *her* to have to constantly shut every cover on every crevice after Max had been through a room. When Livy asked her mother what Max could possibly think lived beneath the bathroom sink, Rosie had said, "Maybe Max doesn't even know, sugar, but better safe than sorry."

What were you supposed to say to logic like that?

Sometimes Livy felt as much an outsider living with her mother and son as she'd felt when she'd first been left in Savannah. Back then she hadn't known how to behave, how to make friends, whom to trust. Then there'd been one magic summer with one magic man...and she'd learned that in truth she could trust no one but herself.

Now the man who had taught her the hardest lesson of her life was back.

Livy cut off those treacherous thoughts and got dressed. For court she always wore a skirt, heels and a jacket. Today she added a bright-red camisole to give the illusion of power.

She glanced into the mirror and stuck out her tongue. She looked scared to death, and she loathed suits. Unfortunately, all the big lawyer boys wore them.

Livy returned to the kitchen just as Max tripped over the rag rug and dumped his dishes into the sink with a crash. "You okay?"

The intensity of the glare she received for being such a *mom* was tempered somewhat by his milk mustache. Livy resisted the urge to wipe it off. With the white foam on his lip, Max looked like her baby again.

Then he asked a typical Max question that reminded her he was no longer any kind of baby. "Mr. Stark said if you believe in something it's true. Is that right?"

Livy hesitated. "What do you think?"

His chin went up; his eyes turned defiant. "I thought that maybe it couldn't hurt to try. Maybe if I believe in something it *would* be true. Like magic."

"Magic isn't any more real than Santa, Max. I wish it were."

He sighed and his chin drooped toward his chest. *Guilt, guilt, guilt.* The word beat in time to the pulse of pain in Livy's head.

Once, Livy herself had believed in magic, but believing hadn't made the magic real. So she'd learned never to believe in anything she couldn't see and hear and touch.

Livy gazed at her son; she gave in to the urge to pull him against her and listen to his heart beat sure and steady; she touched his impossibly soft cheek.

Max was all the magic she needed. No matter who was back in town.

GARRETT WALKED to River Street, bought coffee he didn't need or want, then sat on a bench and watched the Savannah River. Boats flowed by, tourists chattered, the city awoke around him, and Garrett still stared at the water.

I have a son.

He could not seem to get his mind around that fact. Maybe because his son was eight years old—a walking, talking, laughing, falling *person*. Most fathers got to start with a baby and work up. Not him.

For a bonus, his son thought he was *dead*.

Garrett sighed and dumped out his coffee untasted. His heart already pumped too hard and too fast from anger, fear and uncertainty. He didn't need a caffeine jump start.

Why hadn't Livy told him? Had she even tried to find him? Most important, why did she hate him?

He wasn't blameless. He *had* run away. He'd also been a child, at least when dealing with emotions. Because he'd never known love until Livy.

Garrett's mother had taken off when he was a baby. He didn't have a single memory of her. Perhaps he *should* feel abandoned. He'd been told that often enough by counselors and teachers. But how could he feel left when he felt little to nothing at all?

He might have wondered on occasion why she'd gone. Had it been to get away from him? But Garrett had lived with his father, and somehow he doubted his mother had run from a baby.

James, Sr., a no-nonsense, high-profile, corporate attorney, had wanted a son to follow in his footsteps. He'd gotten J.J., instead.

The man had not known what to do with a child who walked around in a cloud of imagination, tripped over his own feet, ran into doors and talked about people who did not exist—except try like hell to change him. Garrett had waited until he was eighteen to run.

But a lifetime of being told he was useless and worthless, that dreams were only dreams and his would never amount to anything, had made Garrett uncertain of what was the truth.

When Livy had told him she loved him, Garrett had run again, knowing he did not deserve a gift as precious as that. And in running he'd made all his father's predictions come true.

The breeze off the river whispered autumn— summer dying, winter coming. The scent of sultry heat fading toward sharp, cool ice, but beneath it all, the tangy whiff of burning leaves and the prophesy of withering daylight.

The rumble of cars over the cobblestone street at Garrett's back made him remember his past. Walking along this very river, taking her hand, wishing things he'd never dared hope for and dreaming more than he'd ever dared to dream.

Touching her skin in the moonlight, gently, reverently, knowing she was the most beautiful being on this earth. Pulling her close, smelling her hair, breathing her name, understanding he held everything in his arms. And knowing in his heart he deserved none of it, but wanting her nevertheless. She had given him strength, made him believe in himself and shared every bit of herself.

Garrett had thought he was coming back to Savannah for the book. He admitted now, he had come back for her.

He still didn't deserve her love. He certainly didn't deserve Max. But he had learned a few things over the past nine years. People rarely got what they deserved—be it good or bad. They quite often got what they fought for, though, and they could earn what they believed in deeply enough.

Livy was different now. Perhaps not the woman he'd once loved, and he had no one to blame but himself. His son, on the other hand, was special. Garrett had seen that the second he looked into Max's eyes. Max was like him, only better, and Garrett wasn't going to allow Max to endure the childhood Garrett had endured. He was going to nourish his son's magic and give him everything J. J. Garrett had longed for.

Garrett breathed the river air one more time, felt the peace of this place he'd been awaiting. As he walked back to Livy's house he made a vow to himself.

He was going to become the father he'd always wanted.

WHEN THE DOORBELL RANG, Livy let out a startled yelp. She wasn't ready. Oh, she was dressed and Max was gone and the house was empty. But she was not ready to see the man again. Not now, maybe never.

As she approached the door, Livy gave herself a quick pep talk. She was stronger, smarter, older. She had everything she needed in her life; she did not need him. J.J. could not hurt her anymore.

She did not love him. He could not touch her and make her do anything. He could not speak to her in that haunting voice and make her dream impossible dreams.

She would fix this. Wasn't she the best family law

attorney in town? If Livy Frasier couldn't fix her own problems, what good was she to anyone else?

Livy opened the door and her breath stopped in her throat, making her chest hurt. He was more beautiful now than he'd been all those years ago. His hair just as black, but longer, his face more defined—a man's face now, with no trace of the boy she'd lost everything to.

Foolish girl. What difference did it make how he looked?

His dark gaze met hers, and she shivered despite the rising heat of the day. The warmth of the sun became a memory; the strength she'd talked herself into, a whisper gone on the wind. This man had been her everything, and when she'd lost him she had nearly lost herself.

Kisses in the moonlight, sex beneath the stars, secret meetings, murmured promises. She'd been so young then, so unbelievably naive and stupid. But she'd never felt anything that strong, or that magical, since. Love that deep destroyed. The girl she'd been then was no more. Thank God.

Tightening her fingers on the doorknob, Livy moved back, the only welcome she could bring herself to give. As he stepped inside, her head spun with memories of other times he'd been here, the occasions he'd snuck up the servants' stairs to her room.

Since this house dated from the mid-1700s, there were also servants' quarters, where Rosie lived, and such antiquities as a front parlor—where, Livy recalled, she'd shared her first French kiss with this man on the chaise longue. There was even a wrought-iron gate around the garden, where once, in the middle of a thunderstorm, he'd put his hot hands all over her icy cold skin and—

"Shall we go into the dining room?" Her voice polite but brittle, Livy hoped he could not tell that her palms had gone damp and she was having a hard time remembering this was business. Business she could manage. The past was beyond her control.

"I'd rather keep it informal." Taking charge, he strolled into the parlor and sat on the damn chaise longue. When he glanced at her, she knew he remembered the same things she did.

Her face flamed and she wanted to hide. Her hardwon self-discipline slipped another notch. If he kept reminding her of the past, she didn't know how she'd make it through the present.

Livy waited for him to speak. That was always best in situations like these. Be patient. Wait for them to spill the beans, tip their hand, talk too much—then pounce. She remained standing, as far away from him as she could get without leaving the room.

"You look…" He hesitated. "Different."

She shrugged. "You could use a haircut."

How she looked was irrelevant. Just as how he looked—spectacular—was not going to make her dreamy-eyed any longer. She had dreamed herself dry long ago.

Livy glanced at her watch. "Can we get down to business?"

"I wouldn't call Max business."

"What *would* you call him?"

"My son."

She winced. "You're so certain?"

"He looks exactly like I did at that age. Size, hair, feet, everything."

The mystery of the blond hair solved, Livy thought. What she said was, "That means nothing."

When he stood, Livy tensed, but he didn't come any closer, merely paced in front of the chaise longue. He wasn't a big man in weight or musculature, but he was tall, much taller than she, and his mien of barely suppressed energy filled the room, pressed on her, made her aware and alive.

He'd always had the gift of being still, yet the force of his personality would rivet attention upon him even in a crowded room. The fact that he couldn't be still now gave voice to his agitation.

In the past few years, Livy had become a master at seeing beneath the surface of anyone. Watching him, she understood that though J.J.'s name might have changed, little else had. She had to remember that. For Max's sake, if not her own.

He stopped pacing, faced her. "Come on, Livy. I can count. And I know you."

"You knew me."

"Fine, I knew you. There was only me for you."

"Too bad that didn't work the other way around."

His jaw tightened. "I never touched another woman in Savannah."

"No, not another woman. For you the mistress was life."

"And that's so terrible? Life?"

She ignored him. He didn't understand. No one ever had. "Adventure, excitement, travel—something new, someone different." She took a deep breath, striving for control, knowing it was lost. "Anywhere but here," she whispered. "Anything but love."

"That's not true."

"Isn't it? I'm not a fool. The morning after I tell you I'll love you forever, you're gone without a trace. I meant little to nothing to you, J.J."

"Garrett," he corrected.

"Fine, *Garrett*," she snapped. To hell with control; with this man, she'd never had any. "So what is it you want from me?"

"First, I'd like to know why my son thinks I'm dead."

"He thinks you're undead."

"Very funny. I want the truth, Livy."

"The truth? J. J. Garrett *is* dead. You're Garrett Stark now."

He frowned, looked at the ceiling, then back at her. "Arguing isn't going to get us anywhere. I want to see my son. I want to know him. I want him to know me."

"No."

"No?" His voice was deadly calm. When had he crossed the room? How had he come to stand only a few steps away? And how could she back up when she was already against the wall? "Just like that? No?"

"Pretty much." She tried to appear unconcerned, even though her heart pounded so loudly she could barely think.

The air between them seemed to hum. She could hear herself breathe, hear him, too. The room had gone hot; her silk camisole stuck to her back. Her hair drifted into her eyes and she shook her head to get it out.

He smelled like sultry nights and sin in the rain. How could she still want him? She had wanted nothing for so long except to keep Max safe. Yet when faced with the most dangerous thing she'd ever known, all she wanted to do was pull him closer and forget all that might keep her sane.

He towered over her, crowded her. His hands, on either side of her head, trapped her. He wasn't touching her anywhere, yet she felt him everywhere.

"You can't deny me my son."

Raising her palms, she braced them against his black-clad chest, prepared to shove him away if she had to. "He's *my* son. And I can do anything I damn well please."

His eyes narrowed. She lifted her chin, daring him. "Then, so can I."

He kissed her, hard—desperately seeking, heedlessly searching. How could she have believed she was stronger now? This man had been her only weakness, and now he taught her all over again that he always would be.

His lips were the same ones that had tempted her with passion, schooled her in sex, whispered hope, promised the impossible.

Instead of shoving him away, her fingers fisted in his shirt, holding him near. His pulse thundered against her wrist, as loud and as fast as her own. His hair brushed her cheek, shaded her face, as his smart, clever mouth captivated, and his touch ignited her soul. The kiss was both everything she remembered and everything she'd ever wanted to forget.

Caged memories tumbled free. Emotions she'd never wanted to experience again burst full blown behind her closed eyelids. The heart she'd hardened to everyone but her son shivered, shook and began to sob.

Livy tore her mouth from his and slapped him with all that she had. ''You're not going to get me to agree this way. You can't see Max.''

The words sounded as hard and cold as she'd wanted them to. As the imprint of her hand on his cheek darkened, so did his eyes. He stepped away, and with his mouth still wet from hers, he took her heart and stomped on it all over again.

''Fine, Counselor, I'll see you in court.''

The slam of the front door reverberated through the wall at her back as she slid into a boneless heap on the floor.

I'll see you in court.

Livy gave a watery, hysterical little laugh. She liked that line a whole lot better when she said it.

CHAPTER FOUR

GARRETT DIDN'T SLOW DOWN until he'd power-walked all the way back to River Street. He was not a man given to bursts of temper, slamming of doors or even the raising of his voice. From his father he'd learned men in their family did not shout, slam or, for that matter, show emotion of any kind. Not anger, not sadness and certainly not love.

Why should he be surprised that the only woman who'd ever coaxed him beyond his inbred reserve toward softer emotions would also be the one to break the taut rein he kept on any hint of temper? Not to say he didn't get angry; he just didn't show it. Prime candidate for an ulcer was Garrett, as Andrew always warned him. Andrew should talk.

Garrett's mind a jumble, he thought crazy things. The craziest of all was that he should turn right around, return to the house where he'd first kissed Livy and kiss her again.

He touched his cheek. It still burned where she'd slapped him. He had no doubt she'd slug him the next time, and he'd deserve it. He had to *think*.

If he didn't play this whole thing right, he would lose any hope of getting near Max in this lifetime. He needed a plan. Plans, though, were not his strong suit;

Garrett liked to go with the flow. But if he had to, he could come up with one. Maybe.

Garrett hurried past the Hyatt Regency Hotel. Some said the tall, concrete structure didn't fit with the quaint, restored nineteenth-century buildings in the river area, but the tourists liked it, as evidenced by the constant stream of them spilling from the back door of the hotel and onto River Street.

Past the Hyatt, Garrett walked in to one of the numerous restaurants. He glanced at his watch and growled. Eight-thirty in the morning. Far too early for a nightcap. His pending ulcer didn't warrant alcohol or coffee. But milk only made him think of Max— his son.

And when he thought of Max, things got all jumbled again. Need and love, longing and hope—they were all mixed up with Livy and always had been. But now they were mixed up with Max, too. Both for J. J. Garrett—a boy who'd known love but once— and Garrett Stark—a man who could only write of it.

Though it was early, a bartender stood behind the bar, preparing for the day. When she lifted a brow his way, Garrett ordered sweet tea, a southern confection he'd always missed whenever he wasn't in the South, and ignored her long look and sultry smile. For reasons unfathomable to Garrett, women found his distracted silences compelling and his gothic demeanor intriguing.

This was convenient when the loneliness overtook him, usually between books, because when he was in the midst of a story his mind was so full of imaginary people, he had no time for real ones. That truth would have ended every relationship he'd ever begun, if his habit of moving on at the first whisper of a new idea hadn't ended it first.

He never lied to anyone. He never promised anything but the moment. He couldn't promise more, because he didn't know how.

Was it fair to fight for his son? Could he promise Max more than that moment? Could he love Max the way the boy deserved to be loved? What if he tried and failed? Garrett was very good at failing.

The bartender returned. "You haven't touched your tea. Anything wrong?"

"Not with the tea."

"Aw, that sounds serious. Can I help?"

She put her elbows on the bar and leaned over with an intent expression upon her face. Garrett got an extraordinary view of her breasts. They were extraordinary breasts.

In any other town he'd have considered the offer. Hell, be real. A day ago he'd have taken the offer. Anything to avoid thinking about the book that wasn't. But today he'd become a father. This morning he'd touched and kissed Livy. Be it better or worse, nothing would ever be the same again.

Though he might never be the parent he hoped to be, he could try. *If* he could get Livy to let him near Max. He'd threatened court. Dare he go that far? Was there another option before things got nasty?

Garrett considered the helpful bartender. "If I had a custody problem, who would be the best person to talk to about it?"

"Custody?" The bartender straightened and glanced at his left hand. "You're married?"

Garrett ignored the question, standing to reach for his wallet. He tossed some money next to his untouched tea and started for the door. He'd find out what he needed to know. He always did. Being a writer had honed his research skills.

"Hey, wait." The bartender followed him the length of the bar. She smiled, friendly this time instead of a come-on, so Garrett smiled back. "One of the cooks had a problem like that. Hold on."

She stepped into the kitchen, and a moment later reappeared with a large, bald man who reminded Garrett of Mr. Clean without the earring.

"Claudio, this is the man looking for advice on a custody problem."

"Talk to Kim Luchetti. She and her partner are the best team in town. Savannah Family Law." He waved vaguely in the direction of town. "They're in the book. Tell Kim, Claudio sent you. She'll take care of everything."

"Thanks." Garrett checked his watch. Why, he had no idea. It wasn't as though he had a clock to punch. Or an idea to write into a book. He rubbed his forehead, craving a cigarette for the first time in five years. Alcohol, cigarettes, caffeine. If his Muse hadn't already fled, she'd be running for her life right about now.

Though he hated to consult an attorney, hated the fact that his first response had been to threaten legal action, just like dear old dad, what could it hurt to call and find out his options?

He needed a plan. This seemed like a good one. Once Garrett knew where he stood, he'd phone Livy; they'd discuss the situation like adults. Everything would be fine.

Why didn't he believe that?

LIVY'S CASE went sour quicker than milk beneath the noonday sun. No surprise there. She could think of nothing but J. J. Garrett now Garrett Stark, who'd returned to haunt her life.

To be honest, her case had gone badly through no fault of hers. Yet she couldn't help but feel on her walk back from court that if her mind had been a little sharper, if she hadn't been hungover from a combination of fear, lack of sleep and shock, then she might not have stood there gaping when the new evidence was revealed, and maybe she could have salvaged something.

Despite her mother's view of lawyers, Livy *did* help people, and she had increased her family law practice to the point that she could turn away cases she did not believe in.

Livy loved the law. The law was cut-and-dried. The law made sense. It gave a semblance of control in a world gone out of control. Still, sometimes life just sucked.

And today was one of those times.

"Another day, another psycho nutcase."

Livy glanced up from her notes on *Bernadette v. Bernadette* to find Kim Luchetti lounging in the doorway. Kim was a paralegal, but in their small office she handled the phones, filing, research and case interviews, which was how she met the psycho nutcases first.

At times Livy felt the two of them were Batman and Robin, the caped law crusaders, fighting for truth, justice and the American Way. Unfortunately, the American Way wasn't all it used to be.

America had been founded on the backs of folks who couldn't quite fit in anywhere else on the earth—outcasts, criminals, people who were very hard to get along with. If they hadn't been, America would have eaten those early settlers alive. As a result, the American Way had become a modern version of "get what you want no matter the cost, or hire a lawyer to get it for you."

"Which psycho nutcase are we talking about?" Livy asked, only momentarily concerned that there was more than one in her caseload.

"Our latest and greatest." Kim kicked off her four-inch spike heels and sprawled in a chair, heedless of her short, mauve skirt. She could have been a fashion model except fate, or a just God, had created her less than five feet tall. She compensated with heels and short skirts, which made her legs look long.

Livy really should hate her, but Kim was a damn fine paralegal and an even better friend. Too bad she was a Yankee. But nobody was perfect.

"Listen to this." As Kim rubbed her hands together, her French manicure caught the fluorescent light and shot off sparks bright enough to blind a gnat. "Guy hauls ass for ten miles with the cops chasing him, sirens blaring, lights flashing. He stops only because he hits a patch of oil and skids into a pig farm.

When he gets out of the car at the cops' request, beer cans tumble out willy-nilly—''

"I don't take cases like that. The guy's an idiot and obviously DUI."

Kim giggled. Only Kim could giggle and make the sound appealing. Was it her height that allowed the giggle, or her bearing and self-confidence that made even a giggle seem so Kim?

She might resemble a black-haired, green-eyed, luscious-bodied Barbie, but she possessed the savvy of the street and brains worthy of a Supreme Court justice. Livy often wondered why Kim had settled for a career as a bridesmaid and not a bride—but if she hadn't, Livy would be out the best paralegal in Georgia.

Folks had often made the mistake of taking Kim at face value. She promptly chewed up such fools and spit them out like sunflower seeds. It really was fun to watch.

Kim giggled a second time, bringing Livy's attention back to the problem at hand. "What's so funny?"

"You're not representing the DUI. Your client is the pig farmer."

"Why is that?"

"Because the pig farmer is Herbert Hoff."

Livy sighed. There was little she could say to that revelation beyond "Great."

Though Livy's specialty was family law, once she handled a family's law, they often saw her as their utility lawyer. In other words, she got called to handle most any legal entanglement her former clients got into because they trusted her. So if Livy believed she could help them, she did. Trust was a terrible thing to waste.

"What's Herb's problem?"

"Seems his prize sow got killed in the accident."

"And?"

"That's a hardship. She would have had litter upon litter..."

"Blah-blah-blah."

"Pain and suffering, lost income." Kim grinned. "God, I love this job."

"Well, that makes one of us."

Kim's smile faded and she sat up, on alert. Livy and Kim had become friends three minutes after Kim had walked into Livy's office for the first time. Livy had been running on empty with too much work and too little time for both the business and her son. Kim had decided Livy needed her, and that had been the end of that.

The friendship was as solid as their partnership, which continually amazed them both. Kim, as a result of her annoying perfection in face, body and brain, had few female friends. Livy had never been comfortable with people her own age. Save one, and look where that had gotten her.

She bit her lip and forced J.J.'s face out of her head. He'd already ruined her morning, she would not let him screw up the afternoon, too.

"Spill it, Counselor. You got a case you don't care for?"

Livy shrugged, then gave it up. *"Bernadette v. Bernadette."* She jabbed a chewed-on fingernail at the file. "These people should never have gotten married, never had kids. Shouldn't there be some kind of law?"

"Against fools and idiots? Yep. Unfortunately, in the great state of Georgia—and every other state I'm aware of—being a moron isn't a crime. What's wrong with your case?"

"I'm representing the wife. Typical story. Husband works late a little too much. Wife goes to see him, catches him with a chickee-poo."

"Blah-blah-blah."

"She wants the house, a car, the kids, plus support and alimony."

Kim spread her hands. "This sounds clear-cut."

"Not quite. She's having an affair with the pool boy, who's almost as young as her eldest son. The best part is, this lovely little bombshell came out in court this morning."

Kim winced, which is exactly what Livy had done when she'd heard about it—from the pool boy after the husband's lawyer had put him on the stand. She *hated* surprises, and two in one day was two too many.

"After you quit grinding your teeth and swearing a blue streak in your head, then what happened?"

Livy smiled. Kim knew her so well. "Turns out that both of them have been behaving this way for years. The wife's only mad now because the latest in the long line of hotties is her cousin."

"Ouch."

"Ouch isn't the half of it."

Sometimes Livy took a case that looked good—

wronged wife, crying children—but when the truth came out, things got ugly.

Who was she kidding? There was no ''sometimes'' about it. The truth was almost always ugly. Still, she did enjoy sorting through the silt and picking out the gold. Every once in a while that gold was Justice.

''You did your best, Livy. Why so glum?''

Livy shook her head. ''My best wasn't good enough. I lost, Kim.''

''Define *lost*.''

''Joint custody.''

''That doesn't sound unreasonable under the circumstances.''

''You're probably right, but tell that to my client.''

Kim raised her perfect brow. ''What about Mom and the pool boy?''

''You sound just like the opposing counsel.''

''At least your client won't have to worry about the father flipping out because he's been denied visitation, so he snatches the kids and disappears.''

Livy's heart stuttered and she put her palm against her chest. ''Wh-why would you say something like that?''

Kim gave her an odd look. ''Are you having a heart attack? You're as pale as one of Rosie's ghosts.''

''I'm fine.'' Livy forced herself to drop her hand and breathe deeply. She hadn't thought about that. J.J. wouldn't...

No, *J.J.* wouldn't. She had no idea what Garrett Stark might do.

''Why do people use their kids for leverage?'' she muttered.

"Because they can."

The two of them sighed as one. Livy didn't know what she'd do without Kim to talk to, Kim to understand things, Kim to keep her grounded and sane. Sometimes Livy was so grateful, she got all weepy. Usually after they hit the Merlot.

Kim always waved off Livy's words, saying "That's what friends are for." Livy wasn't so sure. Since she'd only had one friend before Kim—and as Kim said, boyfriends didn't count because once they weren't boyfriends they were slime, but a girlfriend was a girlfriend forever, if they were any type of friend—Livy decided to believe Kim on this subject.

"Let's talk about happy stuff a minute." Kim smirked. "I'm in love."

Livy managed not to snort. Barely. "You are always in love."

"But this time it's real."

"Uh-huh."

For a smart girl, Kim picked a whole lot of losers. Not that Livy was anyone to judge. Still, Kim should be able to see through the pretty-boy type. Yet she constantly became bored with every single wonder boy within two weeks.

"Who is it this time?" Livy asked.

"Joshua."

Livy rolled her eyes. She couldn't stop herself. Joshua sounded far too pretty already. "You need to catch a clue, Kim. Every guy you've dated has turned out to be a loser with a capital L."

"But they always look like such winners."

"Bingo. Looks like a winner?" Livy made the

shape of an *L* with her thumb and forefinger. "L-o-s-e-r."

"So you're saying I should search for a loser and he'll be a winner?"

"Couldn't hurt."

"I think I'll pass on that Dear Livy advice, thank you. Joshua is gorgeous and tall and blond as a Viking, built like one, too. He works at the conference hotel on the river, in Reservations. He can't be like all the rest. He must have something upstairs to manage that."

"You'd think, wouldn't you." Livy didn't hold out much hope.

From what she'd observed of relationships over the years—and she'd had to observe quite a few in her business—people were attracted to the same type over and over again, regardless of whether that was a mistake or not. It usually took years of dogged determination, or years of therapy, to change type.

When Livy dated, which was rarely, she chose mildly attractive, middle-aged, slightly stuffy men. No dark, dangerous, poetic strangers for her, thank you. And she'd been just fine, until a certain type had come knocking. Which only proved that dogged determination stood for little. Maybe she needed years of therapy, instead. She could start tomorrow.

"How's my angel baby?"

Livy smiled. Kim and Max were buddies. Once upon a time, she had worried about all the women in her son's life, figuring that couldn't be good. Then she'd had the brilliant idea of signing him up for Little League. With all those hardballs and swinging bats—

She started so violently at the memory that Kim reached over and put her hand atop Livy's. "Did he fall off the back porch again?"

"No." Livy frowned. "Or at least not so I could tell. He's begun to hide minor wounds."

"Probably not a bad idea, considering."

Livy frowned. "It *is* a bad idea. Do you know what kind of infection you can get if you don't clean even a paper cut properly?"

"No, but I'm sure you'll tell me as soon as I actually care. Now, getting back to Max—what's he done lately?"

"Stayed out after dark and ended up with a broken forearm."

"Well—" Kim shrugged "—something had to give sooner or later."

Livy, unable to keep still any longer, stood and began to pace behind her desk. Calmly Kim watched her go this way and that. "How can you be so blasé? He broke a bone."

"I got that. Honestly, Livy, he's a boy. My brothers broke bones every damn day." Livy gave her a look. "Well, not every day. But close enough. You know what my mom would say to you? You need another baby. That'll fix you right up. Once you've got two, you won't worry overly much about one."

Though Kim didn't talk about the place she hailed from—"north" was all she said—she had on occasion mentioned her five big brothers. Livy couldn't imagine six children—the worries, the heartache, the medical bills.

"Your mama was just lucky she got y'all fed and bathed."

"I just love how you say mama and y'all." Kim grinned. "Hallelujah, I love the South. Especially southern men." Her green eyes went dreamy and brought to mind images of lazy kitties and sultry Savannah nights.

"Kim, could you focus for a minute?" She did. "Max *broke* his *arm*. I'm at my wits' end."

And not about that, her conscience added. *About his father—a man you think is dead. A man my mother thinks is dead. A man Max thinks is dead.*

That was the thing about lies; they multiplied, until a person forgot what was real and what wasn't. Kind of like magic. Livy rubbed her forehead some more.

"You've got to let him climb trees and jump off things and be a boy." Kim wiggled her fingers and spoke in an exaggerated Transylvanian accent. "Out in the dark where the children of the night howl."

The accent made Livy remember how Max had met J.J. in the first place. He wanted to be undead. She really had to have another talk with him. No matter how many times they discussed fantasy and reality, Max just didn't seem to get it.

"You're as bad as Max. Girls don't break bones? Or stay out after dark? I wish I had one of those."

"I remember sneaking out after dark." Kim wiggled her eyebrows. "But that was in high school."

"Never mind. He's only eight. The world is full of—"

"Psycho nutcases. I know. Still, Livy, you've gotta cut him some slack or he'll never grow up—"

"Normal?"

"At all. Maybe you should check into one of those Big Brother programs. For boys who don't have dads."

"I know what a Big Brother program is," Livy snapped.

Kim, always astute, looked at Livy too closely. "What's the matter with you today?"

"Nothing." There went those multiplying lies again. "Don't you have someone to call and harass?"

"Always." But Kim didn't leave; she just kept staring at Livy with those too-intelligent eyes.

Livy stared back. How long was she going to be able to keep this mess to herself? She resisted the urge to rub her forehead. However long it took.

All she had to do was hold J.J. off until he grew bored and left. That shouldn't be too hard. Leaving was what he did best.

Kim cleared her throat.

"Was there something else?" Livy asked.

"One thing. I had a call from a potential client."

"Other than our pig farmer? It's been a busy day."

"The guy just wanted some initial advice—it may not come to court. Another client recommended us. Remember Claudio from the Irish pub on the river?" When Livy's expression went blank, Kim explained further. "He never knew about his kid, then when he found out, he had to prove he was the father before he could sue for visitation."

A chill touched Livy's neck. "Goose on my grave," she muttered.

Kim was too caught up in her story to listen to Livy's mutters. Besides, Livy muttered a lot.

"This guy's case is a lot like Claudio's. So I told him he should get a copy of the birth certificate, see if he's listed as the father. If not, he'd need to get a blood test, consider a DNA test. But to get those, he'd probably need a court order if the mother was being difficult. Sounded like she was. Once he has proof of parentage, the mother would really have no choice."

"No choice," Livy echoed.

"Funny thing, though. When I told him your name, he hung up. I figured he'd want to get started on the court order right away."

Livy froze. That damn goose was dancing all over the entire family plot. "What was *his* name?" she asked, though she already knew.

"Garrett Stark. I know that name, but I can't remember why. Who is he?"

Livy didn't bother to answer before she ran out the door.

CHAPTER FIVE

GARRETT FIGURED the un-book could wait until tomorrow to be unwritten. It wasn't every day a man discovered he had a son.

Talk about the fickle finger of fate. He still couldn't believe he'd called Livy's office for advice. What kind of name for a firm was Savannah Family Law? Other law firms were called Smith, Smith and Jones, or some variation. Didn't high-powered attorneys live to see their names on the stationery? Apparently not Livy Frasier.

So instead of writing, Garrett spent the morning thinking, something he'd been doing a whole lot of lately. The fact that Livy would rather say Garrett was dead than have him be a father to his son made him feel worthless, useless, a failure. Just like old times.

And just like old times, the urge to run prodded at him. He could go somewhere new and start the book over. A different town could make him forget the shape of Max's face. A few hundred miles and he might forget the scent of Livy's hair.

She wouldn't care. She'd made it perfectly clear that he was an intrusion and she wanted him gone.

But this time he wasn't running. He didn't care what Livy wanted. Garrett needed to know Max.

From what he'd seen and heard that morning, Max needed to know him, too.

Livy loved her son. That was obvious. But she had no idea how to cultivate the boy's magic. In trying to keep him safe, she'd end up crushing his spark, making him like every other boy—and Max was different.

Garrett knew, because he was different, too.

So what was he going to do? Garrett couldn't very well announce to Max that he was his dad and Livy was a liar, and then cart the kid off for a painless and simple blood test. Livy would have Garrett in jail faster than he could say "I want a lawyer."

He'd be within his rights, which would eventually come out anyhow, along with the truth. But did he want to start his relationship with his son the way his own father's relationship had been with him—one of "you do what I say and to hell with your feelings or anyone else's"?

Garrett didn't have to answer that question, even for himself.

After a considering glance at the bottle of Poe's best friend atop his kitchen counter, Garrett carried a book out on the porch, instead. Drinking didn't help, anyway; he'd best nip the habit in the bud.

But a Bud would taste so good right now.

"No more," he said aloud. "You're a father."

Garrett remembered his father sitting on the porch, sipping a martini after work, J.J. hovering nearby, waiting for a look, a word, a minute.

Don't bother me, Junior. I need to unwind.

As far as Garrett could tell, his father had been wound so tightly nothing would have unwound him.

A movement on the sidewalk caught his eye and he stood to get a better view. Livy turned in to his yard and stalked up his walk. Furious, she was muttering unintelligibly as she came up the steps, and didn't see him watching her from the shadow of the eaves.

She was so pretty, even wearing that grave-dirt shade of burial suit. But the flame-red silk beneath the suit made him hope that the Livy he'd known lay sleeping beneath the woman she'd become. His Livy had always worn bright colors against her pale, pale skin.

The memory of that skin beneath the moon, beneath him, made Garrett shift, and the movement brought her attention from the front door to him. Heat flared in her eyes, but not the kind of heat he remembered, not the kind he'd always ached for when the cold loneliness overtook him.

He expected her to scream, throw something, maybe kick him in the shins. Instead, she merely spoke low and clear. "You've got nerve calling my office for help."

"It was a mistake."

"Whatever it was, don't do it again. And stay away from my son."

"Or?"

Her lips tightened. She said nothing.

"You can't keep me away from him—"

"I can. If I call the police and say you're bothering him, who do you think they'll believe?"

"You." He shrugged. "Until I tell them the truth and then prove it."

"Shit," she said, but there was no heat in the word, only a touch of desperation.

"You're scared."

Her gaze shot to his, and he saw that he was right. So he moved closer, and he moved slowly. He had a chance to make her see he meant no harm. If she ran now, he'd be chasing her for a long, long time. "That's okay. I'm scared, too."

She snorted. "You were never scared of anything."

He shook his head. "It only seemed that way. But you... You were the most fearless person I'd ever known."

She backed up a step, narrowing her eyes, and he stopped advancing as he waited for her to flee or fight. The tense readiness of her stance made him think she wanted to kick him now, but she didn't.

"Things change when you have a child. You can't be the same person anymore."

"Why not?"

"Because there's suddenly someone more important than anything or anyone, especially yourself."

"That doesn't explain why you had to become a lawyer and turn stiff as a board."

She glared at him. "I became a lawyer to feed us."

"I can feed you now."

"I don't need you. Max doesn't need you."

No one ever needed him. If he died tomorrow, would anyone give a damn past the funeral? Except for Andrew, because of the loss of that oh-so-special book.

Garrett had thought he'd been living the perfect life. But now he wasn't so sure.

"Maybe you should ask Max if he needs me."

"Why? He's been doing *fine* without you."

"Has he?"

Though it didn't seem possible, she went even stiffer. Her back and neck must hurt something awful every night.

"What's that supposed to mean?"

Better tread lightly here. He shrugged. "Every kid deserves a dad."

"Even kids whose dads don't deserve them?"

Garrett's insecurities returned. He'd learned over the years that most writers functioned with an odd sort of schizophrenia—arrogant enough to believe they could write, yet vulnerable enough to possess the emotions to do it in the first place.

Since this morning, Garrett's schizophrenia had begun to slop over into his life as well as his work. One minute he *knew* he was the best thing for Max, and in the space of an instant and a single wrinkled nose from Livy, he was certain he'd be the worst possible influence on his son.

Garrett sighed. "I'd like a chance, Livy. I won't hurt him."

He was treated to her "too dumb to live" glare, which he was starting to believe she reserved especially for him. "Where have I heard *that* before?"

A single sentence and one night in the garden might have been only yesterday, so clear was the voice of his past.

I won't hurt you, Livy. I swear. I'd cut off my arm before I'd hurt you. Give me a chance. Let me touch you. Let me...

He could say he'd been twenty and foolishly stupid. Seduced by the sight of her atop the grass, the drift of the flowers against her hair, the scent of her skin all around him and the taste of her mouth on his. But the truth didn't make what he'd done forgivable.

Garrett licked dry lips and discovered he could taste her still. Maybe that was why he'd been drinking since he'd come back to Savannah. With whiskey in his mouth he no longer tasted Livy and burned for her.

How could he explain that he'd left so he *wouldn't* hurt her? That he'd known in his heart he would never be good enough to stay.

For months after, his entire body had hurt with loneliness and a desperate desire to return. The only way he'd survived was to write until the blinding fury of need dimmed. He'd put everything he'd felt for her, all that he'd feared and believed, everything he'd left behind, into that first book. He'd done it for her. But she'd never believe him.

"Did you ever try to find me?"

"No." She crossed her arms.

"Why not?"

"I lived on the road for seventeen years. My father was exactly like you. Drift and wander, pick up a job here, sleep over there. You told me your name— something easily changed, as you've proven. But you never told me where you were from, or anything about your past. There would have been no finding you, J.J., even if I'd wanted to try."

Uncertainty swamped him. "Why didn't you want to try?"

"You left me, of your own free will. Why would I drag you back where you didn't want to be, so you could leave Max, too?"

Considering it from her angle, she had a point. Why would she believe he'd stay for the son when he hadn't for the mother? Garrett tried a different tack. "Maybe we should leave our past out of this."

"I don't see how, since the past is Max." Her sigh was long and as full of exhaustion as her eyes now that the heat had burned off. "Why are you here, J.J.? Why don't you leave? It's what you do best."

"Not anymore."

Her withering look revealed how little his words meant, and he couldn't blame her. But he wasn't going to give up. "Don't make me go to court, Livy. You'll lose and you know it."

"Why are you doing this to me?" she shouted, and the anguish in her voice bounced off the cool shadowed porch and into the bright autumn sunlight.

Two tiny old ladies paused amid their afternoon constitutional and glared at Garrett from the sidewalk.

"Ladies." He inclined his head.

They sniffed—as only elderly southern ladies could, making him feel as if his knuckles had been rapped without them ever touching him—then straightened backs stiffer than Livy's and hurried on without answering.

Garrett was trying to get the hang of being a gentleman. But there seemed to be nuances to it that a border Yankee like him couldn't quite fathom.

In the silence that followed, Garrett heard a tiny

hitch in Livy's breath that was almost a sob—would have been a sob for any other woman.

He inched forward, encouraged when she didn't move away. He wanted to touch her so badly his hands hurt. Or maybe they hurt because he was fisting them too tightly in an attempt to keep himself from touching her. Because if he did, he wouldn't be able to stop.

Gentling his voice, Garrett spoke just above a whisper. "I want to see Max. I want to know him. Why is that so hard to believe?"

"You didn't want me, why do you want him?"

"I did want you. Too much. You consumed me, Livy."

"Stop!" She raised her hand, palm out in front of her face. "I don't want to hear this. We're talking about Max."

"Are we?"

She didn't answer. Garrett hadn't really expected her to. "You can't *love* him. You barely know him."

"You're telling me you didn't love him the minute you looked into his eyes?"

She hesitated. "I'm his mother."

"And I'm his father. He's you *and* he's me—equally."

"*Not* equally. I carried him. I bore him. I cried every time he hurt himself. I sweated each time I thought I might lose him."

"I'm sorry. I wish I'd been here then. But I'm here now. He's *us*, Livy." Garrett could no longer stop himself. He grabbed her by the arms and dragged her close. Even when she struggled, even when she finally did kick him in the shins, he didn't let go. Instead, he gave her a tiny shake so she'd listen. "Can't you remember what we were like? The magic we made. The magic is Max."

"Shut up!"

Her voice shook with anger and pain. Her body fairly vibrated beneath his hands. He'd finally pushed her too far, though he wasn't sure how.

"Magic isn't real."

"Oh, that's right. How could I forget? No Santa, no bunny, no damn tooth fairy." He let her go, mad now himself. "You're wrong, and I'm not going to let you raise my son to doubt magic. To doubt all the beauty there is in being a child. He's a kid. He deserves make-believe. Hell, I deserve it, and you could certainly use some."

"Grow up, J.J."

"If being grown up means losing sight of what shines in this world, everything that's a mystery, a maybe or a might, I'll pass. We *made* Max. You and I. Don't tell me that wasn't magic, because I refuse to believe you."

"And I refuse to let you see my son. If you love him as you say, you'll leave him alone. If you ever cared for me at all, you'll go away."

Garrett frowned. "No."

Her lip trembled, so he stepped forward, hand outstretched, but she flinched from his touch and fled down the steps. "Don't take this into court, J.J. Savannah might be bigger than most small towns, but at heart it's smaller than small. Bring this out and you'll only hurt Max."

She turned away, just as his father always had when he'd expected J.J. to fall into line without question. Annoyance rose sharp and bitter. "Don't call me J.J.," he said to her back.

She didn't even turn around. "Don't call me at all."

Garrett watched Livy march away. Everything about her confused him. He'd once known her intimately, understood her completely. With Livy he'd never felt lacking. At least, until she'd told him she loved him and he'd been unable to say the same.

Back then he'd believed he could not love. Love was for other men. Men who knew how to love back.

But from the moment he'd seen his son, Garrett had known there was something special about Max. There'd been an instant connection, a recognition deeper than he'd ever felt before—perhaps that magic both he and Max believed in so deeply.

In Garrett's life, in his work, he'd come to the conclusion that magic was something that happened when you were looking the other way. No explanation, no rules, you couldn't *make* it be.

Magic just was.

So even if Garrett failed, and he probably would, he had to take a chance; he had to find out.

Because maybe love was like that, too.

LIVY'S EYES BURNED, but she blinked fast and hard, refusing to let any tears fall. She'd learned long ago that tears did no one any good. Not that she still didn't indulge on occasion, usually courtesy of Max. But

right now she felt like a good crying jag, courtesy of
J.J.

"Oh, pardon me," she snarled. "Garrett."

Maybe if she refused to think of him as J.J., the
boy she'd loved, but only Garrett, the man he'd become, she would no longer feel so raw.

How could he possibly still have the power to hurt
her? She'd gotten over him years ago, become ad-
justed to the fact that she'd never see him again—
except in the eyes of their son. So why did she want
to sit down on one of the crumbling front steps of the
nearest old house and sob?

The prince had not taken the princess to his castle
and given her her every heart's desire. The knight had
not rescued the damsel in severe distress. The lover
had never loved her.

She rubbed at her eyes. One look at the man and
she was nineteen again. Her heart brimming with first
love, her mind full of him, her body on the edge of
womanhood, waiting for J.J. to make every dream
come true. And he had. For a little while.

Livy blocked out the lingering hum of awareness.
He was handsome. He was tall, dark and strong. He
was also the father of her child. She couldn't be in-
different. But she could be an adult. Adults controlled
themselves. They did not leap into bed with every
person who aroused them.

She and Garrett had been kids. Then she'd had to
grow up. Garrett still hadn't. To him, Max was a
bright, shiny new toy, and he wanted one. But what
happened when he grew bored with Max, as he'd
grown bored with her?

Livy knew all too well, and she'd do whatever she had to do to make certain her son wasn't left devastated when Garrett Stark blew town.

She glanced at her watch. Rosie had a meeting at ghost walk headquarters and would not be home to meet Max after school. If Livy hustled, she could be.

She stepped up her pace, so that when the whirlwind of legs and big feet came around the corner and plowed into her stomach she had to windmill her arms to keep from falling.

Max landed on his butt in someone's front yard. Livy hurried to him. "Oh, baby, I'm sorry."

She leaned down to help just as Max threw his arm up for balance. He caught her in the nose with his cast so hard Livy saw tiny floating black spots. At least she had an excuse for her eyes to be bright with tears.

"Mom! What are you doin' here?"

Holding her nose, waiting for the blood to begin flowing, Livy could still give Max The Look. She'd had so much practice. "What are *you* doing here, young man?"

He ignored the question he didn't want to answer, just as guilty parties always did. "I'm sorry I hit you in the nose again, Mom. I never try to. Stuff like that just happens around me."

"I know." She ruffled his hair. "But that doesn't make it hurt any less."

He squinted, sheepish. "It's not gushin' this time."

"Well, that's something." She pinched the bridge, pleased to find it still straight though sore, then she gazed down at Max and sighed.

He didn't need to answer her question. She had an idea what Max was doing here. The same thing she'd been doing, and she would put a stop to it immediately. Before Max decided Garrett Stark would make a pretty good best friend.

Livy traced a finger along the bumpy surface of his cast. "We have to talk, Max."

"Sure." He grinned. "See how crowded my cast is? I got all the doctors and nurses to sign, then at school everyone wanted to. It was so cool, Mom. No one else has a cast."

Livy shrugged off the guilt his comment engendered. She wasn't the worst mother in town just because her child wore the only cast in school. Intellectually, she knew that. But in her heart? Not so much.

Oblivious to Livy's angst, Max started to walk toward the big white house down the street. Livy caught at his arm and got nothing but cast. Touching that thing was like stroking a gravestone. Livy shivered. "Let's go home, Max."

His face scrunched in confusion. "But...but...I wanted to visit Mr. Stark."

"I figured that out, since you're once again where you're not supposed to be when you're not supposed to be there. Didn't I ground you?"

He hung his head and kicked a stone off the sidewalk. "I wasn't gonna be long."

"Oh, that makes all the difference."

At her sarcasm he glanced up with a scowl. In the way of children, he stuck a knife in her weak spot. "Usually I'm home a while before you get there on

Wednesdays, anyway." Then he twisted it a bit. "It's not like you're there waiting for me."

Guilt, guilt, guilt, pulsed in Livy's head. She did her best, but she always seemed to come up a few hours short. "If no one's home, you're supposed to go to Mrs. Hammond's. How many times have we discussed this?"

Obviously not enough, Livy added to herself.

"But, *Mom,* Jenny always wants to play house." He gave an exaggerated shudder. "And I have to be the husband. She's always saying she loves me, and when she does that I just want to run away as fast as I can."

Like father, like son.

She really had to stop thinking that way or she'd let something slip. Taking hold of Max's unfettered hand, she tugged him in the direction of home. He held back, and with a sigh that only sounded a little exasperated, Livy halted. Max stared at her from eyes so like his father's she had to stop herself from looking away. "What is it, Max?"

"He's a *writer,*" he said, as if that explained everything. "For a job."

As fascinating as a dead bird is to most boys, being a writer must be to Max. Ever since he'd been old enough to hold a crayon, he'd drawn anything that came into his head, and once he could write words, he wrote stories that were far too advanced for a boy his age, causing both pride and concern to war within Livy whenever she read one.

"He's a writer, but he's also a stranger. What have I told you about strangers?"

"But—"

"*What* have I told you?"

He sighed and recited the creed. "They might look nice and talk nice, but that's their job. They could grab you and take you and you'll be gone forevermore."

"And?"

"Then I'll wish I'd listened to my mom."

Livy hated scaring him, but truth was truth. The world was so screwed up. "I want you to stay away from Garrett Stark."

"But—"

"No buts. That's final."

She took his hand, expecting the grudging acquiescence she always got when she put her foot down. Instead, Max yanked away and backed out of Livy's reach. "He's *not* a stranger. If he was gonna take me away, he'd have done it when I snuck in his house."

"You what?" Livy shouted.

A soft gasp made her look up, to find the two little old ladies Garrett had frightened earlier strolling toward them. Max scuttled behind her as Livy stifled a groan.

The Kendall twins—Miss Violet and Miss Viola— had been her granny's best friends. Savannah purebreds and southern gentlewomen, they often tried to get Livy to cease her unladylike lawyering and settle down.

"Olivia Frasier, your grandmama would be horrified to hear you shouting like a fishwife in public."

Miss Violet's genteel voice matched her peach afternoon dress as well as her winter-white shoes matched her hat and her gloves. The summer-white accoutrements had been neatly packed away after the Georgia-Florida football game, no doubt; just as any lady in southern Georgia knew it was inappropriate to wear panty hose until that age-old rivalry had been played out for the season.

"Or shouting anywhere at all, for that matter," Miss Viola continued. Her dress was autumn orange, the accents a perfect taupe. The sisters were identical in face, body and voice. The only way to tell them apart was by the shade of their hair. Miss Violet's was black streaked with gray, while Miss Viola's was gray streaked with black.

"I'm sorry," Livy said. "But there are times when shouting is needed."

"Oh, no, dear, a lady knows how to make folks listen by the tone and not the volume of her voice. It's the courtroom that's ruining you. Our father, the judge, always shouted."

Their father, the judge, had been as deaf as a sixty-year-old rock star. The courtroom had nothing to do with it.

Violet raised her perfectly powdered, white-as-a-daisy-petal, never-been-in-the-sunshine nose. "We just refused to listen when he did. Right, Sister?"

"Hmm?" Viola frowned in the direction of Garrett's house. Livy glanced that way, too, and discovered he watched them from the porch. She cursed beneath her breath.

"Olivia! Such language."

The sisters might be old, but *they* had ears like Irish setters.

Max snickered. He'd come out of hiding and now stood at Livy's side. Max loved it when the sisters took her to task, because that meant they weren't picking on him. Two elderly ladies who'd never been married had no idea what to do with a rambunctious little boy, except tell him to sit still—which for Max was a behavior straight from the realm of impossibility.

Violet glanced at Max and he sobered instantly. She patted him on the head and went back to ignoring him. Max nearly crumpled in relief.

"There's something about that man..." Viola murmured, still staring at Garrett.

"Really?" Violet removed her Coke-bottle glasses, which she never wore unless she absolutely had to, from her winter-white purse, and peered down the street. "He needs a haircut."

"No..."

"He most certainly does, Sister. A disgrace. He looks like one of those guitar players on MTV."

Livy and Max glanced at each other. *MTV?*

"I've seen him before."

Livy almost cursed again but managed to contain herself. Though her granny had been senile at the end and unable to remember J.J. from one day to the next, the sisters remembered the name of their first-grade teacher—and pretty much everything that had ever happened in their considerable lifetimes. Livy didn't think they'd ever seen her and J.J. together, but she couldn't be sure.

"He's a horror writer," Max put in helpfully.

The sisters eyed him as if he were a bug, and Max began to fidget. "A what?"

"He writes books about vampires. But don't worry." Max motioned for them to come closer, then whispered, "He isn't one."

The sisters straightened, glanced at each other, then back at the old white house.

"Hmm." Viola pushed the brim of her hat up a tad. "A writer. Must be why he looks familiar." Livy let out a silent sigh of relief. "And that would explain why he's living in the Alexander place."

"Why?" Max asked.

"It's haunted, child."

"It is not!" Livy exclaimed.

"Don't contradict me, Olivia. Of course it's haunted. All the best houses in Savannah are."

"Is yours?" Max piped up.

"Certainly. The judge stops by every afternoon at three for tea."

Livy resisted the urge to voice her disbelief. The sisters could still box her ears if they were of a mind. But if they were holding regular conversations with their dead daddy, maybe she didn't need to worry that one of them would connect Garrett to J.J. anytime soon. *Maybe.*

As Miss Violet had said, all the good houses were haunted, and all the true Savannahians believed in ghosts. Perhaps that was why Livy had never truly fit in here, even though she'd wanted to.

"Since Daddy started drifting about, have you noticed the former owner doesn't?" Miss Viola asked.

"Of course not, Sister. The judge loathed that man.

Said he was no better than a common horse thief. Why, when Daddy bought the house he was never even told about the ghosts it already had, or that the building had been built right on top of a former cemetery.''

"Well, it's hard not to hit a burial place around here. The way they used to just bury people willy-nilly wherever they pleased. Look at that Jewish cemetery right in the middle of the road.''

"Ahem.'' Livy cleared her throat, hesitated, then couldn't help herself. "They built the road through the cemetery. Not the other way around.''

"Whatever, dear. The point is, Mama got no sleep at all some nights, what with the slamming and scratching and whispering. She finally buried a Bible in the backyard. Oh, Daddy had a fit about that, I'll tell you. Putting a perfectly good King James into the ground. But when the commotion stopped, Mama just smiled and Daddy shut up.''

Miss Violet nodded. "Which proves our point, Olivia. There's no need for a woman to shout or curse. If you're right, you're right, and we so often are. Everything comes out in the end.''

"That's what I'm afraid of,'' Livy muttered. "We'd better get going.''

She'd like to retreat before the sisters got on a roll again. It was so hard to extricate oneself when they were. Unfortunately Max had other ideas.

"So whose ghost lives at Mr. Stark's?''

Livy cast a sharp glance at her son. He stared at Garrett's house with as much awe as he'd said Garrett's name. Strangely enough, Max had never been frightened of ghosts, probably because Rosie spoke of them at breakfast, lunch and dinner as though they were just another friend or relative—a habit most folks who lived in Savannah for very long got into.

Miss Violet squinted at the house once more. "I'm not certain who haunts the Alexander place."

"Maybe an Alexander," Livy said dryly.

Miss Violet gave her a sharp look. Livy tried to appear innocent, but that was more difficult than it seemed when you were guilty. How come so many of her clients had no trouble with it?

Was everyone crazy around here?

Miss Violet tilted her head so she could focus her entire attention on Max. Her huge hat wobbled but didn't fall down. "Hasn't your grandmother told you all the ghost stories? If Rosie insists on being in trade, you'd at least think she'd be good at it."

For the sisters, being a guide was a trade. Of course, being a lawyer was a sin. Unless you were a judge. Somehow that was okay.

"Rosie's the best ghost-walk guide in town." Max defended his favorite person in the world with alacrity.

"I wouldn't know, but I have heard she does her business well."

Miss Violet said "business" with a little tilt to her mouth and twist to her voice that made Livy remember the way the judge had always said "lady of the night." The sisters had never much cared for Rosie. In their eyes, she'd married beneath her—a Yankee carpetbagger, no less.

No matter how many times the two had been told

that Rosie's husband was a *carpenter,* not a *carpet-bagger,* they didn't get it, or perhaps they chose not to. Just as no matter how many times folks reminded them the war was over—a war they hadn't even been alive to see fought—they could still sneer *Yankee* better than Vivien Leigh.

To make matters worse, Rosie had also committed the unpardonable sin of leaving her mother to live alone in her old age. That just wasn't *done* here.

"Rosie would have done better to stay home with her mama than traipse across the country like a hippie."

To Miss Violet, any woman who wore her hair long and didn't do heels was a hippie.

"But then, Rosie was always different."

Miss Viola could put more connotations on the word *different* than Miss Violet could to the word *business.*

Max's eyes narrowed and his mouth tightened. Sometimes he was a little too astute for his own good.

"How's your pet goose?" he asked.

Livy resisted the urge to groan. There'd be no getting away for a while now. The sisters' goose had been a bone of contention between them and Rosie since the day they'd brought it home. According to Rosie, a wild animal should not be a pet, and the twins were exploiting the goose for their own nefarious purposes.

"It's not a pet," Miss Viola snapped.

"More of a decoration, maybe a tourist attraction," Miss Violet clarified. "When Daddy started dropping in for tea, the former owner wasn't the only one who stopped coming around. Our ghost goose went away."

"Daddy never liked that goose, even when he was alive." Miss Viola wrinkled her nose. "Daddy, not the goose."

"That's probably why the goose went away. The judge can be difficult, even though he's dead. So we got a very special, very live goose to make up for the loss of the ghostly one."

"I don't remember hearing about a ghost goose at your house," Livy pointed out.

"The goose was one of the ghosts that horse thief who sold Daddy the house never even mentioned. And it didn't leave when Mama buried the King James." Miss Viola frowned in concentration. "Maybe because geese aren't familiar with the Bible."

"What does this goose do that makes it so special?" Livy had often wondered.

"Stays in the yard and doesn't fly away."

"Well now, Sister," Viola pointed out, "our goose *can't* fly."

"Did you have its wings clipped?" Livy couldn't keep the censure out of her voice. Perhaps Rosie was right about the goose, after all.

"Of course not!" Viola looked insulted. "The poor thing had an accident as a gosling. That's how it ended up being trained in the first place. Our goose would have died in the wild. It's better off here, regardless of what *Rosie* says about exploitation for monetary gain."

Livy sighed. That sounded like Rosie.

"Rosie says you made the whole thing up to get on the ghost-walk tour," Max offered.

The sisters' mouths pruned and their eyes narrowed. Together they turned toward Max.

Livy grabbed his hand. "Gotta go. Nice chatting with y'all."

This time she didn't have to drag Max. He went willingly. Around the corner at any rate. There he stopped dead.

"Old hens."

"Keep a respectful tongue for your elders."

"Why? They don't have a respectful tongue for Rosie."

Livy wasn't sure what to say to that. It always seemed as if she was telling him to behave in one way while the rest of the world behaved in another.

Do unto others. Everyone did—though not in the way the Golden Rule intended.

If you can't say anything nice, don't say anything. The sisters had just ruined that one.

Don't get arrested. Max's grandma visited jail every other week.

Don't cheat, don't lie, don't swear. Livy wasn't even going to think about how many times each day he saw those rules broken.

Did all parents have the same problem? Was anyone else trying to raise decent human beings in an indecent world? Or were they all scrambling to get along the best they could and hoping things would work out fine in the end? Some days Livy did that, too.

"Just do what I say," Livy told Max wearily. "Not

what everyone else does. If someone jumped off a cliff, would you do it, too?''

''You always say that.''

''I always wonder. Let's get out of here before they follow us.''

Max glanced over his shoulder with wide eyes. He appeared more concerned about the sisters than the ghosts.

Livy couldn't blame him.

CHAPTER SIX

ROSIE CAME HOME to an empty house, an uncommon occurrence at 7:00 p.m. Max couldn't *still* be at the neighbor's. Sometimes Livy was late, but she never forgot.

Frowning, Rosie walked through the front hall and glanced into the parlor. No blinking red light signaled a message on the answering machine. Rosie let out a long breath of relief. If Max was in the E.R.—again—someone would have called.

Even when Max's mishaps had Rosie's blood pressure on the rise and her heart palpitating like the wings of a frightened bird trapped within her chest, she kept a cool head for her daughter's sake. Livy could blow a gasket quicker than anyone Rosie had ever seen, and after traumas both Max and Livy needed a sane voice in their world. How Rosie's husband would laugh to hear that these days Rosie was the sane voice.

She sat down on the love seat without bothering to turn on a light, and let the serene darkness soothe her senses. "Ah, Henry, I miss you more every day. I thought it would get easier as time went by, but it hasn't."

Rosie teased Livy that her daddy was up and walking, but in truth, he was gone and at peace. Because if Henry was going to appear to anyone, it would be Rosie, and while she talked to Henry every day, he never talked back. But she felt better for the talking, and that was what counted.

The house creaked and settled around her, a comforting sound, old and familiar. She'd once loathed this house and all that it stood for. With age came truth, if not wisdom.

It had not been the house, or even her parents, that had made her unhappy. Rosie had needed something more than a solid home and a good family could give. She'd found that something in Henry Frasier. Passionate love, pure freedom, the adventure of open skies, open road, open life. The possibilities had astounded her.

She had never been so happy as when she was with that man. The reality of their daughter had almost been an intrusion—for Rosie, anyway. Not that she hadn't loved her child. She had, still did. But Henry had taken one look at Livy and fallen in love. From that moment on, Rosie had been the outsider in her own family.

Most women would be thrilled with a husband who changed diapers, walked the baby at night, did practically everything but feed the child, and Henry even did that once Livy refused the breast at the age of five months—another mother failure on Rosie's mother failure scorecard. Rosie hadn't been complaining. She'd just been…left out.

She'd never wanted to go to college, never been interested in a career. Sure, she'd wanted to want something, and once Henry came to town, she'd wanted him. Then she'd had dreams of being the perfect mother to a brood of children. But she'd only had one, and that one had not wanted to be mothered at all.

Silly to be jealous of your daughter's relationship with her father, but there it was. Livy and Henry had been two of a kind, twins of the soul, and although he'd always loved Rosie—and she'd known it—what he felt for Livy was deeper than love, a kind of connection that went beyond anything Rosie could fathom. And she'd resented it.

So she could understand why Livy stared at her with resentment whenever Rosie and Max shared a joke and a giggle, or just a look without a word. Because Max and Rosie were connected at the soul, too.

Once, Livy had been as full of life as Henry. When he'd died, a good slice of Rosie did, too. But a bigger part of Livy died, and Rosie wasn't sure what to do about that.

When she'd returned to Savannah for good, she'd found her child with a child of her own. Rosie had never questioned Livy's assertion that the baby's father was dead. The sadness in her daughter's eyes, the stiffness of her body, the way she devoted heart and soul to her son—all had made Rosie believe something terrible had happened beyond the loss of Livy's own father.

Rosie had wanted to be a different kind of mother from her own, a woman who had kept a tight rein on a girl who needed freedom and questioned Rosie about everything as if she didn't trust her at all. Rosie hadn't wanted that for Livy, so she'd kept her questions to herself.

She had hoped that by staying in Savannah, in making the three of them a new family, she might forge the relationship she'd always wanted to have with her daughter. But things hadn't worked out as Rosie had hoped.

"Our little girl could sure use you around, Henry. We both could. Sometimes I feel so lost, so adrift and confused—"

"Hey, Rosie, I'm back."

The whisper right behind her head should have made Rosie shriek. At the very least, it should have taken her a minute to figure out who had come calling her name.

But Rosie would know the voice of her darling anywhere. She reached up, yanked him over the back of the love seat and into her lap. Max lay there giggling, so she leaned down and gave him a loud raspberry on his neck, which only made him laugh harder. His flailing cast nearly caught her in the chin, so she gently pinned it down, then tickled him a while.

When Rosie was with Max that lost feeling fled, because at last she'd found her vocation. Despite her aversion to the title, Rosie Cannaught Frasier had been born to be a grandma.

MAX AND ROSIE TUSSLED on the couch, laughing and whispering and rolling about like puppies in the sun. The tug to join them was deep and strong, yet Livy wasn't quite sure how to go about it.

The ease that Rosie and Max had together was beyond Livy. No matter how much she might want to fit in with them, make the two a three, she couldn't—and she knew it.

"Who were you talkin' to, Rosie?"

"Only Grampa, sugar. You wanna say hi?"

Livy snapped on the overhead lights, making Rosie cringe like a vampire who'd been thrown into the sun. "Mama, don't encourage him. He'll never sleep."

Max rolled his eyes. Rosie looked as though she was having a hard time not joining him. Sometimes Livy felt that she had two children instead of one. Especially when she had to constantly bail the elder out of jail—something that hadn't happened in quite a while. Knowing Rosie, this only meant she was planning something exceptionally rare for her next stunt.

"Where were you two?" Rosie asked. "I was getting worried."

Livy made a face. Rosie never worried. That was why Livy did it so well.

"Mom took me to McDonald's." Max knew better than to mention Rosie's archenemies, the Kendell twins, or their poor exploited goose.

Rosie peered at Max, eyes narrowed as she searched for a more recent injury than yesterday's. Usually McDonald's was reserved for trips home from the hospital. Mainly because Livy got as much comfort from a Big Mac as Max did. At this rate, her hips would be the size of Atlanta by next year.

When Rosie's search for new gashes or gaps came up empty, she glanced at Livy. "What happened?"

Livy gave Max a pointed look. He hung his head.

"I wasn't where I was supposed to be when I was supposed to be there."

"Big whoop," Rosie said. Max snorted.

"Mama!" Livy shouted, a touch of hysteria in her voice. Both Rosie and Max stared at her, shocked at the outburst. For a woman who prided herself on control—in all situations but emergency rooms—Livy was having a very hard time keeping herself under control lately. And only she knew why.

Livy closed her eyes, took a deep breath, started the inevitable count to ten and beyond, and the phone shrilled, making her gasp out loud. She opened her eyes and gestured up the stairs. Max went, dragging his feet.

When Rosie made a move to answer the phone, Livy snapped, "Let the machine pick up."

Rosie sat back on the love seat, folded her arms and gave Livy a look that was almost like a mother's.

Kim's voice came out of the machine. "Livy, where in hell are you? What were you thinking to run off like that? You turned off your cell phone again. And you missed an appointment." The sigh that filled the room was long and full of concern. "You'd better call me. Tonight."

Click.

"Sugar, you need to stop grinding your teeth like that or you'll have nothin' left to chew with."

Livy hadn't realized she was grinding. She usually didn't—except when the sound woke her up at night. She sat opposite her mother in a chair on the other side of the knee-high, cherry wood coffee table.

"So where *was* Max?" Rosie plopped her bare feet onto the table.

"Not here."

"I got that. Was he off with Sammy again? Boys will be boys, you know. He needs to run and jump and get a little dirty."

"So I hear."

"And he could use a man in his life."

Livy scowled. Was everyone conspiring against her? "Why don't *you* bring one home for him?"

"A man? Me?" Rosie laughed. "That's not going to happen, sugar."

"Why not? Daddy's been gone a long time. And no matter what you might say, he isn't coming back."

"I know." Rosie shook her head as if Livy confounded her as much as she confounded Livy. "I just like to tease you."

"Tease?"

Rosie shrugged, a bit sheepish. "You make it so easy."

"Well, stop it. I've got enough trouble."

"What kind of trouble? Kim sounded fit to be tied, and that isn't like her."

Livy hesitated. She'd never told her mother about J.J. And her mother had never asked. She'd come home, fallen for Max, settled in, and never once inquired about the baby's father. At the time, Livy had been grateful. She still was.

But if Rosie truly cared about her, wouldn't she have demanded the answers?

Regardless, what good would confiding in her do now?

Livy stood. "I'll take care of it."

"I'm sure you will. Taking care of trouble is what you do best. Sometimes, though, don't you need a shoulder? I've got two."

A memory flitted across Livy's mind of a day long ago and a farmer's field full of people. The summer sun was hot; the breeze cool on her face beneath a big shady tree. Daddy had gone to play volleyball and left her behind. She'd cried on Mama's shoulder, then laid her head in Mama's lap. The flicker of the sun through the leaves danced across her face. With music on the wind, and the taste of Kool-Aid on her tongue, she fell asleep with her mama's fingers stroking her hair. On that day, all had been right in Livy's world.

She had been happy then, but the life she'd led had not prepared her for the way the world was. Her mother had thrown her to the wolves when Livy had needed her the most. Livy had learned that soft memories were merely that—memories of a way of life that didn't exist past childhood.

"Livy?"

Rosie's voice made her shake off the soft memory, along with her hard thoughts.

"I'd better check on Max." Livy started for the stairs.

Her mother's next words stopped her. "People always used to say to me, 'I've never seen a man love a child as much as Henry loves his.'"

Livy winced. "Mama—"

"'If anything happens to her, you'd best dig a grave right next to hers for him.'" Rosie's dark-blue eyes, which were so like Livy's own, held an unaccustomed sadness in their depths. "And they were right. But I'd never have imagined I should dig a grave for you next to his."

"Mama, really."

Rosie ignored her, as Rosie had a habit of doing. "When I came back here you were different. Once there was a light in you that rivaled your father's, and that was saying something. Then it was gone—" She snapped her fingers. "Like a candle snuffed out in a high wind."

"You expected me to be laughing after I lost my father, my grandmother, and was left alone with a baby at nineteen?"

"I didn't say that. Three deaths so close together would be hard on anyone. I told myself you'd get better. You just needed time. But you've had enough time, and you've only gotten worse."

Livy ignored the voice that pointed out she'd been living the lie of J.J.'s death so long she barely felt a twinge when it was brought up. Funny how easily lies could become the truth. And then blow up in your face.

"I know you've never approved of me, Mama, of what I do—"

"That's not what I'm talking about and you know it."

Livy gave an exasperated sigh. "Then what *are* you talking about?"

"I want you to enjoy life. Quit wallowing in the dregs. Quit seeing all the bad things."

"That's my job."

"You can do your job without living it. Without

bringing it home. The world is a great big beautiful playground. Explore it. Experience it. Imagine more—don't settle for less.''

"Be all that I can be? I'm too old for the Marines.''

"You know, if you'd been this sarcastic as a child I'd have smacked you.''

"No, you wouldn't have.''

"Maybe I should now.''

"Too late. Your time for mothering me is past.''

"A mother's time is never past. My mistake was letting you be so long.''

"I don't need this, Mama.''

"And you don't need me. You've made that quite clear. But Max does. If you can't enjoy life, you should at least let Max enjoy his. And if you don't know how, I do.''

Livy had had a busy day. She should go upstairs and let this go. Instead, she lost control yet again.

"You call talking to dead people and telling stories about ghosts 'living'? You think encouraging Max to dream impossible dreams so that he'll end up crushed when he finds out that dreams rarely come true 'good parenting'?''

Rosie stood, the love seat between the two of them. "Who says dreams don't come true? You've got to believe in something, or what's the good of going on?''

"What do you believe in?''

"That someday I'll see Henry again.''

"Floating through the dining room?''

"I don't care, as long as I see him. I believe we'll be together forever someday. I believe that life is full of gifts, and you should take them wherever you find them. Hold on to them tight. Max is a gift I never thought to have, and I'm not going to let you stomp all over his dreams with your combat boots, sir.'' Rosie flicked her a snotty salute.

''Dreams, magic, love, hope. I gave up on fairy tales a long time ago. Isn't it better to know the truth, even if it's hard, even if that makes life less of a jolly romp through time, than to have the truth hit you over the head when you aren't looking? It can destroy you.''

Rosie stared so long that Livy wanted to squirm. Livy had lost her temper and let too much fly free. Rosie might act flaky, but she wasn't. Especially when it came to emotions.

''Is that what happened to you, Livy? Did the bad old truth sideswipe you when you least expected it? Is that why you don't believe in anything anymore? Is that why you refuse to need anyone?''

''I believe in Max. He's all I need.''

Livy walked out of the room, but Rosie's parting shot followed her up the steps.

''Why don't I believe that?''

MAX LAY ON HIS BED and listened to his mom and Rosie argue. He couldn't hear what they were saying, but he'd heard them arguin' enough to know what it sounded like.

The arguments scared him, though Rosie said people argued and that it didn't mean they loved each other any less.

But Sammy's parents had argued a lot and they'd

gotten divorced. Then Sammy's daddy had moved to California, changed his name to Moon Doggie like that guy in the movies Rosie liked, and started surfing for a living. Sammy didn't hear from him anymore, and judging by the names Mrs. Sontag called Mr.— everything *but* Moon Doggie—there wasn't much love left after the arguing.

What would he do if Rosie left? Or what if his mom decided to change her name to Gidget and live in a hut. Max giggled. As if.

He stopped giggling when he heard her footsteps on the stairs. She would come up and punish him now—for his own good. At this rate, he'd be the best boy in four counties.

She stood in the doorway, and he turned on his side, surprised by the odd expression on her face. She looked scared, and he hadn't broken a thing all day.

He sat up. "Mom? You okay?"

"Sure." Her gaze touched his cast, then skipped away.

"You gonna ground me some more?"

"Maybe tomorrow. I've had all the fun I can stand for one day."

Max smiled. Sometimes his mom was almost as funny as Rosie. Usually when she was tired and couldn't seem to help herself.

"You *are* grounded, Max. That means no running around after school. You're to come directly home. Do not pass go. Do not collect two hundred dollars. Got it?"

"I think I know what grounded means by now."

"I'd have thought so, too. You can imagine my

surprise to find you on your way to the Alexander place today.''

''Why were *you* there, Mom?''

She blinked and her face blanched. ''There? Where?''

His mom always repeated questions when she was trying to buy time and think of an answer. Max figured it was a lawyer trick, and he wondered why the judges put up with it.

Max didn't answer her silly questions, just waited patiently for her to spill the truth she liked so much. He shouldn't complain. Other kids' parents lied to them all the time, which made it hard for kids to believe anything they were told by anyone. But Max's mom always laid out the truth, no matter how little he might want to hear it.

Whenever there was a question she didn't want to answer or a truth she wouldn't tell, instead of lying, she ran. And that only happened if he asked questions about his father.

''Time for bed,'' she announced. ''I'll be back in five minutes to tuck you in.''

Until now. Max was so busy puzzling over the strange and sudden change that he didn't realize his mom still stood in the doorway until she said his name.

''Max?''

''Hmm?'' He looked up in time to catch that scared expression again, which bothered him. Moms weren't supposed to be scared of anything—except their babies fallin' and breakin' their necks.

''You're lucky Mr. Stark didn't call the police instead of bringing you home when you broke into his house.''

"I didn't break anything. Except this—'' He held up his cast. "The door was open.''

"You knew it was wrong, didn't you? Just walking into a stranger's house as if it were yours?''

"I figured he was undead. The rules are different then.''

"Why...?'' She shook her head. "Never mind, I really don't want to know why. Just don't go there again. Understand?''

She left the room without waiting for his answer. Which was good, because he wasn't going to give her one. If she could ignore questions, then so could he.

Max wasn't sure why, but he had to see Garrett Stark again. Even if he did end up grounded for life.

CHAPTER SEVEN

AGAIN TURNED OUT to be the next day. Usually school sucked and Max hated it. But after breaking his arm he'd been a hero with his tales of time in the cemetery followed by a trip to X ray.

Just showed how much difference a day could make. One day a hero and the next he was back to being weird Max, the wussy, or any one of a hundred other names. Kids were mean, and some were meaner than others.

Someday he'd be bigger and stronger and smarter than all of them, and then they'd be sorry. Unfortunately, not today.

Even his teacher spoke sharply to him. "Max, quit wool-gathering. I'm over here!" Which caused all the kids to snicker. Max gathered a whole lot of wool. It wasn't that he didn't understand what was going on in class. It was just that what was going on in his head was a whole lot better.

When lunch recess came and Sammy, his best and only friend, snapped, "The only reason you got that cast anyway is 'cause you're such a spasmoid," Max decided he needed school as much as he needed bigger feet.

He walked off the playground when no one was looking and went to make a new best friend.

THE UN-BOOK was better than ever. After Garrett perused his single page, he lit a ceremonial fire, and as it burned he contemplated dancing around the ashtray. If he thought dancing would help, he'd do it. But not even the usual rituals worked these days, so why start a new one?

The only thing that did help was Max, and Garrett figured he had as much chance of seeing his son as he had of finishing the book on time.

But he left the back door open anyway, just in case. After all, the kid seemed to have a knack for turning up exactly where he wasn't supposed to be.

Garrett wandered into the dining room. He'd planned to burn the coffin, or at the very least haul it outside and chop the thing into firewood. But when he put his hands on the wood, he suddenly had the first good idea he'd had in days.

A tablecloth and a vase would make Andrew's joke into Garrett's. He still needed to figure out suitable retaliation for this "gift," but pretending the coffin was a table would be fun. Andrew was so single-minded, he probably wouldn't get it, which would only make things funnier for Garrett.

As if on cue, the phone rang. Sometimes Andrew could be downright spooky, and he didn't even try.

The phone had been ringing on the hour since 8:00 a.m. that morning. His agent was getting nervous. Garrett had no doubt that sooner rather than later he'd have a houseguest he didn't want. What better way to greet Andrew than with a coffee table that doubled as an eternal resting place? Garrett was going to need the latter as soon as Andrew found out the truth, anyway.

He started laughing, and then he couldn't stop. Hysteria did that to a fellow. Maybe if he hid inside the coffin, Andrew would never find him.

Garrett stopped laughing and swiped at his eyes. That wasn't a half-bad thought. Not the hiding, but the getting inside.

New places and new experiences often gave him new ideas. If lying in a coffin wasn't a new place and a new experience, he didn't know what was. Garrett ought to get a doozy of an idea out of this.

Slowly he approached the wooden box, more captivated by his crazy concept with every tick of the clock. What *would* it feel like to lie inside?

Intense curiosity filled him. Garrett hadn't felt such a sweeping need to know in quite a while—that blessed niggling of nosiness that kept him writing hour after hour, day after day, until he uncovered all there was to know in the dark depths of a story and laid the secrets out for everyone, including himself, to examine.

"Well, hell, now I've got to do it," he said as he opened the lid and climbed in.

The coffin had been built for a corpse of years past—when men didn't top six feet. Garrett's knees kept the lid from closing completely.

"Not quite my size, Andrew. So sorry, old chum."

The laughter bubbled up again, but he squelched it. He wanted to absorb the experience. Somehow, someday, in some future book, he'd need to know what being in a coffin felt like, and he might never get another chance to lie in one if he didn't do it now.

"Smells like wet wood," he muttered. His knuckles scraped the side, and he hissed as splinters threatened. "Scratchy. Unfinished." Shifting against the pain in his spine, he winced. "And hard. Could sure use a pillow if not a mattress. Not very restful, but the usual occupant wouldn't notice. If I could get the lid closed, would there be any light in here?"

Garrett twisted and turned until his knees scrunched in sideways. The lid thumped shut. Something clicked. "Oh-oh."

He pushed on the lid. He was stuck, all right. The sound of his heart filled the small area. Was the space actually getting smaller? Or was he getting bigger? Now he *was* hysterical. And hot, cramped, hungry and... He admitted it—scared.

He put some muscle behind his next push. The top jiggled but held. He slammed his palms against the top again and again. Regardless, the coffin remained firmly shut.

"They sure don't build 'em like this anymore." His voice sounded normal, and that calmed him a bit. Too bad the latch was built better than the body. Sunlight streamed through tiny cracks at the corners.

"If I were undead, I'd be dead."

Garrett snorted, then quickly stifled the urge to laugh. He had to squelch it or he might never stop. He also had to stop panicking or he might do something crazy. Make that *crazier*. For a person trapped inside a coffin, any loss of control would be very bad. He needed to *think,* not snicker.

If he could use his legs, he might be able to bust through the top. Unfortunately, he couldn't because he'd crunched his legs in sideways to fit.

Garrett had gotten out of sticky situations before. A lot of them. As a child he'd always been into, on top of or underneath something. His father had said his infernal curiosity would get him killed one day. Looked like James, Sr., was right again.

Panic threatened once more, but this time Garrett quashed it unmercifully. He needed to stay calm to figure a way out. He'd survived worse than this. Worse than this had made him thrive. Facing fear was what Garrett Stark did best, mainly because the J.J. inside him was afraid of a lot.

He wrote about his nightmares so he could own them, then lived life as if there was nothing of this earth that he feared. A lie, but then, Garrett told lies for a living.

In truth, there was one fear he'd never conquer. His fear of failing at everything that mattered. He'd made a good start at letting that fear own him.

Livy hated the ground he walked on. His son thought he was dead. The career that gave him the only sense of worth he'd ever known was about to crash and burn. And Garrett had just discovered what claustrophobia felt like. Maybe he could use that in a book, too. If he lived.

"Breathe deep. Plenty of air. Just not enough room."

Keep calm. Eventually someone would find him. When the smell reached the street.

Garrett cursed and slammed his hands once more against the lid, as if it would actually work this time. Pain was his reward. He rocked the coffin back and forth a while. To no avail. In the distance, the phone began to ring. Andrew was going to be pissed when Garrett turned up dead.

"I'm not going to be too happy about it, either."

He swiped at the sweat tickling his forehead and only ended up scraping his knuckles along the wood, gaining the slivers he'd merely imagined before.

"Whatcha doin'?"

The voice was close enough to make Garrett start. The nervous sweat turned cold.

"Max?"

"Uh-huh."

Garrett's panic receded. He was no longer alone and in imminent danger of dying. But as the fear ebbed, the embarrassment seeped in. Maybe he should just stay in here and die rather than have his son see him like this.

He'd been hoping Max would show up, but he'd had dreams of them doing fun, father-and-son things, so Max could get to know him, come to like him; then eventually Max would love him. But how could a boy ever respect the father he found stuffed in his dining room coffin?

In the end, Garrett didn't have a choice. The latch clicked and the lid lifted. Max peered down at him, sweet face scrunched like a dried-apple doll.

Garrett sat up so fast Max leaped back. The lid of the coffin hit Garrett in the head.

Max giggled. "Stuff like that happens to me all the time."

Rubbing the bump, Garrett stood. "Me, too."

"Really?" Max's smile faded and he cradled his cast with his good hand. "I kinda thought once I grew up I wouldn't be such a loser."

Anger made the bump on Garrett's head hurt more. He gave Max a sharp look. "Who said you were a loser?"

The boy's shoulders slumped. "Everyone. Nobody likes me."

"A whole bunch of people signed your cast."

Max shrugged. "The kids thought it was neat for one day, and then they didn't." He rubbed his finger across the names. "Mostly nurses and doctors signed. They all love me. Mainly, Mom says, because I keep them in business. But nobody likes me just for me. Except Mom and Rosie, and they kind of have to."

"I like you."

Max tilted his head and peered at Garrett through his bright, white bangs. "You do?"

"What's not to like? You can walk and talk and pee on your own, right?" Max snorted. Garrett had heard bathroom humor worked with young males pretty well. Looked as though he'd heard right. "And you're polite," he continued.

"I came into your house without being invited again. That's rude."

"You saved my life. I'll let it slide."

His eyes went wide. "I did?"

Garrett nodded at the coffin. "I was fooling around and I got locked in."

"That sounds like something I'd do. Why'd *you* do it?"

"I wanted to know what it was like. Inside."

"Why?"

"So I could describe it. For a book." Put that way, what he'd done sounded silly. It so often did, which was why Garrett spent most of his time alone.

But Max didn't stare at him as if Garrett had slipped a gear. Instead, the boy eyed the wooden box warily. "What *was* it like?"

"Not bad. Until I realized I couldn't get out." Which reminded Garrett of something. "Hold on," he said to Max, then slipped into the kitchen.

He returned with a hammer and knocked the offending latch off the coffin. "Why would they put one of those on there, anyway?" he murmured.

Max took a single step toward the box, then stopped and slowly turned just his head to regard Garrett with solemn dark eyes. "To keep the wanderers in?"

"Wanderers?"

"Undead. Zombies. Ghouls. Spirit walkers. That stuff."

Since Max appeared dead serious, Garrett kept a straight face. He could remember when the surreal had seemed very real—a year ago when he'd last been writing a book. How he wished the line of reality would blur that way again soon.

"I doubt a latch would be of any use if that stuff really wanted to get out."

The expression Max turned on him stunned Garrett. A smile of joy, eyes full of adoration—the combination pure hope. What had he done to gain such a reward?

"You're not going to tell me there's no such thing as zombies and the rest?"

Suddenly Garrett understood. The boy had his father's imagination as well as his eyes, and Livy was like James, Sr., more than Garrett would have liked. If he hadn't planned to stick around a while for his son before, he certainly would now.

"Why would I tell you that?"

"Because you're a grown-up? And you've lost your angel eyes."

"My angel eyes?"

"Did you ever see a baby babbling to the wall or the ceiling or the air?"

"I haven't seen many babies."

Thanks to Livy. She might be mad at him for leaving, but he was getting madder by the minute that she hadn't found some way to drag him right back. Irrational, but true.

"I haven't, either. But Rosie says babies can still see the angels 'cause they only left 'em a little bit ago. Once they start talkin' and listenin', they stop seein' the angels. Most babies anyway. Some, like me, still see things that other people don't."

Garrett considered his son. "You get to watch a lot of angels, Max?"

Max considered Garrett. Garrett could almost hear the kid wondering if this grown-up could be trusted with the truth. Garrett held his breath.

"Not a single one."

Interesting. "What do you see?"

"Nothin'."

Garrett frowned. "But you said—"

"Sometimes you don't see with these—" He pointed to his eyes. "You know with this—" His finger tapped his temple.

Slowly Garrett nodded. He knew things there, too, and none of them were real. At least, the way the rest of the world judged truth and lies. Max looked at things the way no one else did. Or maybe the way no one did *anymore.* But maybe the way they should again. If they knew how.

That wispy idea he'd first heard in the graveyard, then lost, now hovered like a mist over the river at dawn—a teasing lilting presence just out of his reach.

"When you go off like that, are you knowin' with this?" Max rapped on his forehead with a knuckle.

Poof, went that wisp of a whisper.

At the sight of his son, Garrett couldn't care less. "Uh-huh."

"That's what I thought. Can you teach me to be like you?"

"We already talked about this, Max. I'm still very much un-undead."

"I know. I mean, can you teach me not to be afraid of stupid stuff that isn't there?"

To Garrett there wasn't anything better to be afraid of than what wasn't there. Like his book.

"How do you know I'm not afraid?"

"Are you?"

He couldn't very well admit to his son that he was

scared of just about everything—love, hate, Max, his mother, the next day, the next page, the rest of his life.

Loser.

Garrett's inner voice was downright nasty sometimes.

"Mr. Stark?"

He shook off the voice and smiled at his son. "You can call me Garrett."

"My mom won't like that."

Max's mom didn't like much these days, which made Garrett wonder. "Is it okay for you to be here?"

"Until four." He waved his cast in dismissal of minor annoyances. "Please tell me how not to be afraid. I've never met anyone who knew what I was talkin' about."

Garrett sighed. He'd spent a lifetime with no one who understood all the strange yet wonderful things that went around in his mind and flowed onto the page. Oh, Andrew loved how Garrett's mind worked, but he didn't understand it, or even care to. As long as Garrett kept doing it.

So how could he deny the entreaty in his son's voice, his son's eyes? He couldn't.

"You say you're afraid of stupid stuff that isn't there?"

"All the time."

"But if you think it's there, then, isn't it?"

"No one else knows about it."

"Maybe *they're* stupid then."

Max's mouth made a little *O* of surprise, and Garrett smiled.

"Don't ever discount the magic of your imagination, Max. It's a gift few people have and fewer appreciate."

"That's what Rosie says."

"I'll have to meet Rosie."

"She'll like you. Especially the hair."

"Your mom didn't like it."

"Mom doesn't like much."

"I noticed."

"Yeah." Max sighed. "Did you ever feel like you were dreamin' even when you knew you were awake?"

Garrett loved it when that happened. Those books just wrote themselves. "That's the best time."

"Not when it's scary stuff."

"Define *scary*."

"I feel things…hoverin' just out of my sight. And if I turn around, they'll be gone. But I'll hear 'em laughing."

Garret knew that feeling, too. He hated when that happened.

"You know why I write books?"

"Because you can?"

"There is that." Although not at the moment. "I learned that to make a fear go away you have to own it."

Max appeared intrigued. "How?"

"By facing it."

"How?"

Garrett had to laugh. The kid never stopped with the questions.

"If you're afraid of spiders, pick one up. The dark? Sit in it for a while—it's not so bad. Coffins bother you—" he winked "—hop on in."

"And things that aren't there, even when they are?"

"Write about them, Max. Conquer them in a book and they go away for good."

"I like to write stories."

Garrett smiled and resisted the urge to run his hand over Max's electric-blond hair. How could they be so much alike when they'd only just met?

"Stories are what I do best." He glanced at his cast. "Next to fallin' down, anyways." Max tilted his head and peered at Garrett, hope coming to life in his eyes. "Does writin' about what scares you *really* work?"

"So far. In a book I'm the god of my own little universe. I can take every nightmare and stomp all over it."

"Like Godzilla and Tokyo."

"The fifty-foot woman and every man she could find."

"King Kong and New York City."

"Exactly. Where do you think all those moviemakers get their ideas?"

Max's smile started in his eyes, then spread all over his face. "From things that no one else sees."

"You're not weird or crazy. And you're not alone, Max."

The boy slipped his hand into Garrett's just as he had the first day. "Not anymore."

CHAPTER EIGHT

"YOU NEVER CALLED ME back last night."

Livy shut the door of her office. "Good morning to you, too."

"It's afternoon," Kim pointed out.

Livy glanced at her watch. "You're right. I didn't realize I'd been in court that long. Lucky me."

Kim leaned back in her chair and crossed her arms. "Are you going to tell me what's going on? Or do I have to guess?"

There was no way Kim was ever going to guess this one, and Livy wasn't telling, either.

"Nothing's going on." She breezed through Kim's office and into her own, put her briefcase on the table and yanked out what she wanted. She didn't need to look up to know that Kim had followed her in. "I had to leave early. People do it all the time."

"You don't. Unless there's a dire emergency. What was it this time? Tripped into the river? Fell off the curb? Landed on the neighbor's dog? What?"

"Nothing like that."

"Then it was *Save the crab, Clean up the cobblestones, Preserve our southern heritage,* or *Ghosts are people, too.* What did it cost to bail her out this time?"

"Nothing. Mama hasn't been in jail in over two weeks."

"Oh-oh."

Livy glanced up, and they shared a smile. "That's what I thought. I wonder if I should take her temperature or something."

"I'm sure she's fine. But you aren't."

Livy got interested in her paperwork real quick. Kim knew her too well, and Livy wouldn't be able to keep lying for much longer. But she didn't know if she could ever confide in Kim about this.

"Livy?"

"I have no idea what you're talking about."

"Yes, you do. Why won't you lean on me? That's what I'm here for."

"I thought you were here to answer the phone, file the files and weed out the psycho nutcases to a manageable level."

"Those are only a small part of the Kim Luchetti bonus plan. First I'm your friend, second I'm your partner. Though I'm starting to think it's the other way around for you."

"That's not true." Although Livy knew it was, and not because she didn't want to be a good friend. She wasn't sure how. She gave up pretending to read her notes and searched her mind for a friendly topic. "Uh, how's Joshua?"

"Toast. Don't change the subject. You're acting weird and I want to know why."

"There's nothing to tell you, Kim. I'm tired."

"You're always tired."

"More tired than usual."

"Uh-huh." Kim crossed the room and peered at Livy's face like a surgeon. "You don't look like you've been sleeping well."

That was the understatement of the year. Livy had barely been sleeping at all. Last night had been the worst. The time with Garrett, the argument with Rosie, Max's questions—all had combined for a sleepless night with too much to think about.

Kim straightened, grinning as if she'd had a brilliant idea. "What you need is a night out."

"Oh, no. No, I don't."

Livy knew what a night out with Kim entailed, and she couldn't handle one. Kim always partied as though it was 1999, even though 1999 was long gone. At times her merriment seemed a near frenzy, as if she was trying to forget something but couldn't unless there was enough booze, music and men.

"You do." Kim hiked her hip onto Livy's desk and winked. "Trust me."

"I hate it when people say that."

"That's because you're a lawyer. When people say it to you it means they're guilty."

"And when you say it, you're trying to get me to do something I shouldn't."

"Why shouldn't you go out with a friend like a normal young woman?"

"Because I'm not young and I've never been normal."

"I don't think you were ever young, either."

From behind a closed door in Livy's mind drifted laughter—hers and his—followed by the sudden image of a picnic on a bluff, wine and cheese, then sex in the sun. "Oh, yes," she murmured. "Yes, I was."

"Have you met a man?"

Poof went the image and the laughter.

"Of course not!"

Kim merely smiled, then said in an exaggerated southern accent, "Ms. Livy, you lie badly."

"You keep talking like that around here and someone's going to pop you in the nose."

Kim's smile became a grin. "A man. A real man from the way you're acting. Well, thank God."

"There is *not* a man. I don't like men."

Kim snorted. "That's only because you've been dating wimps for too long."

"This from a woman who dates every village idiot."

Kim's eyes narrowed, but she didn't lose her temper. She never did, and Livy could be very provoking. "You can't make me mad so I'll go away, Livy."

Livy gave Kim's butt a shove, and she slid off the desk. "Don't get mad. Just get lost so I can work."

The phone began to ring. "All right." She tossed her hair, the movement nonchalant. Whenever Livy tried that she resembled a cheerleader on speed. "But only because duty calls."

Kim left Livy's office and picked up the phone. "Savannah Family Law." She listened. Her shoulders stiffened. "What?"

The expression on Kim's face made Livy jump to her feet.

"No, Max isn't here. He's supposed to be there."

She mouthed *school* and Livy's heart lurched. A

parent always thought—or rather hoped—that their
child was relatively safe in school. But in this crazy
world such a hope was foolish.

Livy picked up their second line and dialed her
house. The phone rang until the machine answered.
Weird. Rosie was usually home at this time of day.

Livy hung up and headed for the door. She had a
feeling she knew where Max was—again—and this
time there would be no more Ms. Nice Guy. She
couldn't believe he'd out and out defied her. But she
almost hoped he had. The alternative would be far
worse.

If Max wasn't with his father—

Oh, God. Livy shuddered and refused to entertain
that element of terror until she was forced to.

Kim was right behind Livy when she opened the
outer door. "You stay here, Kim."

"Oh, no, I'm not."

"Someone has to. What if he shows up or calls?"

Kim hesitated. "Where are you going?"

"He's been hanging out with a friend at the old
Alexander place."

"You think he'd ditch school to go there?"

"In a heartbeat."

Kim sighed and stepped back. "I'll stay." She took
Livy's hand and squeezed it tight, and they shared a
look that said more than words.

"Go." Kim shoved Livy out the door. "Call me
as soon as you get there and tell me what's what, or
I'll send the cops."

Livy couldn't talk; her throat was tied in knots. She

nodded, instead. With no time for the leisurely stroll she'd enjoyed yesterday, Livy hailed a cab.

Five minutes later the cab pulled away from the curb and Livy turned to stare at the huge white face of the Alexander mansion. It appeared deserted. Her heart began to thump the cadence of panic again.

Didn't Garrett work at home? If he wasn't here, then where was he? And if he wasn't here, and Max along with him, what would she do next? Call the FBI to report a kidnapping? Would he really steal her son? She of all people should know J.J. always took what he wanted and left.

Livy ran up the walk, climbed the porch steps and rang the bell. All she heard was the echo through the empty house—no movement, no footsteps, nothing. She tried the door, but it was locked.

On the short ride over, Livy had convinced herself she'd find Max and Garrett on the porch, yakking away and drinking iced tea. She'd worked up a righteous snit. In an instant that anger dissolved, leaving a cold sweat behind. Adrenaline made her head buzz and anxiety had her ears ringing.

She tried to talk herself down, but a sob escaped. Horrified, Livy pressed her knuckles to her mouth. She had to calm down and *think*.

Garrett would never hurt Max. That much she knew. Even if he had kidnapped him, he was a hotshot author now; there was nowhere he could hide.

"Unless he's already left the country." Livy started to hyperventilate. "Relax," she ordered. "Just breathe deep or you're going to pass out."

She sat on a nearby chair, put her head between

her knees and talked to herself some more. So what
if they were in Bolivia? Garrett would bring Max
back eventually. A child just wasn't his style, she as-
sured herself once more. The novelty would wear off
quickly enough. He had no idea of all the things he'd
miss out on because of Max. Of course, there wasn't
a single thing Livy had missed that had mattered more
than Max. Because once there'd been Max, nothing
had mattered more than him.

She stood up too fast and swayed. But a good,
brain-jarring shake of her head stopped the vertigo.
She marched down the steps, determined. She was
getting inside this house somehow. If Max had been
here, she'd know it. If Garrett had taken him somewhere, she'd find out where. Then she'd kill the man.

Livy tested every window on her way around the
house. They were all painted shut, so she began to
search for a brick.

Breaking and entering? her mind whispered.

"Whatever it takes," Livy answered. She climbed
the back porch, her gaze searching for a loose, heavy
object and coming to rest upon the half-open back
door.

"But, Officer," she murmured, "the door was
wide-open." Livy pushed it. "And I heard suspicious
sounds from inside."

She walked in, not bothering to listen. *Suspicious*
was a matter of interpretation. Same as *probable
cause*. Right now she didn't care. They could lock
her up forever. Once she found her son.

But the place was as deserted on the inside as it
had appeared from the outside. She even checked the

coffin in the dining room. Empty. Who kept a coffin in the dining room anyway? Or anywhere in a house, for that matter?

"Psycho." She slammed the lid.

Most of the rooms were unoccupied—by people or furniture. One contained a treadmill and a television set. In a second sat a sleeper sofa and nothing else. Another held Garrett's bed, unmade, and his clothes, still in the suitcase.

"Figures."

She could feel him in that room—his spirit amid the rumpled sheets, the imprint of his head on the crumpled pillow.

Something deep down inside her trembled—because she could smell him, the same scent as before, soap over warm skin.

Livy hurried away from his bedroom. Sometimes, when she thought of how deeply she'd loved him, she was mortified. He had been everything, and when he'd left she had felt hollow, empty, dead. The only way to go on had been to forget. But a single moment of weakness, the mere scent of his skin, caused everything to come rushing back.

His office was pristine, and gave her a start. *Had* he packed up and left? If he had, he'd forgotten his laptop. The sight of the machine made her racing heart slow. Though Garrett might leave behind his furniture and clothes, sparse as they were, Livy doubted he'd leave his computer.

She continued her search. The calendar had only one date marked—a big red circle around December 15.

"Wonder what that means."

The phone rang, and she skittered away from the desk. After several rings, she moved closer, picked it up and glanced at the caller ID. *Lawton, Andrew,* followed by a New York area code, then a number. She placed the phone back on the desk, between the laptop and the calendar.

Nothing else cluttered the desktop. After a token flash of guilt, Livy began opening drawers. All she found was a contract for a book, delivery date December 15—aha!—a few yellow legal pads, pens and an address book. The only entries inside were Lawton's, several publishing houses and her own.

She dropped the book back in the drawer. Why on earth had Garrett kept her address all these years? It wasn't as though they exchanged Christmas cards. Livy had believed he'd gone on to the next town, next adventure, next sweet young thing, forgetting Savannah, forgetting her.

But if so, then why had he come back? And why was hers the only woman's name in his book?

"Because he has a little black book for all the ones he wants to call again, that's why."

She opened every drawer, searched every crevice. But there was no little black book. There was nothing else at all.

Where was he? More important, where was her son? Had she been wrong? Was Max even now anywhere but here?

Livy crossed to the window and glanced out, just in time to see the sisters stroll past on their afternoon walk. Must be four o'clock. If all was right in her world, Max would be home from school by now. But life hadn't been right since Garrett returned.

She turned and tripped over a box of books. Several more were scattered about. Why bother to unpack books or clothes? He wasn't staying.

Even the last time, he'd lived out of his duffel bag, not bothering to make the major commitment of hanging up so much as a single sweatshirt. Livy should have figured him out by that quirk alone. Would have if she hadn't been dazzled by everything about him.

Absently she glanced down at the books and saw they were copies of a novel of his. Livy had never read a Garrett Stark book. Her tastes ran more to the law review or the newspaper.

Curious, she picked up his first release. She had read *about* it in the paper. There'd been quite a buzz. His writing had been called a cross between Bram Stoker's and Flannery O'Conner's.

Southern vampires. Livy shook her head. He and Max were certainly a pair.

"You've never read my work."

Livy caught her breath, the startled sound seeming to whirl about the room. He lounged in the doorway, looking for all the world like the southern vampire she'd just been thinking of; only his clipped Yankee voice spoiled the image.

"Where in hell is my son?"

Confusion flickered over his face. "I just walked him home."

Relief made her dizzy; fury alone kept her upright. She glared at him.

Black hair, black eyes, black stubble of beard made

his skin gleam pale. Black clothes accented the long, leanly muscled body. Would he die if she put a stake through his equally black heart?

Doubtful. So she threw his precious book at his beautiful damn face.

GARRETT CAUGHT the book right before it crashed into his nose. Luckily, he'd learned to manage his big hands as well as his huge feet. Fifteen years ago the missile might have split his lip.

"What did I do this time?" he asked.

She goggled at him. "You don't know?"

"Max said he needed to be home by four. No one was there so I took him to the neighbor's." If possible, she appeared more angry, and Garrett got nervous. Had he left his son in the wrong stranger's hands? "Wasn't that right? Max said that's where he should go, and the lady next door agreed."

"It's fine," she snapped. "Though where my mother got to I don't want to know."

"Then, what's the problem? And why are you here?"

"Aargh!" She threw up her hands. "It's Wednesday."

"All day."

"It's September."

"Is that a problem?"

"Does *school* ring any bells? Does *truant* mean anything to you?"

The light dawned. He *was* the idiot Livy's expression branded him. Garrett had been so thrilled to see Max, and not just because he'd wanted out of the coffin, but because he genuinely liked the kid and enjoyed being with him. From what he'd observed, Max felt the same way, too.

Livy still glared at him as if she expected something. "Uh. Sorry. I didn't know."

"What kind of man doesn't know that an eight-year-old should be in school on a Wednesday afternoon?"

Her continuing "too dumb to live" look was getting on Garrett's nerves. When she gazed at him like that, he was back in his father's office, a child again, being told how worthless he was in every aspect of life. Garrett had stopped feeling inferior to the rest of the world years ago. Although his confidence had taken quite a few knocks lately, he wasn't going to let Livy give him any more. He was a big boy now. He knew how to fight back.

"What kind of man?" he asked, voice deceptively mild. "Maybe the kind who's never been around children." He took a step into the room. "A man who was so thrilled to see his son come through the door he couldn't think past the joy of it."

"Perhaps a kidnapping charge might help you to think more clearly."

She made every sentence a threat, every encounter an argument, every day difficult. Annoyance surged through him, and he gave up trying to play nice.

"Try it," he murmured, "and I'll make you very—" he took a step closer "—very—" another step "—sorry."

She was tall, but he was taller, so she had to tilt her head to see into his face. When she did that, the light from the window splashed across her, revealing the lines of strain around her mouth and the deep-down terror in her eyes.

His anger drained away. He dropped the book she'd thrown at him, and the unexpected *thud* made her start violently.

"Shh," he whispered, slowly lifting his hand toward her face, giving her time to step back if she needed to, praying she would not. "You're scared to death, aren't you?"

She kept very still. She didn't move away, though her eyes went wary, wide and dark.

He let his fingertips glide over her cheekbone, across the fine lines. Only the tease of a touch, down to her chin, where he spread his thumb over those tight, tight lips. Her lids fluttered closed. As if against her will, she let out the breath she'd held, on a sigh that was almost surrender.

With her smart mouth shut and her angry eyes closed, he could almost believe it was that long-ago summer come again.

Back then his hands had been hardened by work, callused by tools, scarred from wood and nails. Back then he'd been afraid to touch her for fear he'd scratch her with the roughness of his skin or bruise her with his big, clumsy hands.

Yet when the nicks in his fingers had caught and pulled her hair, she'd merely laughed and put her lips against the cuts, then drawn her tongue along the center of his palm, making him forget any fear, every caution. She'd placed his scarred hands on her perfect body, letting him touch her any way that he liked.

The past and the present blended as his gaze wandered over her. The pulse in her throat throbbed, and he ached to put his mouth there, feel the beat against his tongue. Instead he skimmed his fingers down her neck to her collarbone, barely touching her, and she shivered.

Her hair brushed the back of his hand. The scent, secret summer, aroused him instantly with one gentle drift. The dark, crisp material of her business suit only emphasized the pearly shade of her skin, a texture that was yet the softest thing he'd ever touched.

His hands were no longer rough, hard or clumsy, but he was still so afraid he might hurt her. Hurting her was what he'd wanted to do the least but ended up doing the most.

He should step back, let her go—Max was waiting. And he very nearly did. But she opened her mouth and her breath shook, then her lips trembled. Before he knew it, he was kissing her and every good intention was burned away.

Their last kiss had tasted of anger; this one held the flavor of desperation. Tangy and wild, heedless yet helpless—it tempted him to take all he'd once been given.

While he might not be a gentleman, he *had* acquired some finesse and a little bit of patience over the years. So he gentled his mouth, soothed her trembling lips with his tongue, placed a single finger on the pulse that taunted him and absorbed her heartbeat into his own.

If she'd pushed him away he'd have gone, gladly, because he was falling back in the deep, and sex would only confuse this mess they were in. But tell that to his body. The traitor. All it did was shout for hers.

Hers answered, bumping against him in uncomfortable yet intriguing ways. Her mouth became more frantic. Her fingers pulled at his shirt. Then her hands were against his skin, on his belly, across his chest. He moaned, cursed, and tried to pull away, but she fisted a hand in his hair and yanked him back.

She was too reckless. Something was wrong. And while his big-mouth body screamed, *Take her,* his mind said, *Huge mistake,* and his heart whispered, *Not like this.*

He kissed her softly when she kissed him hard, and he rubbed her back gently while she ran her short nails across the twitching muscles in his stomach. He even murmured soothing nonsense into her hair when she scraped her teeth across his chest.

His lack of response finally penetrated, and she looked at him, wary and uncertain.

Garrett brushed his fingers across her cheek. "Are you going to slap me again?"

The old Livy would have smiled. The new one would have slapped him, just for the hell of it. What neither one of them would ever have done was burst into tears.

CHAPTER NINE

WHEN WAS THE LAST TIME she'd cried like this? Oh, there was the other night when Max was asleep with his brand-new cast. But that hardly counted. She always cried after serious bodily harm to her child. Call her a mother.

But to cry in public was another matter. And to cry in front of Garrett Stark was a sin for which there was no redemption. However, Livy couldn't seem to stop.

Mainly because he said nothing, merely gathered her closer and let her weep as he nuzzled her hair.

Wonder of wonders, she let him. Because she was so cold, she shook, yet when his warmth seeped into her icy skin, little by little the tremors stopped. His smell, though a treacherous, traitorous temptation, would ease her if she just closed her eyes and let herself be eased.

"Hush," he murmured, stroking, soothing. "It's all over now. Nothing to be afraid of anymore."

Little did he know, what scared her the most was him.

Because his strength was a trap and his comfort a lie. She couldn't depend on him; she could only depend on herself. Nothing had changed. Even though it felt as though everything had.

Livy extricated herself from Garrett's arms. He let her go, though she could have sworn he clung just a little. Odd, since she was the one who'd needed comfort. Turning, she scrubbed at her face. She must look lovely right about now.

Garrett was very good at giving comfort. Probably because he'd given it a hundred times before. He'd just never given it to her. She'd had no need of comfort that long-ago summer when the world had been her playground and the future full of promise. She hadn't needed comfort until he'd gone.

She'd continued to hope for months. The one thing that had killed the hope had been crying for him during a twenty-three hour labor and hearing only the sound of her own voice as an answer.

Had it been then that she'd started to hate him? She couldn't remember; she only knew that she did.

She didn't want to face him and see the desire she could still taste reflected all over his face. She wanted him. So what? He was a beautiful man on the outside. He knew what to do with that mouth, those hands, his body. He'd been her first, and she'd heard a woman never forgot that. So far, she'd heard right.

How could she have kissed him like that, touched him as if the intervening years had never been, as if all the pain had never happened, while her child waited for her at home? Because she'd been so afraid, and for a moment Garrett had made the fear go away.

"I have to leave." Livy spun about and ran right into him.

He grabbed her arms to steady her, then held on

when she struggled. "Just wait a minute, Livy. We're not finished."

"We were finished nine years ago."

"The existence of Max says differently."

"Let me go, Garrett."

"Not yet."

Livy stopped struggling. What was the point? He was bigger and stronger than her, and if he chose to keep her here, he could. But that didn't mean she had to like it.

She sneered in his face, and he glowered right back. They stood toe to toe, nearly nose to nose. The only thing in the world right then was the two of them. The moment stretched, long and taut. Deep down where the past lived, she trembled.

"Just what in Sam Hill is going on here, Livy?"

The loud voice made her gasp. Garrett shoved her behind him and faced the man who stood in the darkness of the hall. Garrett stood rigid and ready, like a dog that had been startled over a bone.

Though Livy didn't appreciate the comparison, even if it was her own, his able protection soothed her thundering heart. Despite his new fame and good fortune, Garrett had once lived on the edge. His years of drifting had prepared him for anything, and the sudden realization that no one, nothing, would get through him to hurt her or Max made a warm wash of security flow through her.

"Who are you?" Garrett demanded.

"Step away from Livy."

"I don't think so."

Livy relaxed as the intruder took a few steps into

the room and she recognized him. When Kim had said she'd call the cops, Livy should have known she meant Detective Klein.

Klein had played football for the Citadel, then spent eight years as a Marine—which explained his salt-and-pepper crew cut, as well as his stoic demeanor—before becoming a cop. The man was a mountain, and no one in town messed with him.

"It's okay," Livy began, inching around her brand-new watchdog.

He shoved her right back. No one but Garrett messed with a mountain, it seemed.

"Mister, you'd better stop pushing her, or I'm gonna get testy."

"You'd better tell me how you got in my house and then get right back out."

"Door was open."

Garrett cursed. "I may as well put a revolving entrance out there. Thanks for stopping in. Now you can leave."

Klein laughed, a deep rich sound that Livy loved. He was a good man, a gentle man for all his size, and one terrific cop. From the moment she'd met him, she'd liked him.

Perhaps it was the sadness that always hovered at the edges of his oddly light blue eyes and made her want to pat him on the top of the head, if she could reach it. Or maybe it was the fact that Klein was not a handsome man—not handsome being an understatement.

Livy's gaze touched upon Garrett's long dark hair and the shape of his face against the shadows. She had seen the underside of handsome and it wasn't something she wanted to see again. If the measure of character was the homeliness of a face, then Klein was nearer to sainthood than anyone.

Klein reached behind him, and Garrett tensed, ready to pounce. But the detective only brought out his badge, flipped it open, then shut. "Where's the boy?"

"Home, safe and sound." Garrett relaxed, but not completely. "Why did you call the police, Livy?"

"I didn't." She stepped from behind him, and this time he let her. "Kim?" she asked.

Klein grunted. "She was mighty upset. You had your cell phone off again."

Livy winced. She carried her phone wherever she went, but only remembered to turn it on if she tried to make a call and had no power. With a child like Max, she needed to break that habit.

Klein and Garrett sized each other up. Now they looked like two junkyard dogs circling, preparing to fight over her—that bone again. If Livy didn't do something, she figured they'd start bumping chests and howling at the moon.

She moved closer to Detective Klein. Garrett followed, and she gave him a "get lost" glare, which he ignored.

"What was Max doing here?" Klein asked.

"None of your business." Livy could almost see the hair on the back of Garrett's neck rise, and she wouldn't have been surprised to hear a growl.

His aggressive stance went beyond annoyance with her, irritation over being interrupted or anger at hav-

ing his home invaded against his will. Garrett seemed
to have a problem with authority.

Livy was an expert on that, having bailed her
mother out of jail on countless occasions because of
the same foible. She figured Max got his rebellious
streak from Mama. Looked like the DNA strands for
rebellion had come from both sides of the family.

"Who is this guy?" Klein demanded.

Livy opened her mouth, but Garrett answered, instead. "Garrett Stark."

"I wasn't asking you."

"But I don't mind answering."

Klein ignored him and addressed Livy. "Kim said
you'd come here searching for Max. Why?"

Garrett answered for her again. "Because I'm—"

Livy elbowed Garrett in the ribs—hard. He doubled
over and coughed. Klein's eyes narrowed, his gaze
jumping between the two of them.

"He's Garrett Stark," she said.

"I heard that. So what?"

Garrett's head went up. But a long look from Livy
made him keep quiet. "The horror author," she sup-
plied.

"Good for him. But what does that have to do with
Max?"

"Uh, well, you see…" She fell silent when the
awkwardness of her words and the tension in her
voice made Klein's face tighten in suspicion.

Livy wasn't any good at lying. Perhaps because
she'd spent so much energy on her one big lie, she
had little left for any more. She'd never seen that lack
as anything but an asset. Juries and judges seemed to

sense her sincerity. She did well in court. But in a situation like this... Sometimes Livy wished she could lie as well as the master standing next to her.

Almost as if he heard her secret wish, Garrett touched her elbow. At the jolt of awareness, whatever she'd been meaning to say flew out of her mind, leaving Garrett free to speak for her some more. "Max is interested in writing, so he came to me with questions."

Klein, not an idiot on any scale, continued to stare at each in turn. "I find it hard to believe that Livy Frasier allowed her son to spend time with a stranger."

"I'm not a stranger."

The detective's gaze touched on Garrett's hand cupping Livy's elbow, then raised to her face. "Funny, that's just what I was thinking."

Livy didn't want Klein thinking anything. The man was like a bloodhound when it came to the scent of a secret.

"Max left school in the middle of the day," Livy blurted.

Klein slowly nodded. "Which would explain why Kim was nuts when I called the office."

Livy stepped away from Garrett, her inner radar beeping like a beacon at Klein's words. "What do you mean *you* called the office? I thought Kim called you."

"Didn't say that."

"Don't play stalwart cop with me, Klein. Why did you call?" The detective sighed, shuffled his feet, and Livy knew. "What did she do this time?"

"Who?" Garrett asked.

"My mother." Livy didn't spare Garrett a glance, but kept her eyes on Klein. Something in his gaze unnerved her, and suddenly Livy wished she hadn't moved away from Garrett's touch, because she was cold again and he'd been so hot. The fact that she longed for the comfort she'd only just discovered him capable of, made her speak too sharply.

"What happened?"

"You'd better come to the station with me, Livy."

The funny black spots she'd seen earlier on the porch were back, and this time they were dancing. Unfortunately, there was no convenient chair for her to sit in, so the world did a nasty dip and twirl.

Someone caught her by the shoulders. Even with her eyes closed, Livy knew Klein, not Garrett, had steadied her. The detective's hands were strong yet fumbling. Gentle enough, but not the hands of a man who wanted anything more than to keep her from breaking her nose.

"Tell her what happened before she faints," Garrett snarled.

"I never faint."

"You could have fooled me."

She opened her eyes, forced the black spots away, and glared at Garrett. "Shut up."

"She's okay now, Klein. You can get your hands off of her."

Klein peered into Livy's face with a half smile. "I don't think I will just yet. What's going on here, Livy? I've never seen you this jumpy, and with you that's saying quite a bit."

"Nothing's going on," Garrett said.

"That's what they all say. Now, let the lady answer. Why are you so upset?"

"Is my mother all right?"

"She's in jail," Klein answered.

Livy slumped with relief. Rosie wouldn't be in jail if she was hurt or dying. "So all's right with the world."

"Your mother's in jail a lot?" Garrett's voice was full of surprise and a healthy dose of wonder. That figured. Only Garrett would think a jailhouse gramma fascinating.

"Define *a lot*."

Both Livy and Klein laughed. She must have looked better, because he let her go, though he didn't move away.

Klein sobered first. No surprise there. Though he had a beautiful laugh, he didn't use it often enough.

"It's a bit more serious than usual this time," he said. "You need to come with me now, Livy. I'll drive you."

"You'll have to. I took a cab."

"I'll take you," Garrett offered. "We can talk in the car."

Livy didn't even bother to look at him. "We were through."

His hand on her arm was as gentle as his voice. "We've never been through, and you know it."

Livy sighed. If only he'd been rough and demanding; she would have been able to resist. She did, however, move away from his touch. "Detective, I'll be right out."

"Yeah, beat it," Garrett said.

Klein eyed Garrett as he might a perpetrator caught red-handed. "Butt out, pretty boy."

Livy stifled a smile. "It's all right, Klein."

The detective glanced at Livy. "You sure?"

"I'm sure. Two minutes, and I'll be there."

Klein still didn't move until Livy gave him a tiny push. Garrett stared at her with a puzzled expression on his face, but said nothing.

"I have to go," she reminded him.

"Let me go with you."

She laughed. "I've been dealing with Mama for years. I don't need your help."

"You've never needed anyone's help."

"That's not true. Once, I needed yours."

He had the grace to wince. "I'm here now."

"Now is too late."

"If you don't need me, then you don't need the cop, either."

"If the cop offers his help, I'll take it. Klein is one of the good guys."

"Which makes me one of the bad?"

Livy had had enough. Dealing with a truant Max, a disappearing mother and a reappearing dead lover was too much for one woman to stand in a week. "You're behaving like a jealous boyfriend, and you have no right."

"What rights do I have when it comes to you?"

"None."

A flicker of hurt crossed his face, but she couldn't afford to let that affect her.

"You're the mother of my child, Livy. I can't forget that. I can't stop thinking about it—"

His voice was low and urgent; his words made something slick and weighty rumble within her.

"I didn't get to feel him kick. I never touched him beneath your skin. I missed all of it. How do you think that makes me feel?"

"Maybe the way I felt when you left me behind?"

Again he had the grace to wince, but he wouldn't drop the issue. "How did you feel?"

"Alone, betrayed, worthless."

Those three words made the anger return, and Livy held on to it, let the feeling grow. She'd been angry at Garrett for a very long time. Anger was an emotion she understood. What she did not understand was the resurgence of lust for him, and the hint of something stronger, deeper and much more dangerous that she refused to put a name to.

She could shove his body away with her hands, but to end this connection between them she would have to use words.

"I meant nothing to you then. I don't understand why you give a damn now."

The words fell between them, shattering any momentary bond they'd shared. His face went white, and she almost felt bad. Until she remembered who she was dealing with.

"You believe that?"

"Of course I believe that." Livy started for the door.

"You couldn't be further from the truth."

She hesitated; something in his voice made her

want to believe, want to turn around and begin again what had never truly ended.

Then a horn honked on the street, and the phone began to ring, a startling shriek. Livy's inertia vanished, and she left Garrett behind as easily as he'd once left her.

DESPERATE FOR a distraction to keep him from doing something more foolish than he already had, Garrett answered the phone. How foolish was that?

"I've been calling every hour on the hour," Andrew began.

"Was that you? And here I thought all that ringing had to be the ghosts."

"Is that what the book is about? Ghosts?"

Garrett shrugged. "Okay."

Silence descended on the other end of the line. In Andrew's case silence was rarely good.

"I'm coming down there."

"Would you quit with that? I do not need a sitter. I especially do not need someone with an imagination deficit hanging around. You'll frighten off all the creative ghostly vibrations."

Not to mention the Muse he'd completely forgotten about the moment his son had walked into the house.

"I suppose you're going to tell me the house I rented you is haunted."

"From what I hear, all the houses in Savannah are haunted." Which only proved how far gone his sensitivity was. He hadn't felt a thing but lonely since he'd moved into this place. If anyone should feel a ghost, that someone should be Garrett Stark.

"You do know there's no such thing as ghosts, don't you, Garrett?"

"You do know there's more to this world than what we see, don't you, Andrew?"

"Of course. There's the money I haven't made yet."

Sometimes Garrett wondered if Andrew was kidding when he said stuff like that. Probably not.

If ghosts existed, Andrew would never see one because his world was confined to the tunnel of his vision, which made Garrett and him the perfect team. Because Garrett's inner world was so large and unwieldy, he often had a hard time addressing the realities of life. Of course, his inner world was nonexistent lately, but Garrett would just keep that to himself.

If it wasn't for Andrew, he'd no doubt still be writing with the stub of pencil he'd sharpened with his pocketknife, on a legal pad he'd skipped breakfast to buy, in the middle of a grungy apartment in Miami.

Those days had been tough, but there were times Garrett missed the cold hard bite of life. He wasn't quite sure anymore how to get back some of the edge he'd had in the beginning. Another thing that had led him back here.

"You sound almost normal," Andrew murmured. "But there's something wrong. I can smell it from here."

"That's not me. Have you been chewing up editors and stashing their mangled bodies in the closet again? You really have to stop that."

"You never let me have any fun."

The silence that followed their teasing spoke louder than any words. Andrew was worried, which only made two of them.

"What is this book about, Garrett?"

"I'll let you know."

"What?"

The panic in that single word made Garrett do something he hadn't done in a long, long time. He lied—straight out and with no remorse. There was no reason Andrew should improve his ulcer until he had to.

"I'm superstitious about this one. I don't want to talk about the book until it's done."

"Oh. Okay."

Though Andrew didn't understand things that were weird and spooky, he understood people who were. Or at least pretended to. Authors had all sorts of superstitions, eccentricities and routines that they used to convince themselves the work would come out all right. Andrew knew better than to mess with any one of them.

"Then I guess I won't keep you." Andrew still didn't sound convinced that Garrett wasn't dancing naked beneath the full moon, when he should be working like a good boy.

"And maybe you could stop calling me all the time?"

If Garrett had actually been writing, the phone would have driven him batshit. As it was—the phone was driving him batshit.

He should probably turn it off, but then he'd have

no contact with the outside world at all, such that it was.

"All right. I'll stop calling. I'm just a little worried."

At times Andrew was the mother Garrett had never had.

"Relax. Have I ever let you down?"

"Not yet." Andrew sighed. "Of course now would not be the time to start."

That was what Garrett liked about Andrew. The man could always be counted on to leave him in the cheeriest of moods.

Garret hung up. The utter stillness of the house did not make him want to write, as it was supposed to. Instead, without Andrew for a distraction, what Garrett wanted to forget he could only remember.

Livy.

An autumn wind casted through the window, ruffling his hair with the scent of the river, stirring moist cool night across his face. Still he burned for her, deep down where no breeze could ever cool him.

Because of the ghosts in his past that wouldn't stop haunting him, Garrett had rarely looked back. Instead, he'd always looked forward—next town, next book, next adventure. Because whenever he had looked back, Garrett had seen Livy and ached for her.

Why did he keep teasing himself with tiny tastes of a woman who despised him? For that matter, why did she keep giving him small sips? To torment him? Or because she could no more stop the pull of the past than he could.

The joy he'd once found in Savannah had been the

deepest he'd ever known. Yet this time all joy seemed lost to him—except when he gazed into the face of his son.

He should focus on Max, leave Livy alone. But he knew that no matter his good intentions, if she let him touch her he would. Then he'd lose himself in Livy the way he had the last time until he'd become afraid there would soon be nothing left of himself.

She didn't believe he'd ever cared for her. She thought she'd meant nothing. She couldn't be further from the truth.

To save himself he'd run away, and had ended up losing more than he'd ever imagined when he'd left a part of himself behind.

Livy said she didn't need him. Once, Garrett had said such things, too. It had taken him years to realize that sometimes what he said he needed the least was what he really wanted the most.

Could that be true of Livy, as well?

CHAPTER TEN

As soon as Livy snapped her seat belt into place, Klein put the car into gear. Although she would have liked nothing better than to lean her head back against the seat and rest, Livy didn't have the time or the luxury. What else was new?

"What's the charge this time? Civil disobedience? Creating a public nuisance? Littering? Soliciting? What?"

Klein gave her a slow sideways glance. "Theft."

"No way." Livy's response was automatic. "Impossible. My mother is the least covetous person I know. What on earth would she steal?"

That slow glance came again, but this time Klein's lips twitched. "A goose."

"Shit. She didn't."

"So she says. The sisters say otherwise."

Livy should have known this was coming. She should have expected it. Her mother had been fuming over the sisters' ghost goose for months now, and she hadn't been fuming silently. Everyone in Savannah knew how Rosie Frasier felt about that goose. What should have surprised Livy was that Rosie had waited this long to take action.

"What, exactly, do the sisters say?"

Klein didn't answer right away, instead concentrated on the road as he negotiated a one-way square.

Savannah was beautiful, ancient and special. But the historical section was difficult to navigate. There were no cross streets, only square upon square. To get from one side to the other, a driver needed to be familiar with the streets, then drive up some, down others and around and around at times. Which made it much easier to walk, if you had the time.

At last Klein came out of the one-way roundabout and returned his attention to Livy. "Rosie felt the goose was being exploited."

"Tell me something I don't know. With her, someone's always being exploited."

"She called for its emancipation."

"And?"

"The sisters say she emancipated it."

"I was afraid of that. She'll give it back."

"You really think so?"

Livy opened her mouth, shut it again, then scratched her nose. "We could pay for it?"

"That would work with any other goose. But the reason the sisters are so mad, the reason they're pressing criminal charges..."

"Besides the fact that they've got the feud of their lifetime going with Rosie?"

"Besides that, I hear this goose is exceptionally rare."

Livy started seeing those black flecks again. Only this time they were shaped like dollar signs. "How rare? Give me numbers, Klein."

"Not money rare. Trained rare."

"Trained?" Livy scoffed. "The thing stays in the yard. I'll buy them a poodle."

But Klein was already shaking his head. "They want their goose back. Nothing else will do. So your mother had better cough up one trained Christmas goose quick."

"You can bet she will if I have to give her the Heimlich myself."

Klein slowed to the curb. Livy's gaze went from her darkened home to the lights next door. "I should probably leave him here rather than drag him off to see Gramma in jail. But if I don't take Max with me, I won't have any time with him today."

"I don't think it'll scar him for life to see Rosie in jail. Might help him to understand where she spends so much of her time."

"Let's hope so." Livy shoved open the car door.

"Does Max know?"

She glanced back at Klein, puzzled. "What?"

"That Stark is his father."

Could a person's heart really stop? For an instant, Livy thought hers just might. Then she slammed the door shut with unnecessary force. "W-why would you say that? Max's father is d-d-dead."

"You never stutter unless you're lying. You can't fool me, Livy. I detect things for a living."

"When did you detect this?"

"A minute after I met the man. You noticed I didn't like him."

"I wondered what your problem was. I didn't think you'd suddenly come down with a case of undying love for me."

He gave her a soft smile. "Not that you wouldn't be worth it, Counselor, but I make a much better friend than a lover."

The sadness in his voice caused Livy to pause a minute. But Klein shook his head, a nearly imperceptible movement. He would not talk about himself. He never did.

"How did you know?" Livy asked.

Klein lifted his huge hand and tapped a surprisingly long, elegant finger to his cheekbone. "Max has his father's eyes."

And here Livy thought she was being ultrasensitive. "Is it that obvious?"

"Not to someone who isn't used to looking beneath the surface. Once I noticed that, I noticed other things. The way Stark touched you." Klein shrugged and stared out his window, as if seeing something a long way off. "How you leaned into him when he did. What was between you is too intimate to be new. It didn't take Sherlock Holmes to deduce you've got a big lie on your hands." He shifted so he could look her in the face, and the odd dreamy expression was gone. "Max doesn't know, does he."

Livy rested her head against the cool glass pane of the window. "No."

"When are you going to tell him?"

"I wasn't planning to."

"Ever?"

Klein's voice was so incredulous she straightened and looked at him. "You don't know J.J."

"No, I don't. Who the hell is J.J.?"

"His pen name is Garrett Stark. His real name is

J. J. Garrett. He specializes in running off in the night. I'm not going to let Max get attached to his long-lost daddy so he can be crushed when the man finds a new and better toy.''

Klein was skeptical. "You think Stark would do that?''

Livy threw up her hands. "I don't know. I'm obviously no great judge of character. I didn't think he'd leave before, so I was the one left holding the baby.''

What *had* she really known about the man she'd loved? Not much. They'd been little more than children, caught up in a whirl of new emotions and each other. They had shared their bodies and their dreams. But Livy had not shared her past and J.J. had not shared his.

"True enough,'' Klein murmured, obviously thinking of something else. "You should still tell Max.''

"Why should I tell him? Wouldn't it be better for Max if he continued to think his father's dead rather than to lose him?''

"There's a difference between dying and leaving, Livy.''

"Is there? I've experienced both, and as the one left behind I have to say they felt the same to me.'' She blinked to keep the heated tears in her eyes from dripping down her face. "Devastating.''

Klein patted her shoulder, awkwardly, like a big puppy that couldn't quite control his limbs. But he meant well.

Livy cleared her throat. Klein yanked his hand away. Back to business once again.

"One problem at a time,'' Livy stated. "Right now

I can't think of anything but Mama and her golden goose.''

Klein nodded, allowing the topic of Garrett Stark to drop, though she still sensed his disapproval hovering and heavy within the tight confines of the car.

"That's understandable. Grab Max, and we'll see to one problem at a time.''

LUCKY FOR MAX his gramma was in trouble again, which took the heat off of him. He'd known he was in for it the moment he'd walked away from school. But an afternoon learnin' how to stomp on the fears that haunted him was worth a whole lot of time in his room.

Even though his mom said, "I'll talk to you later, mister," and the spark in her eyes showed she wouldn't forget, she didn't start yellin' at him in front of the Hammonds like he'd expected. Not that she yelled much, but he figured if there was ever a time for yellin', the time was now.

They traveled in silence to the police station, which was okay with Max. The less said about anything the better.

Detective Klein parked in his space, and together the three of them went inside. Max had liked Detective Klein the first time he'd met him. He looked like that droopy dog Duke on the *Nick at Night* show about the oil-rich hillbillies. How could you not feel warm and fuzzy about a guy as sad as that?

Max liked the old shows on *Nick at Night* almost as much as he liked the old horror movies on Saturday afternoons. And his mom smiled a whole lot more

when she found him watchin' the story about a man
named Jed.

Turned out they were lucky Detective Klein was
along, because the policeman at the front desk didn't
want to let Max in to see Rosie. He'd never gotten to
see her in jail before, and while he loved her bunches,
he really wanted to see what she looked like behind
bars.

The detective eyed Max and winked. Max glanced
at his mom, who seemed real nervous and jumpy, but
she was starin' at the wall and not at him, so he
grinned and winked back. Detective Klein liked
kids—kids knew that sort of thing—and he was nice,
deep down where nice counted. Max heard that in his
voice.

The detective returned his attention to the policeman. "You go get some coffee while I take care of
a few things."

The other man didn't seem happy, but he went.
Max figured that happened for Detective Klein a lot.
He was huge. What would it be like to be so big no
one picked on you? Max thought he might like it.

"Livy?"

Klein stared at Max's mom with a frown so deep,
the lines between his eyes and around his mouth were
like crevices in a rock. Max peered back and forth
between the two of them. Something was up here.
Had his mom told Detective Klein about Max skipping school? Were they really taking Max to jail, and
Rosie wasn't even here?

No, his mom would never lie to him. She'd say
right out, "You're busted, buddy. Off to jail you go."

Besides, Max wasn't scared of jail. Rosie had told him all about it, and from her point of view the place sounded like one big slumber party.

Still, when they got back where the prisoners stayed, Max breathed a sigh of relief to hear Rosie's voice coming from behind the bars.

"They say Renee Rondolia, his simple, lost soul denied final rites, wanders on moonless winter evenings throughout Savannah. When you hear the cool river wind whistling through the trees, glance out your window or perhaps down a shadowed city street, then you might see his large, hulking figure coming for you."

Max hurried past the other two, ignoring his mom's urgent, "Max!" as well as her hand, which snatched for his shoulder. He'd gotten so used to avoiding that hand, he didn't even have to think about it. But he did trip over his big toe and slam into the bars, catching himself with his free hand before he got a nose full of iron. His cast skidded along the bars as if they were a xylophone.

He pressed his face through the opening and grinned at Rosie. She was surrounded by several women dressed pretty weird—which was saying a lot, considering how Rosie dressed. Right now she wore big, loose, orangey-red pants that looked like something out of an Arabian Nights movie and a T-shirt that said, *It's as bad as you think and they are out to get you.*

"Hey, Rosie! Are you guys havin' a slumber party?"

Her smile made him warm all over. *No one* had a

gramma like Rosie. "Hey yourself, sugar. I was just telling a story to pass our time."

He took in the brightly painted faces and really short skirts of the ladies. One of them wore a leopard bra, though why she had on a bra and no shirt, Max couldn't quite figure. Still, it was pretty, in a jungle sort of way.

"Like your boots," he told that lady, because her boots matched her bra, and she must have searched all over Georgia to find something like that.

"Thanks." She winked and cracked her gum louder than Max had ever heard. He smiled back, and that was when his mom caught up to him.

"Mama, what are you doing in there?" She glared at Klein. "Why is she in with the regular population?"

"She *is* the regular population. This time around she's garnered more than a nuisance charge."

"It's nonsense, and you know it."

"I'm not the judge. You can tell him all about it tomorrow at the hearing."

"I don't want any special privileges, Livy." Rosie stood and joined them on her side of the bars. "Besides, I don't like to be alone, and the girls wanted a story."

"Rosie tells the best stories," Max put in, uncertain why his mom was mad about the pretty ladies. They looked ready for Halloween, and Max loved Halloween. On that one night, magic walked all over the place.

"My stories aren't half as good as yours." Rosie put her fingertip to his nose and flicked it.

"The one you were tellin' sounded good. Who's Renee Rondolia and why was his soul lost?"

"Mama," Livy warned.

Rosie gave her an impatient glance. "He's going to hear about Renee eventually. Everyone does. The story is as much a part of Savannah as the river."

"He doesn't need to know now. That legend scared the sh—" His mom glanced at him, then pursed her lips. "The pants off of me when I was eighteen."

If something scared the sh—pants off his mom, Max really wanted to hear about it.

"I'll only ask Sammy and find out tomorrow," he pointed out.

His mom glared at Rosie, and Klein, too, when he snorted, then she turned to Max. "Fine. I'll tell you." Rosie rolled her eyes behind Mom's back, but Max knew better than to laugh. "A long time ago there was a man named Renee and he was simple—"

"What's simple?"

"Not the brightest crayon," Rosie put in. "If you know what I mean."

"Ah." Max nodded. "Like Sammy. Two cans short of a six-pack."

"Max!" His mom groaned. "Where do you get this stuff?"

He shrugged. "Around."

"That's what I was afraid of." She pushed on her eyelids as if they hurt. After a deep breath, she dropped her hand. "Anyway, Renee was slow. When a girl turned up dead, the town blamed him. He died. They buried him in the marsh and that's where he stayed. Got it?"

Max squinted at his mom, then turned to Rosie with his eyebrows raised.

"She sure knows how to take the fun out of a good story, doesn't she?" Rosie said.

"I'll say."

"Never mind, you two." Mom sounded real annoyed, so Max kept his mouth shut. He was still on her list, and he didn't need to make her any madder at him than she already was. If he was really lucky, the missing goose would be all the trouble Mom could handle for one night and maybe a few days, too.

Sometimes Max wondered if Rosie tried to get in trouble so in comparison the things Max did wouldn't seem so bad. That would be just like Rosie.

"Klein, I want her out of this cell."

"I like it in here."

"And we want more bedtime stories," said the lady who seemed to be wearing a shiny purple bathing suit with orange shorts over top. Except the shorts might fit Max, even though the lady was a whole lot bigger.

"Mama, where's the goose?"

"Goose?" Rosie batted her eyelashes and Max laughed.

"Max, stand over there!" His mom pointed to the corner.

"Come on, kid." Klein led him away.

"What's goin' on?" Max whispered urgently.

"Just listen and don't interrupt. You can find out a lot that way."

"Tell me where you put the goose, Mama. Then I'll give it back and this will all go away."

"No can do, sugar."

"Why the hell not!" Mom shouted.

The place went quiet.

"Oh-oh," Max murmured, as Rosie's cheery smile went south.

"Watch your mouth, Olivia. I may not be the usual mother, but I am your mother."

"You tell her, Rosie!" The bra-and-boots lady punched her fist high in the air. The other ladies did the same. "Yeah!"

Max almost felt sorry for his mom. She hadn't had a good day. He could tell by the way her mouth kept pinching together and her forehead was all scrunched. Rosie could be a real pain when she tried. Though Max had to say she didn't even seem to be trying today.

"I'm sorry." Mom rubbed between her eyes. "But this could get serious if you don't give the thing back."

"I didn't say I had it."

"Mama, we both know you have it."

"What happened to innocent until proven guilty?"

"Got me." Mom sighed. "I'll be back in the morning to go to the hearing with you. I'm hoping that if you sleep on this you'll come to your senses tomorrow."

"You can always hope."

"But I won't hold my breath."

"That's my girl."

Max relaxed. Rosie was smiling. Mom had stopped

rubbing her forehead and chewing on the inside of her lip. Things were okay again—or as okay as they'd get while Rosie was in jail.

But Mom would get her out. She always did.

CHAPTER ELEVEN

HOW AM I GOING to get her out this time?

The question beat in Livy's brain the entire way home. All of Rosie's other legal entanglements had been settled with a small fine and a bit of community service, something Rosie loved anyway.

Folks in Savannah knew Rosie Frasier. She was eccentric in a city where eccentricity was relished. She meant no harm, and therefore serious charges had never been pressed. Of course, she'd never gone head to head with the sisters before.

Livy unlocked the door and stepped into the darkened house, Max hugging her side. Livy didn't like to come home to an empty place. It always made her feel lonely. From the way Max kept her skirt clenched in his fist, he wasn't a huge fan of an empty dark house, either. What a surprise.

"Hungry, baby?" she asked.

He shook his head. She knew what he was up to with the absence of the usual chatter. As a toddler, Max had always thought that if he couldn't see Livy, she couldn't see him. During hide-and-seek he would toss a blanket over his head and believe he was hidden. In the same vein, he no doubt hoped that by keeping quiet he could make her forget he was there, or at the least, what he had done.

Not tonight.

Livy followed Max upstairs, then straightened his room while he got in his pajamas and brushed his teeth. There were books tumbling out of his bookcase again. She needed to buy a bigger one or at least buy another. He had drawings taped all over his walls, and a few had fallen down. She replaced them with new tape, finishing just as Max returned from the bathroom.

Once he climbed into bed, Livy sat on the edge and traced her fingers through his long bangs. "Haircut time again," she murmured.

"I could grow it long like Mr. Stark." He gasped, slapped both hands over his face, a movement made difficult by the cast on one arm, then slouched beneath the covers.

Livy shook her head. Even if he had succeeded in getting her mind off his truancy, the first words out of his mouth would only have brought everything right back. Which showed Livy how enthralled by Garrett Max was already.

She pulled his hands away, fingers brushing the hard cold weight of his cast and flinching. His eyes were closed so tight his face wrinkled with the force of it. She drew her fingertip down his nose.

"Open up, Max. We're going to talk and there's no getting out of it tonight."

He sighed and opened his eyes. Her heart twisted and turned. Max *did* have his father's eyes. She'd always known they shared a color. But she'd never realized genetics could be found in the tilt of an eyebrow, the cloud of regret that darkened brown to black and a single shade of expression as Max waited for the ax to fall. His father had looked at her like that a lot since he'd come back to Savannah.

Livy rubbed her forehead some more, uncertain what to do or say. Small gentle hands pulled hers away from her face. Max leaned so close she could see flecks of black in the dark brown of his eyes. Then he climbed into her lap and tucked his head beneath her chin.

"Sorry, Mom," he whispered.

His words, his tone, his dear sweet face tempted Livy to let the entire incident go, because she found her throat so choked with love she didn't know if she *could* scold him. But she coughed and forced herself to do what had to be done.

"You scared me again, Max. What were you thinking to walk away from school?"

"Everyone was being mean to me."

Anger surged through Livy at his words. Max didn't have many friends. Since she didn't have many herself, Livy wasn't sure what to tell him. Kids picked on anyone smaller and younger. Survival of the fittest began in elementary school.

"Kids are mean, baby."

"Don't call me baby, Mom. It's embarrassing."

"Sorry."

How long would it be before he told her not to kiss him good-night, not to walk him to school the first day, not to be seen anywhere near him? Sooner than she was ready for, no doubt.

"Even Sammy was mean today."

"That's too bad."

Livy tried to make her voice sympathetic but firm. Max couldn't think that just because kids were being kids that meant he could walk off school grounds and wander at will.

He was going to have to learn to deal with mean kids, or at least learn not to care what they said. But it was hard to sound unconcerned when what she wanted to do was march down to school, grab every mean kid by his mean ear and twist until he was crying on the outside the way her son was crying on the inside.

She'd end up in jail, but she'd be smiling. Maybe that was why Rosie so often laughed when behind bars. She'd stood up for what she believed in—no matter how silly what she believed in might be—but whatever happened, Rosie could face it laughing because she'd done the right thing.

Livy cradled her son and slowly rocked him as she always had when he was a baby and upset. Once a mother, always a mother, she'd found. Give any mommy a baby and every single one did the baby sway. Even with a baby who did not want to be called a baby anymore.

Livy kissed Max's hair. How was she supposed to know what was right for him or what was wrong? She didn't even know that for herself. What if she made a mistake and ended up hurting him worse than any bump or bruise ever had?

"You're going to have to get used to mean kids.

They're all over the place. And when they grow up, they only get meaner.''

"Mr. Stark isn't.''

A matter of opinion, Livy thought. She'd been hurt more by Mr. Stark than anyone.

"He told me things, Mom.''

Livy stilled. She was going to be in jail with Mama soon, because she just might kill Garrett if he'd told Max—

"He told me how not to be afraid.''

Her breath came out in a rush. One hurdle avoided, another right in her path. "What are you so afraid of? I don't understand.''

"But he did.''

Silence filled the room. She could hear Max breathing, loud, through his mouth as he always did when he was nervous.

He extricated himself from her lap, her arms, her protection, and Livy tried not to cling, but she did. How could a stranger walk into her son's life and understand him when she could not? Even if the stranger wasn't really a stranger, to Max he was.

Her son sat on the bed, no longer touching her. He was as tired as she, his dark eyes huge in his pale little face. She should tuck him in and let the mystery go unsolved, but she couldn't.

"What did he understand?''

"Every time I try to tell you what scares me, I can see by your face you have no clue what I mean.'' Livy started to explain, but he cut her off. "If I say there's a closet monster, you say, 'No, there isn't,' like that's supposed to make it go away. When I told

Mr. Stark about the dark and the night and the mist, he got it.''

"He would," she muttered.

"I know." His voice excited, Max's face was filled with wonder, and Livy was glad he'd missed her sarcasm. "He knew exactly what I meant about things that aren't really there. You can tell me all you want that if I can't see something it isn't real, but it's real to me. Just because you say it can't be, Mom, doesn't mean that it isn't.''

From the moment he could speak, Max had questioned everything. Annoying as that could be sometimes, maybe it wasn't the worst thing. Livy had always hoped the first time anyone offered him a joint, or the latest equivalent, Max would sneer "No way!" with the same enthusiasm he'd always said it to her.

"What exactly did Mr. Stark tell you about your fears?''

"That I need to own them.''

"How much does it cost?''

Max laughed. "Not own like that. I take my shadows and I make them real in a story. Then I crush them, and they aren't so scary anymore. Because I won.''

"I still don't get it.''

Max grabbed a piece of paper from his nightstand. "Here." He shoved the paper into her hands. "At Mrs. Hammond's while I was waiting for you, I tried it, and I do feel better.''

Livy glanced at the story. Max had written "The Closet Monster" at the top of the page. At the bottom he'd drawn a gaping black hole of a closet, so large it loomed over the tiny bed and tinier blond boy who cowered beneath it. In between the title and the drawing was a story.

"Go ahead, Mom. You can read it." Max patted her knee as if she were a sad, pathetic dweeb. "Maybe then you'll understand."

There was a boy named Max and he had a closet monster. Every time his mom closed the door the monster grew bigger. Max tried to keep the door open, because what you can see is better than what you can't, but his mom always shoved all the doors shut whenever his back was turned. So the monster grew and grew.

Which explained the constant open state of the closet door, if nothing else.

Max spent a lot of nights sleeping under his bed.

"Max, you don't sleep under the bed, do you?"
He ducked his head. "Only sometimes. Keep readin', Mom."

But one night he got tired of the floor, and he decided that it was his room and he was going to take it back, and the closet, too. So instead of hiding under the covers or under the bed, he marched across the floor and punched that monster right in his nose. And *poof*, the closet mon-

ster became a big black raincoat. Max slammed
the door and slept on the bed forever and ever
more.

"Well?" Max's eyes were bright with newfound
knowledge, as well as a confidence Livy had never
seen there before.

"It's a wonderful story. But I still don't see how
it helps. There's no such thing as a closet monster,
and there never was."

Max groaned. "Mom. You have to admit it's there
before you can make it go away. Like ghosts. Rosie
says the people who make peace with the ghosts in
their house, the ones who talk to them and invite them
to stay as long as they behave, are the people who
can live with them without any trouble."

Livy didn't know what to say to logic like that,
which was no logic at all. What she'd been telling Max
since he was old enough to understand hadn't done a
bit of good. He still believed in vampires and zombies
and all sorts of dark, creepy imaginings as much as
her mother believed in the ghosts of Savannah.

Livy threw up her hands in defeat. So why not face
the monster and own it? Why not invite a ghost to
stay? She would never have thought to suggest anything of the kind, yet Garrett had known immediately
what his son had needed to feel safe.

Jealousy reared its ugly head. She'd raised this
child, been everything to him and he to her, yet one
week in town and his undead dad had become his
new best friend.

Livy stood and lifted the covers. Max dove beneath

and snuggled against the pillow with a tired, contented sigh. "It'll be nice not to see that silver-toothed closet monster anymore."

Livy kissed him on the forehead. "I bet it will."

Her jealousy dissolved at the sight of his peaceful, sleepy smile. She couldn't stay angry over something that made Max so happy and kept him from sleeping beneath the bed.

"Tomorrow I'm going to write about the goblins in the bathroom mirror."

"Excellent choice." Livy snapped off the light. "'Night, Max. Love you always."

"'Night, Mom. Love you, too."

"Max?"

"Mmm?"

He was almost out, but she had to make one final point. Even if she was a clueless moron, she was still his mother. "Stay in school."

He mumbled something that sounded like "Do my best," and turned over.

Livy frowned into the darkness. He must have said, "Yes, yes, yes," though she doubted it.

For a moment she watched him sleep, a small lumpy figure in a big old bed. Once asleep, a hurricane couldn't wake him, but many nights it took some time for Max to find dreamland. Now that the closet monster was gone, sleep seemed to come more easily.

Livy wished she could conquer her fears as easily. The old house creaked and moaned. Ghosts, if you were of a mind to believe that. For Livy, the creaks were made by old wood and the moans came from the wind through the attic. Still, the sounds were lonely, and she didn't like them. Tonight she could use some comfort, though she knew that for her there was no comfort to be had.

She backed out of Max's room and headed for her own, just as the phone began to clamor.

GARRETT HAD WAITED as long as he could. He'd wandered his house, peering into each room as if through Livy's eyes. He had to say, this kind of behavior didn't look good. He must appear a terminal bachelor who couldn't stay in one place for more than a minute. Funny, that was what he was.

After eating corn chips and salsa for dinner, Garrett had walked into his office, then walked right back out when his computer laughed at him. Although he might have an astounding imagination, he knew his computer hadn't literally laughed. Still, Garrett had heard it just the same.

So he'd taken his beer and his cell phone onto the porch, where the laughter only echoed in his mind.

Max had made the panic recede for most of the day. Now it was back, pulsing in Garrett's belly. He might not be able to write the book he so desperately needed to; he could very well blow the chance he'd been working toward all of his career.

Then he'd be a failure *and* a loser. No big surprise there. All authors waited for the day when the world at large would suddenly figure out they were a fraud, that they couldn't *really* write. That day might come for Garrett sooner than he'd ever believed.

He took a swig of his beer and stared out at the night. Oh, sure here and there he heard the rattle of an idea, like old bones shaking about in the giant empty of his brain. But when he tried to focus, to get something exact, that idea would be gone quicker than time.

Maybe a cemetery walk would help. Garrett had yet to stroll through Bonaventure Cemetery, located outside Savannah proper. From what he'd heard and read, if he couldn't find a spooky idea while wandering out there, he'd never find one.

A grand old forest graveyard, Bonaventure had once been a great plantation during the colonial era. It was most famous recently for its statue of the bird girl that became an icon of Savannah after gracing the cover of the book *Midnight in the Garden of Good and Evil.* The statue had been removed and placed in a nearby museum to protect her from vandals and thieves. The new world once again ruining the ancient and fair.

Despite the encroachment, Bonaventure still possessed more character than most cemeteries. At night the azalea bushes did not shine with bright spots of color, but rather shivered beneath the stately oak trees draped with silver-gray moss.

It was said that on certain evenings a ghostly dinner party ensued atop the ruins of the former mansion. If you listened hard enough and you believed, you would hear music, laughter and the whip of the flames that had burned the mansion to the ground while the revelers continued their party on the lawn. When the roof crashed in, the guests had thrown their empty wineglasses against one of those oak tees. The shatter of crystal still echoed through time.

Garrett gave a delighted shiver. He *had* to see the place. He finished his beer, set the bottle on the porch next to his chair, then hesitated, cradling his cell phone in one hand, as he tried to talk himself out of calling Livy.

For the sake of the book that wasn't, he needed to get in his car, drive out to Bonaventure and wander the ruins for as long as it took to get a really good idea. That might be days, but too bad. The situation was becoming desperate. Bonaventure meant "good fortune" in Spanish, and Garrett could really use some right now.

But until he knew what had happened with his son and his son's mother, he couldn't concentrate, so Garrett punched in the phone number he hadn't called in nine years but had never forgotten.

Even though he'd lived next door back then, he'd still ended every night by calling Livy. She'd said she wanted his voice to be the last thing she heard so it would follow her into the dark of the night. Livy hadn't known that her voice would follow him through the empty darkness of many nights to follow.

Her phone rang on the other end, a shrill happy sound in contrast to the muted pulse of loneliness in his heart. But when she picked up, her voice a breathless "Hello?" Garrett's heart thudded faster. Suddenly he had no idea what to say.

"Hello?" she said again, impatient now.

"Hello." Silence filled the line. He could see her standing next to her bed, holding the phone to her ear, frowning so hard her pretty face wrinkled. There was no question she knew his voice. That was what the silence was all about as she tried to decide if she should slam the phone down now or later.

"Don't hang up," he murmured. "Please. I only wanted to make sure everything was all right."

"We're fine." Though her voice was wary, not friendly, it wasn't unfriendly, either.

"Your mother?"

"In jail. She stole a goose and she won't give it back."

Garrett couldn't help it. He laughed. Amazingly, Livy laughed, too. He was so startled he stopped laughing so he could listen to her.

She laughed exactly as she always had, with abandon and joy. The sound was a bit rusty, and she stopped too soon, when she realized she was alone in her laughter, but the joy was still in her. Suddenly Garrett was determined to dig through the present all the way back to that past.

"I always loved to hear you laugh."

She didn't answer, but she didn't tell him to shut up, either. He was making incredible progress. Something had changed, he could feel it, but he wasn't sure what. She should still be furious at him for the scare he'd given her, albeit unintentionally. Instead, she was letting him talk, joke, even bring up the past she'd forbidden him to mention.

"I haven't had much to laugh about in a long time," she admitted.

"Your mother sounds pretty funny."

"She's a joke a minute," Livy said wryly. "But you don't have to live with her."

Livy had a problem with her mother. Easy for him

to understand, since he had problems of his own with his father. Garrett decided not to press a new issue when there were so many old ones to chose from.

"Max is a wonder," he began. "Some of the things he says are so original, so bright and brilliant...I don't know how you can't smile, if not laugh all the time."

An impatient exhale was followed by silence. He'd said something wrong. Garrett waited for the *click* of the disconnect. Instead, he heard "Thank you," in a grudging though sincere tone.

"What did I do?"

"You gave Max a way to conquer his fears. Though I can't say your method makes the least bit of sense to me, I'm happy he's happy. I've never been of any use when he talks to me about things that go bump in the night."

"It was my pleasure." Garrett hesitated, unsure if he had the right to any request, least of all the one he was compelled to make. "I hope you didn't punish him for visiting me."

"He scared me to death!"

"I know. But he was scared, too. I don't want to tell you how to raise him. I don't want to horn in where I don't belong, but—"

"I didn't punish him," she interrupted. She sounded as surprised about it as he was. "I should ground him until he's twenty-five, but that doesn't seem to work very well with Max."

"Why?" Grounding had never worked with Garrett, either, because he always for—

"He forgets." Garrett's lips curved in the cool, quiet darkness of the Savannah night. "He doesn't mean to disobey me. For a day, maybe two, Max is exactly where he belongs. Then something wonderful comes by—on the wind, in the grass, across his brain like a breeze, and he's gone. When I find him, he blinks at me like Mister Magoo. He has no idea what it is he's done that's made me insane.''

"I was that way, too.''

"How can something so capricious be carried in the genes?''

"My father would say it certainly didn't come from him.''

The sentence dropped between them. Another long silence ensued. Garrett wished he hadn't brought up his father. The memories always put a damper on any happiness he might have found.

"You never mentioned your father. You never mentioned your past at all.''

"Because it was past.'' He heard the ice in his voice.

Livy heard something more. "You don't like him.''

"I don't *have* to like him. He's my father.''

"Sounds like a line directly out of your father's mouth.''

For an imagination-deficient attorney, Livy was mighty perceptive.

Garrett grunted and Livy chuckled. Not a full-blown laugh, but he liked the sound almost as well. Maybe if he could laugh about James, Sr. he might feel better all around. But he wasn't that emotionally healthy.

"Max wrote a great story about his closet monster."

Well, at least someone is writing something great, Garrett thought.

"Sometimes I have no idea what to do with him." The laughter had gone out of Livy's voice; the sadness that seemed to characterize her since he'd come back was evident. "I don't understand him. But you knew right off what he needed."

"Because I needed it once, too. Still do."

"You're afraid of closet monsters?"

"Not anymore. My fears are adult fears now, but none the less invisible and full of teeth."

"What are you afraid of, Garrett?"

The night wind ruffled his hair, the past whispered along his neck, memories sprang to life unbidden and he shivered at the knowledge of all that he feared.

"I'm afraid I'll never be the writer everyone expects me to be. That I'll never find a woman as wonderful as the girl I left behind. That I'll never be the father my son deserves. But you know what I'm afraid of the most, Livy?"

"What?" Livy's voice was hoarse, perhaps with unspoken fears of her own.

"That I'll never even get the chance to try."

The *click* he'd been expecting all along shocked him now. Garrett listened until he heard the dial tone. Then he got up and drove to the place called "Good Fortune," wondering if he'd ever find any of his own.

CHAPTER TWELVE

"WE'VE GOT TROUBLE," Kim whispered.

"Mmm?" Livy didn't look up; she was too busy trying to find some precedent, any precedent, on goose stealing. She needed this case thrown out, not sent to trial. Because at trial they'd lose. Unfortunately, there weren't any goose-stealing precedents to be had. Big surprise there.

Kim's whisper went urgent. "Judge McFie trouble."

"What?"

Livy glanced at Kim, who nodded toward the bench. Livy followed her gaze. They were in trouble, all right. Judge Lamont McFie was presiding. The last time Rosie had gone in front of him, her fine had doubled and he'd promised on the next occurrence to make an example of her for all the other degenerates to consider. Rosie might be a lot of things, but a degenerate wasn't one of them.

"Double damn," Livy muttered.

She was not up for any dips and turns this morning, no arguments or surprises. She'd spent another nearly sleepless night, this time thinking about Garrett's call and the sincerity in his voice when he'd spoken of Max. Parental insecurity was something she could identify with, and Garrett's had made him far too appealing.

Once she'd fallen asleep she'd dreamed just the way she always used to after J.J. called. As a result she'd overslept, awakening aroused from those dreams and annoyed that she'd had them at all.

Too little sex. That's what it was. She could not still be attracted to the man who had crushed her heart. She *would* not be.

To top everything off, when she'd delivered Max to school, he'd put his nose to hers and stared deeply into her eyes. "Bring Rosie home for me, Mom. I know you can do it. You're the best."

Livy took a deep breath and laid her hand over her chest, where it hurt. Max didn't ask for much, so why had he asked for something she wasn't sure she'd be able to give him? Livy didn't want to see his face when she told him she'd failed and his beloved Rosie was in jail for goosenapping.

"Calm down." Kim patted her arm. "There's no proof your mother did this. No one saw her. She didn't confess." Livy just raised her eyebrows, an expression Kim ignored. "Even Judge McFie can't lock her up on the basis of circumstantial evidence and a crazy reputation."

"I hope you're right. But I wouldn't bet the farm on it."

"Me, neither."

Not only was Judge McFie fed up with Rosie, but he was fed up with a lot of people—and the system as it stood today. Having worn the robes of his trade for nigh onto forty years, he dispensed his own brand of justice, believing the bench was a place for the men who were closest to God. Of course, the joke around the courthouse was that McFie was closer to God than anyone by virtue of age alone.

Just then the side entrance of the court opened and Rosie waltzed out.

"Doggone it!" Livy exclaimed.

Once again her mother had not dressed in the dove-gray coat dress Livy had bought for court appearances. Instead she looked as if she'd borrowed clothes from her slumber party pals. The neon-orange halter top was made only minimally less risqué by the addition of a bright-red blouse for a jacket. Her combat boots set off the black leather skirt, which hugged her hips, thighs and calves nicely. She'd released her hair from the usual braid, so the kinky tresses swirled about her shoulders like a black-and-white flag.

"At least she didn't wear the T-shirt that says *Ninety-nine Percent Of Lawyers Give The Rest A Bad Name,*" Kim pointed out. "I don't think the judge would find it as funny as I did."

"This is going to be a very long morning," Livy groaned.

A commotion at the back of the court drew everyone's attention. The assistant district attorney had arrived, and he had friends.

"Oh, no." Livy resisted the urge to put her head down on the table and hide.

Viola and Violet were dressed for the occasion in morning frocks of blue and gray. No hats for the courtroom, or gloves at this time of day, but their matching pumps clipped on the hardwood floor as they approached.

"This is a hearing," Livy stated to no one in particular. "*They* don't have to be here."

"Did you really think they'd miss this?" Kim asked.

"Mama, why did you have to steal their goose?"

"Didn't," Rosie said out of the side of her mouth like an actor in a bad Mafia movie, before she took a seat at Livy's side.

The assistant district attorney, a young man who was probably the son of the son of someone the sisters had dated, tried to usher "the people" to the area reserved for spectators when court was in session. But the two women were having none of it.

Instead, they marched right up to the defense table. "Rosie Cannaught, you're gonna get yours now," Miss Violet trilled.

"What am I getting?" Rosie asked.

"A trip to jail."

"Had one. No, make that ten." She snickered and Kim joined in.

"Stop it," Livy ordered through her teeth.

"You know, they probably hid the goose just to get me in trouble."

"She keeps saying that." Miss Violet leaned down and shouted, "Where's my goose, hippie?" in Rosie's face.

Rosie went for the throat, but Livy grabbed her around the waist and hauled her back into the chair. "Mama! Not now."

"Later?"

"Maybe," Livy promised. The sisters were starting to get on her nerves, and Rosie had had to put up with them for a lot longer than she had. Whatever happened to the "ladies don't shout" rule? Obviously, that rule only applied to other ladies.

"Did you see that?" Miss Viola asked the judge. "She tried to kill Sister. A menace, that's what she is and always has been. She should be locked away from decent people."

"That remains to be decided," the judge said, though he appeared exasperated. "Let's get started."

The assistant DA tried again to send the sisters to the gallery. They ignored him, sitting at the prosecution's table as if they belonged there. From the expression on the baby lawyer's face, he didn't have the gumption to make them move. Livy really couldn't fault him.

"What's the charge?" McFie asked.

"The people charge the defendant under the Criminal Code of Georgia, section 16-8-20. Livestock theft, Your Honor."

McFie snorted. "Haven't heard that one in a while. Felony or misdemeanor?"

"Felony."

Kim cursed and Livy glanced her way. Kim had a mind that retained legal statutes the way a tape recorder retained sound. She'd clearly read section 16-8-20, and it wasn't good.

"What?" Livy whispered.

"Felony livestock theft is punishable by one to ten, and a fine of ten thousand dollars." Now Livy cursed.

"But to be classified as a felony, the fair market value of the animal has to be over one hundred dollars."

"I object," Livy said.

Judge McFie looked down his nose at Rosie, then turned his piercing eyes toward Livy. "About what?"

"Fair market value has to be over one hundred dollars for a felony livestock theft."

The judge glanced at the assistant DA for an explanation. "It cost that much to train this goose, Your Honor."

Since the judge was looking her way again, Livy resisted the urge to rub her forehead. "What do you have to say now, Counselor?"

"No one saw her take it. She says she didn't take it." Livy shrugged. "No proof but hearsay, Your Honor. I request my client be released immediately. This entire matter is a joke."

"With her, it usually is." McFie turned his gaze back to Rosie. "Give up the goose, Rosie, and this will all go away."

"Your Honor!" Livy said, shocked. He had no right to treat Rosie as if she were guilty. It was completely against the rules.

But before she could object, Rosie stood up. "I take the Fifth."

"Mama!" Livy pulled her back down.

"What?"

"If you want me to help you, you need to keep quiet unless I ask you to talk. We've been over this."

Rosie smiled and patted her cheek. "I know, sugar, but I just can't keep quiet. Especially when something's so wrong."

"Rosie," the judge said in a warning tone.

"Just because it's legal doesn't make it right."

"It does in my world," the judge thundered.

"Well, pardon me for saying so, but your world is screwed up."

"You need to watch your tone, or I'll hold you in contempt."

"Contempt." Rosie laughed. "Now, that would be a first."

Livy fought the urge to scream mindlessly or bang her head against the table. She didn't think Judge McFie would appreciate either behavior from the defense attorney. Instead, she watched as he turned a frightening shade of purple.

"That's it!" For an old man, he could shout loud enough to rattle a window. "Take her back where you got her. Until she plays by my rules, she'll be a guest of the city. I don't care how long it takes—you'll learn that the law isn't something to laugh about."

The judge banged his gavel and fled the room as though afraid he'd throttle Rosie if he stayed another moment. Livy could sympathize.

The bailiff appeared immediately and took Rosie's arm. Rosie glanced at Livy. "Nice try, sugar."

Livy had a headache and it wasn't even 10:00 a.m. "You know, I should let you rot."

Rosie didn't appear scared. She never did. That was one of the problems with Rosie. Instead, she winked, unabashed, and grinned. "But you won't."

"I promised Max I'd bring you home."

Rosie's smile froze, then fell. "I guess you'll have

to do something, then. Since you promised Max.''
She gave a short nod and left docilely with the bailiff.

Such docile behavior disturbed Livy. Rosie might
not act scared, but perhaps the seriousness of all this
had finally hit her. And as much as Rosie annoyed
Livy, she didn't want her mother to go to jail scared.

Though she'd been planning to return to the office
and talk to Rosie later, Livy changed her plans right
then and there. ''I'll be in to talk to you as soon as I
get things straightened out with Kim,'' she called.

Despite Livy's words, Rosie kept walking without
saying anything more, until she walked by the sisters
anyway.

''We won!'' Miss Violet jeered. Miss Viola just
laughed as if she'd never stop. Even the assistant DA
smiled. Livy wanted to walk over and knock their
heads together. She should have known Rosie didn't
need any help.

''How do you figure that, since you're still short
one goose?''

The dawn of realization on the sisters' faces was
priceless. When they turned on the lawyer, the two
sounded like a gaggle of what they were so worried
about.

Livy frowned as her mother left the courtroom, still
too subdued. After that parting shot, Rosie should be
grinning. She loved to cause trouble.

''Kim?''

Livy's partner appeared at her elbow. ''Let me
guess. Reschedule everything that can be rescheduled.
Start researching obscure and bizarre livestock prec-

edents. Cancel all meetings after four o'clock. Anything else?"

"Find that goose."

Kim drew her long black hair into a "get down to business" ponytail. "I was afraid you were going to say that."

ROSIE PACED her empty jail cell. All her pals had been bailed out before dawn. They punched a different time clock than the rest of the world and needed to get their beauty sleep come sunup. Kind of like the vampires Max was so interested in.

For a change Max wasn't the problem. Livy was. To be truthful, she'd always been something of a problem. From the moment she was born, Rosie had loved her, but she'd never known how to say it or show it, because Livy had never needed her love, never needed her. That kind of stuff preyed on a mother's mind. Even a mother as liberal as Rosie.

"Well, I'm sick of it," she muttered, and kicked at the iron bars.

"Sick of jail already?" Livy appeared on the other side with a baby-faced officer who held the key.

"Hey, sweetcakes." Rosie smiled at the officer on duty with as much enthusiasm as she could muster. She couldn't recall his name, but all the young ones treated her like the mother they'd always wanted. Why couldn't her daughter want the same? The boy smiled back and opened the door to let Livy inside, then disappeared.

"Tell me where the golden goose is, Mama, and I can get you out of here in an hour."

"Are you on my side or theirs?" Rosie demanded.

"I just want you out of here."

"You didn't answer the question. Sometimes, Livy, you are such a—a—a lawyer."

Livy narrowed her eyes. "Lucky for you, since you need one so often."

Rosie turned away, shocked to find tears burning. It had never bothered her before that she and Livy didn't see eye-to-eye on anything. They were different.

Rosie and her mother had been different, too. It was the way of families, the way of mothers and daughters, that often they did not get along. Even more common was that they might want to get along, yet had no idea how.

"Just once," she managed to say, "I'd like my daughter to stick up for me."

"Once? I go to court with you every single time."

"You defend me, but with a wink and a nudge. How do you think that looks? What does it make people think?"

"Since when have you given a rat's behind what something looks like or what anyone thinks, including me?"

"I care what you think. I always have."

Rosie turned, and Livy frowned at the evidence of her struggle with tears. Her daughter's face, then her voice, gentled. "You're not acting like yourself, Mama. Are you afraid I won't get you out?"

"Of course not. I trust you."

"You do?"

The surprise in her voice grated on Rosie's already

raw nerves. "Why wouldn't I trust you? You promised Max, didn't you? That makes it as good as done."

Why it bugged Rosie so much that Livy wasn't getting her out because *she* wanted her out but because Max did, Rosie didn't know. But there it was.

"For some reason, everything you say today sounds sarcastic."

"Weird, huh?"

Livy sighed. So did Rosie. This wasn't going well. Typical of every conversation they'd ever had.

"Unfortunately, Mama, the judge is going to see this as theft pure and simple."

This is where they differed, or had since Rosie had come back to Savannah and discovered the Livy she knew buried beneath this legalized stranger.

"Nothing's pure and simple. Cut-and-dried. Black or white. Life is often a dirty mess. But sometimes it can be full of colors and light and such beauty it makes you gasp. If you only open your eyes, your mind and your heart."

"Don't start that stuff with me now. The happy days of freedom are over. They fell out of the sky."

Rosie flinched. "You have such a way with words, sugar."

"I'm sorry. That was…uncalled for."

Livy rubbed at her forehead. The gesture always made Rosie want to hold her close and kiss it better. How had her dancing little girl become this sad-eyed woman who seemed to have a constant headache?

Rosie never pressed, but maybe she should have ferreted Livy's problems into the open, the way her own mother always tried. Rosie had resented what she considered nosiness. But what *she* had resented might be just what Livy needed.

Or, at least, what she needed right now. For the past several days Livy had been more stressed than usual, and that was saying quite a bit. Something was going on. Call it a mother's intuition, which she should have made use of before now.

"You've been angry for so long." Rosie took a step closer. "I don't think you know how not to be anymore. And scared, too, about Max." She put her hand on Livy's shoulder and rubbed. The muscles were as hard as stones and vibrated with tension. "I wish you'd trust me. Talk to me. Let me help you."

For a minute Rosie caught a glimpse of hope in Livy's eyes, before it was smothered behind the cool blue once more. She stepped away from Rosie's comforting touch.

"You help me daily, Mama, and I'm grateful."

Rosie curled her fingers together to keep from reaching out again. "I'm your mother. I don't want you to be grateful."

"Then, what do you want?"

"I guess I always wanted you to need me. But you never needed anyone except your father."

Anger flared where the hope had been. It was an expression Rosie was used to seeing in her daughter's eyes. But that didn't make it any easier to face.

"That's not true. I needed you once, but you weren't there."

Rosie put a hand over her heart. "Bull's-eye again, Livy."

"And I'm sorry again." Rub, rub, rub on the fore-head. "I don't want to hurt you. I don't mean to. Do we have to talk about the past? Dredge up everything that can't be changed? I don't know how to talk to you. I never did."

"And I'm sorry for that. I always dreamed of a glorious relationship with my daughter, the relationship I wanted with my mother and never had." She threw up her hands. "But look at us."

"Ever since Daddy died, you've tried to change me. Telling me what I'm doing wrong—with my work, with Max, with everything. Nothing is ever right enough for you."

Was that true? Rosie hadn't meant to become her own mother all over again.

"I just want you to be happy. You *were* happy once."

"Yeah, I was," Livy whispered, almost to herself.

"So find that happiness again."

Livy's gaze flicked to Rosie's and she shook her head. "It's gone."

"You're sure?"

"Very." But she didn't appear so.

"Sometimes what we think is gone is just waiting for us to come full circle. Like your father. He's not really gone, sugar. He's only waiting."

And for the first time in a very long time, Livy didn't argue with her mother.

LIVY MADE IT HOME by four. Barely. Another case had gone sour on her. She was beginning to wonder if she was cursed.

Once, she'd thought the law could give her the security she needed to survive. If she upheld the law, the truth, stood for those who could not stand for themselves, didn't that make her stronger, she who had always been so weak? Upholding the law gave her control, or so Livy had thought. She was starting to understand that control was an illusion. Especially when emotions were involved.

Nothing's pure and simple. Cut-and-dried. Black or white. Life is often a dirty mess.

When had Rosie become Savannah's psychiatrist?

Livy put her briefcase on the table in the hall, then kicked her heels against the wall. She'd felt bad all day. Her mother had wanted to talk. Livy just hadn't been able to. She'd spent too many years keeping to herself, managing as best she could. She didn't talk about anything personal, mainly because she didn't have anything personal to talk about, and she liked it that way.

But suddenly her entire life was one big soap opera, every little thing a throbbing personal problem. She might trust Kim with some of it, but she needed Kim focused on work. One of them had to be.

Though Livy should have stayed late and worked on an appeal, until Rosie was free, late was no longer an option. It was going to be a hardship to keep up with work and Rosie and Max. In all honesty, Livy didn't think she'd be able to manage it.

Mrs. Hammond didn't mind helping in an emergency, but she'd made it clear from the first she didn't want Max over every day after school and sometimes at night and on the weekends, too. Livy couldn't blame her. After the first trip to the E.R., she was surprised Mrs. Hammond hadn't moved out of the neighborhood.

Livy wished she didn't have to work all these hours. The guilt ate at her every time she arrived home after Max had fallen asleep. But the law waited on no one, and neither did the bills she had to pay.

Feet pounded up the porch steps. Max tripped in the door. His cast bashed against the wall. Livy winced.

"Hey, ba— I mean, Max. How's that arm?"

He waved it about like a prizefighter. Several dents marred the surface already. "Great. You know having this means a lot less bruises on my arm."

"I bet."

He looked around. "Where's Rosie?"

"Well..." Livy hesitated. Why was it so hard to tell him she'd failed.

"Jail, huh? That's okay, Mom. You did your best. It'll all work out."

He trotted off to the kitchen in pursuit of food, and that was that. Max didn't mention Rosie for the rest of the evening, except in the "God bless" portion of his prayers.

Because in Max's mind his mom would take care of everything. He trusted her. Just as Rosie trusted her. Hell, *everybody* trusted her. Livy Frasier stood for justice and truth.

Too bad she was a big fat liar.

Exhausted, Livy went to bed right after Max. She hoped tonight, unlike last night, she'd be able to sleep. Though with all the things she had to think about, all the areas of her life that were unraveling, she had a feeling her hope would be merely that. Livy punched her pillow a few times and settled in.

Her exhaustion made her drift in a hazy place between asleep and awake, a subconscious world where thoughts came as fast and easy as memories of the past.

Rosie had said things come full circle. She'd meant love and happiness. She could have as easily meant justice and punishment. What goes around comes around, and Livy was pretty certain something was coming for her.

As if an echo of her thoughts, a *thump* sounded on the servants' stairs.

"Only the house," she murmured. "Too many memories."

Garrett's phone call last night had made her think all day about things she'd believed forgotten. How he had once snuck up those stairs to spend each twilight in her bed.

It had been easy. She'd given him the key.

A key he had never returned.

Livy sat up, suddenly wide-awake. At least that particular memory kept her from screaming when he stepped into the room and quietly closed, then locked, the door.

CHAPTER THIRTEEN

LIVY DIDN'T APPEAR surprised to see him, which threw Garrett off his game.

After she'd hung up on him, he didn't figure another phone call was advised. Appearing on her doorstep would probably get the door slammed on his toe. Besides, he didn't want Livy sneering at him with Max around.

So he'd stood outside and waited until all the lights went out, just the way he always used to. He'd devised a plan: unlock the door, slip upstairs, don't scare her to death, talk fast before she threw him out.

But when he saw her sitting in bed as if waiting for him, just as she always used to, he froze and every word of the speech he'd planned flew out of his head, even as all his blood pooled lower.

Everything he'd felt for her returned, slamming into him with the force of a Missouri ice storm and leaving him just as breathless. For a short time she'd been all he'd ever wanted, ever dreamed of, and so he'd been unable to stay. Because he knew he'd ruin the beauty of them eventually.

Whatever he touched he broke; whatever he cared about he crushed; when things mattered the most, he failed. Just look at the un-book.

"What are you doing here?" she asked.

Garret swallowed. Throat treacherously empty of moisture, he nearly choked. Against the navy-blue pillowcase, her butterscotch hair shone. Once, her sheets had been crisp and white, soothing to lay upon in the heat of a Georgia summer night. But the dark blue suited the woman she'd become and matched her eyes, though Garrett doubted she cared about such frivolities.

"We have to talk—" he began.

"I know." He gaped at her easy acquiescence. "Did you think I'd disagree? Although I'd have preferred to wait until daylight to do this..." She shrugged and threw back the covers.

His eyes, traitors that they were, scanned her form with interest while she moved to her armoire and pulled out a robe.

She used to sleep in a skimpy T-shirt and silk panties. For years the merest thought of her long legs peeking from beneath the cotton had gotten him hard at the most inappropriate times.

Her sleeping attire was still cotton, but flowed about her ankles when she walked. As she lifted her arms and thrust them into the robe, the cotton tightened along her breasts, much fuller now because of him, because of Max.

Garrett turned and moved to the window. Getting hard at inappropriate times did not seem to be a problem of just his youth.

He smelled her first, a haunting hint of spice, even before he heard the *swish* of her robe and nightgown. She stood at his side and stared out the window, too.

Garrett fought not to turn and take her in his arms and make her forget talking while they did anything but.

"I'm going to give you a chance." Her words, coming so soon on the heels of his lascivious thoughts made him start.

"At what?"

He felt her look in his direction, but even in the shadows he did not want to risk her seeing how she affected him, so he kept staring out the window, hands crossed over his interest.

"At getting to know your son."

So much for nonchalance; his head jerked toward her as hope sprang to life within him. "Really?"

"I'm not a sadist, Garrett. I wouldn't hold out Max, then snatch him away and laugh. Even though I should."

"You've been adamant that I didn't deserve a minute with him. Why now?"

She struggled with her words a moment before blurting, "I need help. My mother's in jail, and she's not getting out for a while. I can't be home every day at four, and someone has to be. I could hire a nanny, but—" She paused as if she didn't want to continue.

"But?"

Livy pursed her lips, then looked away. "I think Max needs you."

"Don't sound so happy about it."

"It would be my preference for you to go away and never come back, forget where Savannah is, forget Max exists. But you aren't going to."

"Damn right."

"The two of you connected in a way he and I never have." She sounded sad.

Garrett touched her arm, and she glanced at him. Even in the darkness, he saw the uncertainty in her eyes, and suddenly he wanted to comfort more than ravish. "Max loves you."

"He has to. I'm Mommy. But he doesn't understand me, any more than I understand him. You do. I never thought blood meant so much." She shrugged and sidestepped, effectively removing his hand from her arm. "Max could use a man in his life."

"What about your friend Klein?" Garrett couldn't resist asking. Jealousy burned, even when he had no right. The man had taken an instant dislike to him, and Garrett figured that was because he had an extreme liking for Livy.

"He *is* my friend and a good one."

"Only a friend?"

Livy narrowed her eyes. "Not that it's any of your business, but yes, he's just a friend. I've needed friends like him lately. He's also a colleague and damn good cop. Klein figured out that you were Max's father."

Surprise smothered the jealousy. "How could he know that?"

"He said you and Max have the same eyes."

Pride surged through Garrett, until he saw the shadows dance across Livy's face. The urge came again to take her in his arms, no longer sexual, but there just the same. "Livy, I—"

She held up her hand, seemed to struggle for words. "We'll make an agreement. You can see Max on the condition that you don't tell him who you are.''

The lightness in his heart that was hope, darkened. ''Ever?''

''I didn't say that. Let's just wait awhile. Give all of us a chance to get used to this.''

Garrett nodded slowly as understanding dawned. ''You think I'm going to run off again, and you don't want Max hurt.''

''Is that unreasonable? Just tell me if it is and I can hire a nanny.''

Garrett's emotions had been up and down and all around so many times since he'd come into this room that he was starting to feel like a trolley on the streets of San Francisco.

Once again he'd been judged inadequate before he'd had a chance to try. That made him angry, though Livy had every right to distrust him. And even as the anger burned, so did the fear. What if he *did* mess up? This was his son, not a book.

''I only want what's best for Max. If you think that my being just his friend, for now, is what's best, all right. I agree.''

''Great.'' Livy held out her hand to shake.

Garrett stared at it in disbelief. ''You're kidding right?''

''What?''

''I'm not going to shake hands like Max is a deal you brokered. He's a child. Our child.''

Her hand fell back to her side. ''I'm not likely to forget that.''

''You did before.''

"No." She crossed her arms over her breasts, hugged herself as if she were cold, though the room felt far too warm to him. "I've never forgotten. Never. Not one minute of any day, nor most of the nights. He was always yours. Forever ours. Why do you think I'm so angry?"

"Tell me. Make me understand."

Her sigh wavered in the middle, and suddenly Garrett understood that the shadows in her eyes had been lurking tears. He reached out, but she backed away. "Don't touch me." She laughed, a watery sound, and sat in a rocking chair surrounded by the night. "Even now, when you touch me I can't think. I can only feel and remember."

He caught his breath at her admission, but now was not the time to explore what they'd once felt, what they might feel again. When had he started to hope for a second chance with Livy? When she'd offered him a first chance with his son?

"Did I ever tell you about my father?" she began.

"Max mentioned it."

"He did?" She shrugged. "Good. Then, I don't have to. I adored him and he left me. Forever. My mother dumped me here, and she was off on some great adventure before Daddy was even cold."

Which explained her problem with her mother, and the reason she'd needed Garrett so much back then. She'd frightened him with that need, with the depth of her love. He'd been terrified he'd never be worthy of such a bright and shining gift, so he'd run, and ended up nearly missing the greatest gift he could ever imagine.

"I loved you so much." The intensity in her voice made his heart leap with hope. Until he heard the past in those words. She'd *loved* him. Until he'd ruined it.

"You broke my heart," she whispered, and stared down at her hands, twisting, twisting in her lap.

As if the sight disturbed her, she pulled them apart, cleared her throat and soldiered on. "The day after I said I loved you for the first time, I came skipping up the stairs to your room, and you were gone. I just stood there. I couldn't believe what I was seeing. The place was empty of everything but an old, plaid shirt you'd tossed across a chair. I felt like I was in a trance. I put the shirt on, and I could smell you." She took a deep breath, as if living that moment all over again. "Then your landlady walked in, said you'd packed, paid, and you weren't coming back."

Livy lifted her face, and her eyes shone bright in the silver light of the half-moon. He made a move toward her, but she held up her hand. "No. I need to finish." She rocked back and forth a few times. The floor creaked, an agitated sound that matched her mood. "I still didn't believe it. I *loved* you. Then I found out I was pregnant—"

"Livy, I—"

"Be quiet! You need to hear this." She paused again.

He wanted to tell her to stop, that this was hurting her, hurting him. But she was right; he needed to know what he'd done.

"I was happy when I found out. Everything that had been good about us would come alive in the child. And how could you not come back when there was a baby? Of course, that made no sense. You didn't know about the baby. You'd left *me*. For months I wore your shirt to bed.'' Her voice wavered; so did her lip. ''As long as I had that shirt, I had hope. So I kept hoping, until…''

''Until?''

''Max was born. He was early and too small. The labor was long and, damn it, it hurt. I think more so because I was completely alone.''

Garrett closed his eyes. He was *such* an asshole.

''The day I was supposed to leave the hospital, I put on your shirt again, and it wasn't good enough. The shirt wasn't you, and I finally believed that you weren't coming back. I couldn't keep waiting and hoping forever. When my father died, I mourned, but the mourning ended. When you left me of your own free will, it killed me from the inside out. I didn't want that for Max. When my hope died, so did you. And it was easier that way.''

''Until I showed up undead.''

''Exactly.''

She had every right to hate him. Hell, he hated himself. The fact that he hadn't known what a mess he'd left behind didn't make his leaving any less an act of pure cowardice.

Garrett had believed himself incapable of loving her the way she needed to be loved. He'd feared the disillusionment in her eyes when she realized he wasn't the man she'd hoped for. He'd believed that in leaving he was doing the right thing, the only thing he could do. What he hadn't realized was that for Livy, leaving was the worst thing he could have done.

"So now you know what it was like for me when you left. I'm not proud of how much I needed you. How completely destroyed I was to lose you."

"You sound embarrassed."

"I am! I was. I trusted you. Foolishly, and I paid the price. You were a weakness. One I won't repeat."

"So love is a weakness. I'd heard it was strength."

She made a derisive sound. "I love Max. He's my weakness. He's the only person whose loss would destroy me utterly. I can't afford to love anyone else the way I loved you. I don't have the strength anymore."

He hadn't seen this much emotion from Livy since he'd returned. Though she didn't want him to touch her, he had to.

Garrett crossed the room and knelt next to her chair. Warily she stared at him;, he could almost see her shrinking back against the wood.

"You're selling yourself short. After what you just told me, I think you're the strongest woman I've ever known."

She shook her head; her hair tumbled across her cheek. Garrett brushed it away, and when his fingers slid along her skin she shivered. His body shuddered in response, and he gritted his teeth against the shaft of lust that spiked through him. No matter the inappropriateness, the incongruity of wanting her always, he couldn't help that he did.

"You protected Max from the world, from himself, from me. You did whatever you had to do for him. I'd thank you, but I have no right."

He tucked her hair behind her ear and lowered his

hand toward his side. She shifted, most likely uncomfortable on the hard wooden seat, and his fingertips grazed her thigh. The heat of her skin scalded through two light layers of cotton.

He froze. So did she. When their eyes met, he saw his desire mirrored in her. Still, he knew better than to take what had not been offered. Slowly, carefully, he removed his hand. But she caught him before he could escape.

"Garrett?" she whispered. "Why is it still the way it always was?"

If it was *exactly* the same, she'd be calling him J.J. He took an instant to be glad she wasn't. If she thought him that boy yet, he'd never get past all the mistakes he'd made to become this man.

"Is it the same?"

She pressed the palm of his hand to the inside of her thigh. "Isn't it?"

"Oh, yeah" slipped past his lips before he could stop it. At least she smiled, so he didn't feel too much like an adolescent.

He wasn't sure what she wanted; was afraid to go too fast, make a bigger mistake than ever before. But touching her felt too good to give up, so he let the warmth of her skin soothe him, even as the possibilities awakened.

Staring into her eyes, he was compelled to tell her a little of his heart. "You consumed me then. You consume me now. I can't think past the memories of you that I don't even have."

She slid forward on the chair. His fingers were suddenly full of nightgown, and her knee was bare. He felt like a kid, uncertain where to put his hands, where to look, what to do.

Looping her arms around his neck, she urged him closer, so that he knelt between her legs; her thighs skimmed his hips and their faces were mere inches apart.

"Tell me," she murmured, and her breath brushed his chin.

"Huh?"

She smiled again and worked her fingers against the length of his hair. "About those memories of me."

"Oh." He closed his eyes, focused on the brain in his head, and not the one farther down that seemed to have a mind of its own right now. "This chair. I see you here with Max. It's the middle of the night, and you're rocking him. Then he starts to cry." He opened his eyes and found her staring at him in wonder, so he continued.

"You've got a gown like this, with buttons down the front, so you open them, but only so far." Hesitantly, he reached forward and pressed one finger to a point just above her belly. The muscles of her stomach jumped, and she made a sound deep in her throat that tugged at him much lower than his belly.

"And you open the gown, then you feed him from your breast." He lifted his eyes and caught hers. "It's the most beautiful memory that I don't have."

Her breath came as fast and hard as his own. Holding his gaze, she removed her hands from his neck and pushed aside her robe, then unfastened her gown. Silky white skin appeared between the buttons.

"To here?" she murmured.

Slowly he reached out, popped one more button. "More like...here."

She opened her arms, inviting him back. Though this time it wasn't love for her, it was for him, and he could deny her nothing, because he'd denied her everything before.

LIVY WANTED GARRETT still and she was tired of fighting it. Why should she? She was an adult. So was he. They'd had a child together. Why put off the inevitable?

Though she'd had a quick, breathy fantasy of tumbling him onto the carpet and having sex right there, he was having none of it. In fact, he took his sweet time just kissing her, touching her face, murmuring her name. He was different, yet somehow the same.

His large, gentle hands along her back soothed, even as his lips enticed. Cool air caressed her skin through the gap in her gown. The same air chilled her knees and the contrast of that chill with the heat of him made her shudder.

His mouth moved away and she pulled it right back. In the past they'd often "made out" for hours until both of them were so enflamed with the possibilities they couldn't think straight. Right now, she did not want to think.

He suckled her lips, played a bit with her tongue. His strong hands warmed her knees, then his thumbs discovered the muscles of her inner thighs. She'd never known how responsive those muscles could be until they leaped and quivered beneath his touch.

He'd learned new tricks in the years he'd been gone. She could care less where or how; she only cared that he had. His clever fingers shimmied under the lace of her panties, ran along the line of skin where her hip and her leg joined. His thumbs tested the curves of her hipbones, before he somehow divested her of her underwear while she was enjoying what his mouth did to her ear.

Her robe hung off her arms, and she shrugged it aside impatiently, the movement only making the gap in her gown gape wider. The buttons tugged beneath her breasts, tight, uncomfortable, and she raised her hand to release them, but his were already there. The front opened and his palm skimmed over her. Once, his hands had scraped along her skin and she'd loved the contrast of rough upon soft.

Now those hands had healed, and while they weren't soft, they weren't rough, either. Still, they made her arch, offering more, offering all that she had. When the chair rocked, the softness of her slid against the hardness of him.

Her gasp of shock became a moan of arousal when he lifted the weight of a breast and closed his mouth over the peak. Gently he rolled her nipple with his tongue as he rocked the chair, rocked them both.

Desperate for more, she reached for his buckle, but there wasn't one. His black cotton trousers opened easily, and she touched him now the way she'd always touched him then.

He raised his dark head, and their eyes met. She saw something in his gaze she'd never seen there before, and she hesitated. His lips tilted a bit and he stilled her hand.

"Wait," he murmured, then fumbled about.

Her body aflame, she wanted to scream, *I've been waiting nine years.*

But when he produced a condom, sheathed himself, then leaned over and gently kissed her lips, she had to smile, too.

"Once bitten," she whispered.

"Twice shy."

This time when she guided him to her, he went with a sigh that shivered over her damp skin. He bent his head, nuzzling her breast, and his hair drifted and tickled along her neck, adding sensation upon sensation.

They rocked together fast and frantic, then slower, easier, until they both struggled for control—it was too good to end too soon. But at last he suckled once, pushed against her, tight and hard, then went still. The pulse and release, so deep, so strong, caused answering waves in her that seemed to reach all the way back in time.

Before she'd caught her breath, he rearranged their clothes, lifted her into his arms and carried her to the bed, where he laid her gently on top, then followed her down. When the bed creaked, he laughed.

"What?"

"I have fond memories of that creak."

She was amazed to find herself smiling, when before those memories had only made her want to cry. "Me, too."

"Why don't we make some more?"

He parted her gown, lowered his head to her quivering belly, placing an openmouthed kiss just below her navel. When he looked up the length of her body, the sight of that familiar face brought a rush of intense memories and the echo of fierce emotions.

Perhaps replacing old painful thoughts with new and ardent ones would heal her lingering pain. Maybe to exorcise J.J., she merely needed to work Garrett out of her system. What could it hurt?

"Why don't we?" she asked, and tossed her gown to the floor with the rest of her clothes.

Then she made short work of the rest of his.

CHAPTER FOURTEEN

LIVY AWOKE ALONE, and for a moment it was a long-ago summer night and J.J. had just snuck out the back way, then across the yard to his own room. He'd call her soon and they'd talk before they fell asleep.

Then a cool, autumn-scented breeze through the window brought her back to the present only seconds before Max's sleepy murmur made her remember what she had just done.

In the past nine years she'd rarely had sex, and she'd never much liked it. Livy had come to believe the lack was in her, but in the space of a single instant in Garrett's arms, she'd understood that the lack had merely been of him.

The knowledge frightened her, because not only were the sexual feelings the same, but he was the same, despite a change in name. Be he J. J. Garrett or Garrett Stark, he wouldn't stay. He wasn't capable of it.

This time he'd been careful. She would be careful, too. She'd guard her heart, which shouldn't be that hard. She wanted him still because they'd never finished what they'd started. What they'd had was left undone. So they'd finish it. On her terms this time.

A shuffle in the hallway made her scramble for her

robe. If Max came in with a nightmare he'd wonder why her clothes were all over the floor. But when she found her robe, it was tangled in Garrett's shirt. He must not have left as she'd thought.

She stepped through the door and saw him standing, barefoot and bare chested, in the doorway to Max's room. Concerned that Max had needed her and she'd slept right through his call, Livy hurried to join Garrett. But he merely stared, transfixed at the sight of his son fast asleep.

The love on his face was so plain and so true a little part of Livy's heart broke off at the sight. She had never considered that a father might love his child with the same unconscious devotion a mother would.

Just because Livy had carried him and borne him did not make Max any less his father's child. Genetics stated half and half. Still, she'd been unwilling to give up any part of Max at all. But that expression on Garrett's face made sharing Max a little less hard than it had been yesterday.

Garrett glanced her way, then back at Max, as if he couldn't keep his eyes from the sight. When she leaned in the doorway, he took her hand, and she let him.

The night hovered around them, blue-black and cool, the sound of their son's gentle snore a music that connected them by more than their hands, more than a past, more than any future they might imagine. Embarrassment over what had happened between them seemed silly when they shared a son. As a result the moment was peaceful, pure and lovely. Livy found herself wishing for more of them.

"He's magic," Garrett whispered. "A miracle I don't deserve."

Once, she would have agreed, but now she knew the truth. "Nobody deserves a gift like Max."

"Is that why you protect him so obsessively?"

Her peace fled on the silent night. She might have had a few warm feelings about Garrett after spending some quality time in bed with him, but that didn't mean he could tell her how to raise her son, even if Max was his son, too.

She'd been listening to everyone's opinion on her overprotectiveness since Max had made his appearance in this world. Rosie, Kim, doctors, nurses, even Klein thought she hovered. Too bad. If hovering kept Max safe, she'd hover until she crashed. Unfortunately, hovering hadn't seemed to do much good, as the size of Max's medical file could attest.

Livy tugged free of Garrett's hand and walked back to her room. After a last, lingering glance at Max, he followed. She shut the door behind him and placed her back against the wood.

"I protect Max because I know how easily life can be snatched away."

Garrett picked up his shirt from the floor. "You can't control fate, Livy."

"Watch me."

As he shrugged into the garment, Livy found herself distracted by the play of muscles across his lean chest. She'd always been partial to a tall, runner's physique—a bias courtesy of this very man, no doubt—so she moved across the room, sitting on the bed to keep away from temptation.

He bent again and straightened, socks in hand, then sat at her side. When her hip rolled into his, she gritted her teeth against the lust such a simple movement caused. Getting Garrett out of her system was one thing. Becoming a nymphomaniac was another. How could she be annoyed with him and aroused by him at the very same time?

Livy went to stand in front of the window, pointedly ignoring the rocking chair. Garrett draped his socks over one knee and contemplated her face, reminding her of one of the reasons she had loved him. When he listened, he listened completely, with all of his attention. For a young girl who had gone from being the apple of her father's eye to the ignored child of the town eccentric, such attention had made her feel important, special and cared for. But Livy knew better than to fall for the same trick twice.

"I do the best I can." Even to Livy's own ears, she sounded defensive.

"And I have no business prying. You're right." He shrugged and returned his attention to his socks. "It's just...I was the same way as a kid. Tripped up every step, fell down every hill, broken this, sprained that."

"And what did *your* parents do?"

"My mother left when I was two."

Livy blinked. She had never heard a word about his mother, but she hadn't expected to hear this. "I'm sorry."

"She chose to leave, so I can understand some of your anger at me. I've felt a certain anger toward her myself on occasion. But for the most part, when I think of my mother I have little recollection of her."

A wave of sympathy washed over Livy at the thought of a little boy all alone. "And your father, what did he do?"

Garrett stared at his socks again, as if seeing into the past. "Told me what a klutz I was. Tried to make me a man."

"He what?"

He glanced up, and though his eyes were still cloudy with the memories, his face had gone hard. "My father was a high-powered, corporate attorney."

Oh-oh, Livy thought. *That explains his distaste for my profession.*

"I was an embarrassment to him. Never good enough, never right enough, never smart enough, never athletic enough."

"You were a child. You were exactly the way you were supposed to be."

"Tell James, Sr. He wasn't impressed."

"Let me get this straight—your father told you you didn't measure up?"

"Every day of my life. Until I left."

"What does he say now?"

"I have no idea."

"You don't talk to him?"

"I gave up trying to please Daddy the day I caught a bus out of town. I'm not saying I don't hear his voice now and again." His mouth twisted in self-mockery. "'J.J., everything you touch, you break. Everything you care about, you crush. When things matter the most, you fail.'"

Horrified, Livy could only stare at him. She had known none of this. No wonder he had always seemed haunted. Even when he'd laughed, there'd been secrets in his eyes. He had drawn her in that way. His loneliness had called to her own. Maybe it was better that she had not known the reasons for Garrett's inner turmoil, because she only would have loved him more.

Livy had lived a golden childhood. Though Rosie didn't approve of her job, her demeanor or her mothering skills, Livy had always known her mother loved her. Still, she could understand Garrett's fear of never being enough for anyone.

"In my work I've discovered a lot of men who don't deserve to be fathers. Yours is one of them."

Garrett shrugged. "He was right about some things. I do have a habit of running when things get tough and failing under pressure."

"When have you failed?"

"I failed you. I failed my son. Right now, I'm supposed to be done with the book of a lifetime and I haven't even started. Looks like my father wasn't so dumb after all."

"If you let his voice continue to haunt you, he's won."

"He won years ago. When a beautiful girl told me she loved me and I couldn't love her back. I knew I'd never be good enough, or right enough, or just…" He spread his beautiful hands wide. "Enough for her. So I ran."

He was repeating the same words his father had always said to him. She wondered if he knew how affected he'd been by the emotional abuse of his

childhood. When had he come to believe he wasn't
enough for anyone, even himself?

"You're here now," she said gently.

"I believe you told me now is too late."

A lot of things she'd said in anger were sounding
a bit bitchy coming back at her. Rosie thought Livy
believed the worst of people. In her job, that usually
saved time. But maybe she'd allowed her past and her
work to dictate too much. She couldn't say she for-
gave Garrett; that would be a lie and she'd lied
enough already. But she could give him his chance
with Max unfettered. The two of them deserved it.

"It's not too late for you and Max. He needs you
and you're here. From what you're telling me, you
could be just what he needs at this stage in his life.
How *did* you grow out of your klutzy phase, anyway?"

"Once there wasn't someone looking over my
shoulder, trying to change everything about me,
pointing out every pitfall before I even got there..."
He raised an eyebrow, and Livy winced. "I grew out
of it on my own."

"You're telling me to let Max be Max."

"I'm not telling you anything, Livy, except that
you look beautiful with the moon on your hair."

Before she could stop herself, Livy touched her
hair. She could almost feel the soft light of the moon.
J.J. had often murmured poetic phrases that had
charmed her girlish heart. Tonight Garrett charmed
her woman's soul. She could tell him that she was
too old for such things now, but that would be another
lie, and she'd had far too little charm in her life.

"Max is your son," he said. "You do what you think is best."

"He's your son, too." She rubbed her forehead. "I'm starting to think that maybe I don't know what's best for him after all."

"My life isn't Max's life. Thank God. Once you think it's all right to tell him the truth, I promise he'll always know his father loves him. That's something I can't say about myself. I don't want the same for Max."

"Didn't anyone ever tell you they loved you?"

He crossed the floor, silent in stocking feet, and stood close enough so that the moon shaded them both. Her breath caught as she saw again that strange flicker in his eyes she could not place. She braced herself for a torrent of feelings when he kissed her and touched her as she wanted him to. But he merely brushed his lips along her brow, tucked her hair behind her ear and murmured, "You told me, Livy. You were the only one."

"I'VE GOT A STORY about the closet monster and a story about the goblins in the bathroom mirror."

Max sat so close to Garrett on the couch he was practically in his lap. Garrett had discovered over this past week with Max that if the child wasn't in his pocket he was trying to get there.

Starved for his son's voice, his warmth, the sweet drift of white-blond hair, the little-boy scent of heated sunshine and dry grass, Garrett didn't mind. Everything about Max fascinated him.

So much so that he hadn't thought of the un-book

at all, and his Muse might be dead for all he cared. Even Andrew seemed to have dropped off the face of the earth. A fact that would concern Garrett if he could work up concern about anything other than Max—and Max's mom.

Livy had suspended Max's two-week jail term on condition that he stay with Garrett after school and not wander off. No problem there. The two of them were exactly where they wanted to be. Together.

Garrett shifted just a little, and Max climbed right into his lap, then opened the sketchbook Garrett had given him. "Do you think these goblins are goblin-y enough?"

He took in the blue Magic Marker blobs that seemed to be climbing right out of the gray crayon mirror. Max was really good at visualizing what frightened him. Almost as good as he was at articulating it. For eight, Max was amazingly bright. Garrett tried not to pump out his chest and preen. But he couldn't help it. His son had to be the smartest kid in the whole world.

"Very goblin-y," he answered. "I can see why you wanted to keep an eye on that mirror at all times. I wouldn't want any of those coming at me when I had my pants down."

"'Zactly. Mom would never understand." He nodded sagely. "It's a guy thing."

"Definitely."

Livy wouldn't like to hear that, but truth was truth, and some things *were* guy things. Like eating ice cream in your underwear, or pizza without plates. Drinking milk right from the carton. *We don't need no stinkin' glass!* Or watching cartoons and drag racing at the same time—that was what that little extra box on the TV was for, anyway—while you listened to the radio.

"Once I got the goblins done, I was going to work on the zombies in the basement, but I got a better idea."

"What's that?"

Surreptitiously, Garrett tipped Max back until his son lay against his arm, his head tucked against Garrett's chest. Without even thinking, Max snuggled. Garrett's heart thundered with a love so deep he could barely keep it to himself. But he'd made a promise—one that was getting harder and harder to obey the more deeply he fell in love with his son.

"There's something that's always scared me, and I want to make a story about it before I do the basement zombies."

"You're worried about something worse than monsters, zombies or goblins?"

"Lots worse." His voice quivered, and Garrett's arms tightened around him.

"What is it, big guy?"

Max giggled. "I'm not big like you."

"I was little once."

Max twisted to look into Garrett's face. "You were?" he breathed.

Garrett had promised not to tell Max he was his father, but he hadn't promised not to tell him anything else. Max needed to know that he wasn't a freak, that the way he was, was the way he was supposed to be, and that in the end everything came out all right. Or near enough.

"I was very small. Then when I hit high school, boom, I shot up. One summer I grew four inches and that fall another two."

Max stuck out his feet. "I suppose your feet grew, too."

"No, I think that's when my body caught up with my feet. I didn't trip so much after that."

"You tripped?"

"You know, Max, everyone does."

He held up his cast. "Not like I do."

"That's because you're special."

"I am?"

"Didn't you know that?"

"Mom says, and Rosie, too. But they have to."

"And I don't?"

"No. You're just some guy."

Garrett winced. He hated being "just some guy."

"But you're my friend. I wish you could be my daddy."

"Me, too," Garrett whispered, his lips against Max's hair.

Despite the poignancy of the moment, Max was suddenly done cuddling. He leaped off Garrett's lap, leaving him feeling cold and empty, then tumbled to the floor to write his newest, biggest fear in earnest.

"Half an hour and we have to get back," Garrett reminded him.

Max merely grunted. He was busy.

Livy had worked several late nights. Her mother's case was at a standstill and some of her other cases weren't going well, either. Not that she talked about work with him, or much else. But Garrett knew what a person looked like when the work wasn't going well. He still saw that person in his mirror every morning, though he no longer cared so much.

Each afternoon Garrett met Max at his house. They went to Garrett's place, where they did guy things until dark. Then Garrett would bring his son home so he could be in bed by eight-thirty.

Most often Livy arrived just as they did, but sometimes she showed up after Max was asleep. The guilt in her eyes saddened Garrett, and he'd tried to lighten it by telling her some of the funny things Max had done or said. But it didn't seem to help.

Some nights she was so tired she went right to bed, and Garret wandered home, taking a detour through any cemetery he could find—major or minor. So far not a single idea had jumped up and bit him. Oh, well. What did a book matter when he had Max in the daylight and sometimes Livy all night?

Because there were nights when they'd watch Max sleep, then she'd pull him into her room and they'd make love. He'd lose himself in the taste of her skin and the scent of her hair and the flow of her hands along his body. Then he'd hold her in his arms, and she'd sleep as he watched her face shift beneath the shadows of the moon.

On nights like those Garrett felt as if he were part of a family—until he had to walk home alone in the cool drift of dawn.

She had no idea he loved her. No idea that he always had, or that he always would. Garrett had come to terms with his feelings the first night she'd welcomed him into her body, then her bed. Just because he hadn't been able to tell her all those years ago didn't make his love nonexistent.

Just as telling her now would not make her believe him, even if he could manage to say the words he'd never said before. She'd think he was saying them because of Max. Then he'd lose her, lose him, lose this. So while he often felt lonely, even as she lay in his arms, legs all tangled with his, breath warm and sweet on his skin, he'd keep his mouth shut, keep his love to himself and do his damnedest to make her love him all over again.

"HEY, LIVY, wake up!"

Livy almost slammed her nose into the desk when her chin slipped off her hand. She *had* been sleeping.

And dreaming again of him.

"You all right?" Kim sat on the desk, leaned over to peer into her face.

"Fine." Livy shoved at her hip. "Get off my desk."

"But I look so good on it." Before she jumped off, Kim posed like a sex kitten from a forties calendar. "If I didn't know better I'd think you were having wild and crazy sex all night long the way you keep falling asleep at your desk."

"Who says I'm not?"

"We've had this discussion, and you said you didn't like men." Kim snorted. "Besides, if you were getting that much, you'd be smiling more often."

Livy smiled now, and Kim's eyes sharpened. So

she stopped and turned her attention to the file on her blotter. Kim was too smart. That was why Livy had purposely frowned whenever she felt like grinning.

It wasn't hard to find something to frown about around there; all she had to do was open up a case file. But inside, even when she was frowning, even when she went home tired and found out she'd missed seeing Max again and the guilt hovered, deep down she was happy, as she hadn't been for a long, long time.

If Garrett hung around, as he seemed bent on doing, soon enough she'd have to tell Max the truth, and everyone else, too. For now, she wanted to enjoy this uncommon stretch of E.R.-free life. Whatever Garrett was doing with Max, it seemed to be working. There hadn't been a new mark on her son since Garrett took over.

For just a while longer she wanted to have Garrett to herself. Once everyone knew the truth, they'd all be under heavy Savannah scrutiny. Once Rosie came home, the fun would be over.

Livy didn't want to think about that. In fact, she was tempted to throw Rosie to the wolf sisters just so she could keep Garrett in her bed.

Had the sex been this good last time? She would have remembered. But while she could recall every nuance of what she'd felt for him, the intensity of her love, the depth of her need—the sex? Livy gave a mental shrug. Adequate. Maybe neither one of them had known what in hell they were doing back then. But Garrett certainly knew what he was doing now.

"You're smiling. That file isn't funny. What's up with you?"

"Sometimes you gotta laugh or you'll cry."

"Sometimes," Kim agreed. "What do you want to cry over today? Rosie?"

Livy glanced at her watch. "I'd better run over and see her. Have you checked with Judge McFie's office? When can we get another appearance?"

"Next week."

"Have you found out anything about the goose?"

Kim was shaking her head before Livy finished the question. "If Rosie took that goose, she hid it better than they hid Tut's tomb. Do you think you can get her to give it back?"

Livy merely rolled her eyes.

"Then what are you going to do?"

"Throw her on the mercy of the court?"

"That should work." Kim giggled. "Not."

"I'll try to think of something." Livy glanced at the file in front of her again. "I should never have taken on Jeremy Dubouis as a client. I should have known an easy divorce only meant trouble later. Maybe I should recommend another lawyer."

"He'll just keep calling you. He likes you. And he's harmless."

"But lucrative."

"What did he do this time?"

"Played the bongos on the lawn."

"He did that last week."

"In his jockstrap."

"Oh." Kim's lips trembled. "Well, that's new."

Livy hesitated. Something had been bothering her

since that first night in Garrett's arms. Since he'd told her about his past, she'd been thinking a lot about that little boy whom no one had loved. And about herself. How she reacted to people, what she believed of them and how she acted on those beliefs.

"Kim, do you think I believe the worst of people before I even give them a chance?"

"You've been talking to Rosie."

"Not today."

"Maybe you do." At the expression on Livy's face, she rushed on. "But I can't blame you, Livy. Look at your job. What choice do you have? Like you said— Dubouis had trouble written all over him from the moment he walked in the office. That's the truth. I'm the same way. So is Klein. The only person I know who loves everyone on contact is Max, and he's a kid. He'll grow out of it."

"When he gets burned one too many times," Livy murmured.

"It has to happen."

Livy only hoped it didn't happen to her baby the way it had happened to her. She didn't want Max betrayed by the person he loved the most.

CHAPTER FIFTEEN

"I DON'T HAVE the goose. That's my story and I'm sticking to it."

Rosie seemed none the worse for her week in the slammer. In fact, her cell had the air of a hotel suite. Friends had brought colorful blankets and pillows for her bed, books, CDs for her Discman and countless other presents. The police, who'd known and loved her for years, had ignored it all.

While once this might have annoyed Livy, now she was merely glad her mother was happy in jail. She might be there quite a while.

"I have to be honest, Mama, I don't know what I'm going to do for you."

"Defend me. It's my word against theirs."

"Unfortunately, theirs is going to hold more weight."

"Why? Why is their word better than mine?"

Livy looked Rosie over—from her unbound, fly-away hair, past the slogan *They're Not Hot Flashes. They're Power Surges* across her chest, the hot-pink spandex tights, down to the purple ballet slippers that matched the wings of the hummingbird in her tattoo—and she had a revelation.

If she believed in justice, her client was innocent.

Livy might think Rosie had stolen—make that emancipated—the goose, but if Rosie stuck to her story, then so should Livy.

"Their word *isn't* better than yours."

Rosie began to pace the confines of her cell, arms waving with the force of her annoyance. "Exactly. But because of how I dress, what I believe, who I married, Tweedle Dee and Tweedle Dum are going to win?"

"Not if I have anything to say about it."

Ready to roll, Rosie came up short and gaped at Livy. "What did you say?"

"I said, they're not going to win. You've got the best lawyer in town in your corner."

Confusion took the place of surprise. "But you think I'm silly."

"Silly? Mama, I think you're nuts. But I love you anyway."

"You do?"

"You thought I didn't?"

"Sugar—" Rosie flopped down on her bed "—I figured you were going to hate me forever for leaving you behind."

Livy flinched. "Hate? Now you're being silly. You're my mother."

"But I didn't act like one, and you've never forgiven me."

"I'm starting to think that maybe I've been a bit…rigid about some things."

"Rigid." Rosie snorted. "That's a good word."

"Maybe you should tell me why you felt compelled to leave."

A darkness settled over Rosie's cheery face. "What good would that do now?"

Livy joined her mother on the single bed. "One thing I've learned in this job of mine—people do things that don't make sense. But they usually have a reason that makes sense. In their mind, anyhow. I'd like to know your reason."

Rosie stared into Livy's eyes searchingly. Then she sighed and glanced away. "I didn't leave *you*. Well, I did, but not the way you think. I had to get away from the memory of him, which appeared every time I saw you."

"I don't look like Daddy at all."

Rosie's smile was sad. "It's the expression. The way you tilt your head sometimes. The way you used to laugh. You and Henry were so much a part of each other, and I was always on the outside looking in." She held up her hand when Livy began to protest. "That's the way it was, and I didn't mind." She flipped her wrist in a careless gesture. "Much, anyway. Wherever there was Henry there was Livy. So when he was gone and there was you but no him...I couldn't bear it, Livy. I had to run."

Livy had had the same problem every time she'd looked into Max's eyes. But there'd been nowhere for her to run. All she'd been able to do was bury her pain and her fear beneath layers of anger, then devote all of her love to her son. Hover over him, keep him safe, attempt to control the uncontrollable.

"Silly how the past can affect every little thing," she murmured.

Rosie put her arm around Livy and tugged her

close. Livy's head rested naturally on her mother's shoulder, a place it hadn't been for far too long. "Let's forget about the past and start over. Look forward, and the whole world looks with you."

"You ought to put that on a T-shirt."

"Maybe I will, sugar. Maybe I will."

GARRETT AND MAX turned up the walk and found Livy sitting on the porch with a glass of wine.

"Mom!" Max dropped Garrett's hand and sprinted for her arms.

Garrett followed more slowly, watching them both, letting the love lap at him and try to draw him under.

Livy glanced up, and the memory of several nights in each other's arms flickered in her eyes. Garrett went under gladly. She might be different, but in many ways Livy was still the same. Even if she hadn't been the mother of his child, he wouldn't be able to resist her any more now than he had back then.

"Hi," she said, her voice a bit hoarse, as if she'd been crying, but he could see no other evidence of it.

"Hi."

Max stared back and forth between the two of them and his bright eyes sharpened. "Mom, can Garrett have some wine?"

She raised a brow. "Would you like some?"

Garrett's Poe imitation had stopped as soon as he'd begun watching Max. He hadn't had a drink since, hadn't even wanted one beyond the Kool-Aid or milk he'd shared with his son. But right now, wine and Livy sounded like a very good idea.

"Sure." He sat in the chair next to hers.

"I'll get it," Max announced, and stumbled into the house.

"Wait, I'll—" Livy started to get up.

Garrett put his hand on her arm. "Let him."

"But he'll break the glass or spill the wine."

"Let him," he repeated.

"Drop the bottle...cut his foot, his hand, an artery."

Garrett laughed. "Let it go, Livy. He'll be fine. He hasn't broken anything—not a glass, bottle, table or himself in weeks."

She settled back with a tired sigh and swirled her wine around and around in the glass. "And I'm grateful, Garrett."

"I didn't do anything."

"You're good for him. He's safe with you. You don't know how much that means to me. To know that he's safe."

"I just let him be a kid. And while he's being one, I get to be one, too."

"You can't imagine the terrible things I fear for him."

"I can't? You *haven't* read my books." She smiled. "Maybe you should do what Max and I do. Imagine the worst thing that could possibly occur." She flinched. "Then figure out exactly what you'd do if the worst thing happened. You feel more in control then. Not so much at the mercy of fate, even if you are."

"I like control."

Garrett's lips twitched. "I didn't notice."

It was an indication of the change in their relation-

ship that she merely wrinkled her nose at his sarcasm
and did not throw her wine in his face.

"The worst thing." She leaned back, sipping her
wine, staring at the descending night. "Losing Max—
in any way. That's the worst."

"And what can you do about that?"

"Protect him always, the best that I can."

"Which is what you're doing, Livy. So relax. Live
a little. Kick back."

"I thought I was."

He looked her over. She'd taken off her shoes and
her stockings, but she still wore the business suit.
Why did that turn him on? Maybe because she'd unbuttoned the blouse, and he could see a tiny *V* of flesh
between the panels of prissy white cotton? Or because
he knew just how soft the skin beneath that skirt
would be if he ran his fingers under the hem and—

"Here you go, Garrett."

Lust dissolved in the space of an instant. Max stood
at his elbow, plastic juice cup filled to the brim with
bloodred wine. Tongue between his teeth, he concentrated on the ripples each step made in the tiny lake
at the top of the cup.

"Thanks, pal." Garrett took the cup and brought
his mouth over to sip out the excess. "Great idea for
a container. Now I won't have to worry about breaking a glass outside and getting your mom mad at
me."

Max grinned. "That's what I thought."

"Good thought." Livy turned her head. "Excellent
choice."

Max practically preened beneath their combined

praise. Garrett's and Livy's eyes met, and they shared a smile. He was so in love with her, Garrett could barely keep it to himself, and so terrified he'd blow it he could barely think straight in her presence.

He'd tried to show her how he felt with his body, hoping for a miracle, praying she'd love him again. But so far, all she'd asked of him had been his help with Max and his presence in her bed.

He ought to be ecstatic. What man wouldn't be? He had his son during the day and the woman of his dreams most nights. No strings. But Garrett wanted more. He wanted Livy, Max and himself to be a family. He wasn't exactly sure, though, how to go about that. Maybe by acting like a family?

Garrett sat up so fast he almost spilled his wine. Max giggled. "You're going to get in trouble."

Most likely. Garrett took a healthy gulp as he refined his spectacular idea. "I heard there's a crab boil at Old Fort Jackson tomorrow."

He could tell by the way Livy's brows knitted that she was going to say no. Then Max jumped up and down. "I've never gone to a crab boil, and I love Old Fort Jackson. Remember, Mom, how they fire that cannon sometimes? We haven't done anything fun in forever. Can we go? All of us together?"

Livy's brow smoothed and her eyes filled with a love so deep and pure Garrett's own eyes watered.

"Why not?" She upended her wineglass, draining the contents.

For a minute Garrett thought she might smash the glass against a nearby tree, just as all the legends said those Bonaventure ghosts did. Behavior like that would be so un-Livy he wasn't sure what he'd do. But instead, she smiled at him almost the way she used to and murmured, "Let's live a little."

And he had hopes that the joy he saw flickering to life in her smile would soon reach all the way to her eyes.

EVEN THOUGH RAIN was predicted at some point, Saturday dawned bright and warm—a perfect Savannah autumn day.

Garrett picked up Livy and Max as promised in the early afternoon. His car was a surprise—a family-man minivan that did not fit the image of the J.J. she'd known or the Garrett he'd become. A lot of things about him did not fit her image, and it was those things that were causing her to lose sleep at night, even more than the lovemaking she'd begun to crave.

"Interesting car." Livy buckled her seat belt before glancing over her shoulder to make sure Max had done the same.

"Garrett, your seat belt," Max urged. "You don't want to know what you'd look like if you went through the windshield."

Garrett raised an eyebrow at Livy, then pulled what appeared to be a virgin seat belt across his chest. He didn't even have to say what he was thinking. She knew.

Max sounded like a nervous little old man. Once, Livy would have hoped that his parroting of her dire predictions meant he'd take proper care of himself. Now she knew that Max and care did not go together in the same sentence, and there was little she could do about it.

Her son's chatter, about his stories and the monsters he had foiled within them, filled the silence on the trip to the fort.

Situated three miles outside of Savannah, Fort Jackson was the oldest standing fort in Georgia and had once been the headquarters of all river batteries. The brick structure was surrounded by a tidal moat, making it appear even more ancient than it was.

After Garrett parked the van, the three of them walked about. Max bounced here and there, so excited he couldn't keep still, while Livy and Garrett trailed behind. Livy felt so at ease with Garrett she finally gave in to the urge to slide her hand into his.

They ate crab until they nearly burst, then Max trotted off toward a band that played in the distance— old music, tunes she didn't recognize but liked just the same. As she and Garrett wandered along an ancient stone wall in the wake of their son, she got an inkling of what it might feel like to be a family, and she wanted it so badly she ached, not only for Max but for herself.

To add to her confusion, the promised rain poured down as if from nowhere. The scene looked like something out of a silent movie. People fled in every direction at high speed as the band continued to play.

Livy started forward, planning to take Max's hand and lead him back to the van. But Garrett stopped her, one hand on her arm, one word whispered low. "Look."

Max, being Max, began to dance. It was the

sweetest thing she'd ever seen, and though the blasted voice that had been with her since Max had been laid in her arms—a helpless bundle given over to her protection—whispered, *He's going to slip on the stone and spill his brains out on the street,* she kept her mouth shut and watched the magic of her son dancing in rain.

Then Garrett joined him, and she caught her breath. Hand in hand, they did a jig—the same crazy two-step—then laughed and threw back their heads to drink of the water pouring from the sky.

The band played faster, the musicians laughing, too, at the wonder of Max. Livy hugged herself against the chill of the rain as it drenched her to the skin. She shivered as Garrett's shirt became plastered to his chest, the curves and dips she'd touched with her fingers, tasted with her tongue, both familiar and enticingly new.

The song ended. By now the fort was deserted and the rain was coming down in sheets. With no reason to run, as they were already soaked, the three of them meandered toward the minivan. Somehow the afternoon had given way to dusk. The streetlights came to life, capturing Livy and Garrett in a starburst, and suddenly it was another night, another storm, another streetlight.

She glanced at Garrett and he kissed her, just as he had all those years ago. That night she'd snuck out, gone walking with J.J., and the storm had caught them unaware. Soaked and laughing, he'd twirled her to face him underneath a streetlight, then he'd kissed her until she could think of nothing but that mouth, those hands, his body. They'd tumbled into the garden, fallen on the wet summer grass, and he'd become her first right there beneath the sky as the rain flowed over them both.

Unable to stop the tide of memories, the wash of feelings, she let go of everything she'd held back, even when he was deep inside her. Her tears mixed with the raindrops that ran down her cheeks as she realized she still loved him as much now as she had then.

Because he was the same. And that meant he would leave.

CHAPTER SIXTEEN

MAX MIGHT BE A KID but he wasn't dumb. Something was going on with Garrett and his mom. He just couldn't figure out what.

Sometimes his mom seemed to not like Garrett at all; then other times, right now, for instance, she seemed to like him a whole lot.

He'd never seen anyone kiss that way. Not even on television. If he didn't know better he'd think his mom and Garrett had done a lot of kissing before.

A few people walked by and smiled, which made Max smile, too. Garrett and his mom acted as if there was no one else in the world but them, standing there kissin' in the rain under the light. If Max were a girl he might think it was romantic.

Max rolled his eyes and made a gagging noise, even though no one was watching. It was the principle. Kissing was yucky!

Almost as if she'd heard him, his mom shoved Garrett away and stared at him with wide eyes. Max frowned. She looked scared, and he didn't like that, so he inched forward, ready to step between the two of them and do... Well, he wasn't sure what. Detective Klein would know. Max would have to figure it out as he went along, just like Indiana Jones.

Then Garrett did something that made Max stop in his tracks. He reached out and ran a thumb down her cheek, along one of the raindrops that looked like a tear but couldn't be because his mom only cried when Max got hurt. Her face got all funny, then Max wanted to cry himself and he didn't know why.

"Hush," Garret whispered, and Max's mom's bottom lip wobbled.

"Hey!" he shouted, and both of them jumped apart as if lightning had struck nearby.

Then all of a sudden everything was the same again, and Max wondered if he'd really seen something weird, or if he'd seen that kiss at all. His mom grabbed his hand and yanked him toward the car, and nobody talked about anything but crabs and rainstorms all the way home.

Max was thinkin' all the way there. He'd been hopin' and prayin' and even writin' a story about Garrett bein' his dad. If Garrett fell in love with Max's mom, the dream would come true. Max was so scared he'd jinx it just by wantin' it so bad he could barely keep still. Luckily, his mom thought he had ants in his pants because he was all wet.

Even if Max hadn't liked Garrett bunches, he'd still consider asking him to be his dad, because he couldn't remember the last time his mom had smiled with her mouth so that the happy reached all the way to her eyes. As much as he wanted Garrett to be his dad, Max wanted his mom to be happy. And he'd never, ever, seen his mom kiss anyone except him, so Garrett must be special.

"Mom?" he interrupted in the middle of a chatty

sentence about crab cakes. She talked a lot when she was nervous.

The glance she turned toward him was wary. Most likely she didn't want him to talk about the kiss, but he couldn't help it.

"Now that you've kissed Garrett, shouldn't you get married before the baby comes?"

Her face turned white, which made Max nervous and he started to babble. "Because Joey Caldwell's sister kissed a boy and then she had baby."

He glanced at Garrett, who looked like he was grinding his teeth the way Mom always did when she was really mad, and Max figured he'd somehow stumbled hip-deep in dog do.

"I don't think you should play at Joey's anymore, Max," his mom said.

"I don't. He's one of the mean kids."

"Good. Just because I kissed Mr. Stark doesn't mean I'm having a baby. There's a bit more to it than that."

Garrett snorted, which earned him a glare that Max was glad he hadn't gotten.

"We'll talk about the particulars of babies later. In private."

Then she and Mr. Stark glanced at each other. In the rearview mirror Max saw the look in their eyes and it made him frown.

Something was going on with his mom and Garrett Stark. He just couldn't figure out what.

GARRETT WAITED DOWNSTAIRS while Livy gave Max a bath and put the boy to bed. He'd found an extra

pair of shorts in his car—he always kept something
for emergencies—but there'd been no shirt. So he'd
looped the towel Livy had tossed him around his neck
and waited for her to come back.

Quicker than he'd expected, her footsteps descended and a sad sigh preceded her into the room.

She stopped dead when she spotted him in front of
the fireplace, and her gaze skirted over, then away
from, his chest. Her obvious attraction to him stirred
Garrett. At least they had sex, if nothing else. He
should accept that and be happy, but he couldn't. Not
anymore.

"That was quick."

She nodded and sat on the couch. "The excitement,
the chill, then the warm bath. He was asleep as soon
as I poured him into bed."

Livy rubbed her arms as if she were just as chilled.
Her hair was still damp. She'd scooped it off her neck
in a ponytail, though several tendrils escaped to frame
her face and dust her neck. She wore a flannel nightshirt that reached past her knees and fuzzy slippers
he wanted to feel against his calves.

Garrett sighed. He had it bad. Why did he keep
fighting it?

He sat next to her on the couch, and when she
would have scooted away, he tugged her close. "Lean
on me, Livy. I wouldn't mind."

"I haven't leaned on anyone for a long time."

"Just because you haven't doesn't mean you
shouldn't."

"What if I lean on you and you move away? I'll
fall again."

He let her go because she kept trying to get free, even though his arms felt empty without her. "Is that what you're so afraid of? That you'll need me and I'll be gone?"

She shrugged but didn't answer.

"You don't trust me, and I can't blame you, even though it pisses me off. You share Max, you share your body, but you share none of yourself."

"I'm no good at that."

"You could be if you tried."

She sighed, sad still. "Maybe I should. Here—" She pulled a piece of paper out of the pocket of her nightshirt. "Read this. Max gave it to me before he fell asleep. It's one of his fear series."

Garrett glanced at the neat but childish handwriting: "'What I Want More than Christmas.'" He raised his gaze. "Catchy title."

Livy merely smiled and motioned for him to continue reading:

The boy named Max was scared of one thing more than anything else. He was afraid he'd never have a dad because he wasn't good enough for one. He was a bad boy, though he didn't try to be. No matter what he did he broke things, and sometimes even himself. So he couldn't say he was surprised when no dad seemed to want him.

But one day a man came to Savannah and he was so much like the perfect dad Max couldn't believe his luck. And all he wanted, even more than Christmas, was for Garrett Stark to be his

real daddy. So he believed it with all his heart
and he wished for it, too. He even prayed a bit.
And what he wanted the most happened.

Garrett's eyes burned, so he blinked at the paper a
while as if he were still reading, until the burning
went away a little. Then he looked up to find Livy's
eyes wet, also.

"What makes me the perfect dad?"

"Who could be more perfect than you, since you
are?"

"Probably anyone."

"Why would you say that?" She threw up her
hands. "You've been nothing but wonderful with him
since you got here. You want me to talk to you—talk
to *me,* Garrett."

"I can't write," he blurted.

There. He'd actually said it to another human being
and not just an empty room. Amazingly, the world
did not stop turning. Imagine that.

"Since when?"

"Since before I came here."

"So why did you come here?"

"I thought maybe *this* place, where it all started
for me, would help."

Her lips tightened. "You came here for the book."

"Even if I did, it didn't do a damn bit of good."

"Ever have this problem before?"

"Not this bad. But then, I always—" He stopped.

She narrowed her eyes suspiciously. "What do you
do when you can't write?"

He didn't want to tell her. But he didn't want to lie, either. There had been enough of that already.

"I move on. New book, new town. If the town's wrong, the book won't come. So I move. It's always worked before."

"But not this time."

"There's something. I keep hearing a story, but I just can't quite get it. My mind's too full of Max. Too full of you. And the longer I'm here, the less I care about the book. The more I know of Max, the less I care about a career that was once everything to me—and I'm scared."

Livy stared at him as if she hadn't seen him before, as if she wasn't sure she was seeing him correctly now. "Why is that?"

"Because if I fail at the only thing I've ever been able to do right, how can I expect to be a decent father to Max? Something I have no example of, no experience at, no calling for whatsoever."

"Pretty much like every father or mother ever made."

He blinked. True enough. What was she getting at?

"You love him."

"More than I ever thought I could love anyone. And if you think it's better that he never know the truth, all right. I'll agree, and I'll leave if you think I should. I'll never come back. I'll never bother either of you again." He held her gaze, fought not to bemoan all he'd said, all he'd given up.

"Why do you think he's better off with no one than with you?"

"You've only been telling me that since I got here."

"Maybe I was wrong."

He shook his head.

"Writing's all I know, Livy. If I can't do that, I'm no one. Max is better off with someone."

"You're an idiot." She took his hand and put her lips to his palm the way she always used to. When she would have released him, he clung, and she let him. "You're Max's father, and that's someone enough for me. We'll tell him the truth as soon as I get his gramma out of jail." Her lips twisted. "Again."

THE FOLLOWING WEEK was a good week, full of a family life Livy had never expected to enjoy with the man she'd never thought to see again. She didn't want the week to end.

Because even though Max had literally chosen his father to be his father, for Max to get what he wanted Livy would have to live up to her lie. She was terrified Max was going to despise her for it.

But one problem at a time.

At the end of that perfect week, Livy and Kim once again awaited Judge McFie in court. He'd fined Rosie one thousand dollars on the contempt charge, and today they would finish the interrupted proceedings.

"Has Rosie told you where she hid the golden goose?" Kim asked.

"She didn't take it."

"Right." Kim's eyes widened as she caught sight of something behind Livy.

Livy craned her neck to see Rosie—or a woman who resembled Rosie—entering court. Hair braided demurely, she wore the court dress Livy had purchased years ago. The garment appeared brand-new—never worn, because it hadn't been. She'd even put on panty hose—a torture device straight from the Inquisition, according to Rosie—and pumps—shoes "invented by sadistic men."

"What's gotten into her?" Kim murmured.

"A sense of decorum?"

"I wouldn't count on it."

Livy and Rosie's relationship was better than it had ever been. Amazing what a little truth and a two-week separation could do for a family tie. Though they'd probably never see eye-to-eye on everything, Livy could live with that. Once you knew that someone loved you, you could live with a lot.

Rosie took her place at their table and gave Livy a kiss. There'd also been a lot more touching and kissing than Livy was used to from her mother, but she was adapting and had only had her nose crushed by an unexpected embrace the first three times.

"What gives, Mama?"

"Compromise. I hear that sometimes if you give a little, you get a whole lot."

The click of high heels and the twitter of twin voices approached. This time the assistant district attorney managed to keep the sisters on their own side of the room, though their glares reached all the way across, and so did their words.

"That getup isn't going to work, Rosie," Violet

called. "You can change your clothes, but you can't change the stripes on a zebra."

"What zebra?" Viola asked. "When was there a zebra?"

Rosie just raised her eyebrows at Livy and folded her hands on the table.

Though Livy should have been glad Rosie had taken her advice and dressed for the occasion, seeing her lively mother like this made her think of retired nuns and cane-wielding grannies. Livy didn't like it. Rosie was more Rosie wearing a banner on her chest and sandals on her feet.

"Thanks for trying, Mama. But next time, wear what you want, okay?"

"Next time? Who said there was going to be a next time?"

"If there isn't, I'll never have any fun in my job."

Rosie grinned and patted Livy's cheek. "Sugar, that's the nicest thing anyone's ever said to me."

"What has gotten into the two of you?" Kim demanded. "Has there been an invasion of the body snatchers that I don't know about?"

"No," Livy answered. "I just realized how much I love my mama."

"About time," Kim muttered.

Since Kim was right, Livy let it go.

"See?" Rosie squeezed Livy's hand. "Give a little, get a whole lot."

Judge McFie entered and sat at his bench. "I guess we're about to find out just how well that works," Livy said.

"Got a goose?" he demanded before anyone could

say a word. He narrowed his eyes behind his thick glasses and peered about the room. "Where's Rosie?"

"Right here." Rosie raised her hand and waved at him.

He scowled. "What are you up to?"

"She's trying to pretend she's normal, but we all know better," Violet answered.

"I object." Livy stood.

"To what?" McFie continued to peer and scowl.

"To the assumption that Rosie isn't normal and they are."

The sisters' gasp was loud in the sudden silence. Then they both began to talk at once.

But the judge thundered, "Quiet!" and amazingly they were. "I want to hear this. Go on, Counselor."

Livy glanced at Kim, who gave her the high sign, and Rosie, who gave her a smile. Livy wanted to make this point for her mother. Rosie deserved justice. Everyone did.

Though Livy had gone into law for some measure of control, lately she'd begun think that the more you tried to control things, the less control you had. And while this should have turned her off the job she'd always loved, instead she saw the law in a whole new light. Because justice—fairness, equality, decency—while at times as much of an illusion as control, was still worth fighting for.

Livy approached the bench. "This case is about one woman's word against the word of two others. Three women, who, as everyone knows, do not get along."

"Our word against *hers,*" Viola stated. "Whose are you going to believe?"

Livy remained silent and just looked at the judge. McFie glared at the sisters. Since he was older than their father, they subsided, though they grumbled words no one could make out. Livy took the small favor and ran with it.

"Sure, Rosie has been complaining about that goose to everyone who would listen. She *said* she was going to do something, although she never said what. Even if she said she was going to take it, that doesn't mean she did. I've been saying I was going to throttle her for years, and she's still breathing."

The judge didn't think she was funny, so Livy cut to the chase.

"Rosie says she didn't take that goose. The sisters say she did." Livy tossed her hands up and shrugged. "Who will you believe? The sisters, because their father was a judge, instead of Rosie, because hers wasn't? So Rosie dresses strange and believes in ghosts. So what? If you want to get technical, so do they."

The sisters gasped again, but this time no one listened. Livy pressed her advantage and positioned herself in front of the sisters' table.

"They've got a trained goose and a father who comes for tea, despite the fact that he's buried in the family plot. Not too odd in Savannah. Eccentric. And that's fine. In fact, it's good. Part of the ambience around here."

The judge nodded, so Livy kept on talking as she walked toward Rosie. "I'm not saying my mother doesn't drive me crazy with her causes and her crusades. But that's her right. She's my mother.''

She winked at Rosie before turning back to the judge. "How she dresses, what she believes in, how she chooses to live her life, has nothing to do with her word or its weight in a courtroom. In America everyone's word weighs the same. That's why it's America. She's innocent until *proven* guilty. *Proven.* And I've seen no proof here. So if you're sitting for justice, for truth and right, for the American Way…'' Kim snorted. Maybe she *had* gone too far, so Livy finished quickly. "Then you have to release Rosie Frasier. Today.''

As she sat down, the utterance "Cool!" floated from the back of the room. A glance over her shoulder revealed that Klein sat right behind her. Since she couldn't imagine him saying "Cool!" with quite that level of enthusiasm, Livy nodded a greeting, then looked farther afield.

Max and Garrett had snuck into the cheap seats near the door. The proceedings had started late, leaving them time to arrive after school let out.

Garrett's dark eyes, intent on her face, made Livy remember a few other family things that had been going on all week. She was glad she hadn't known he was watching her or she wouldn't have been able to think straight.

She was also glad Max had caught her little speech. It was one of her best. He'd heard her defend his precious Rosie. Now if only he could see justice in action. She returned her attention to the frowning Judge McFie.

"Your Honor, if I could speak?" The assistant DA stood.

"This is only a hearing, junior, not the trial. Though Ms. Frasier seems to have made an excellent stab at a closing statement, regardless."

"But it's only fair—"

"I think the people have said enough."

"But—"

"Sit!"

Someone in the back snickered. Funny, but it didn't sound like Max, and she doubted Klein even knew how. Livy stifled a smile.

"While I have to say that Mrs. Frasier's antics have been a constant thorn in my side, as well as the side of every judge in Savannah, I must also concede that Ms. Frasier is right. I have no business making a decision based on my level of annoyance, however high that level might be. Justice is what we're here for. Justice will prevail. Without witnesses or proof, I see no reason to charge Mrs. Frasier under section 16-8-20 of the Criminal Code of Georgia, neither felony nor misdemeanor. Therefore, Mrs. Frasier is released." He slammed his gavel with extreme force and fled the room.

"Wasn't that fun?" Rosie stood up.

"I enjoyed it," Kim remarked.

Livy took Rosie's face between her hands and kissed both her cheeks. "Nice job, Mama."

"Me? Sugar, that was all you. And I must say, your daddy would be proud."

Livy raised one eyebrow. "Of a lawyer?"

"Of you. Justice. Now, that would have been right up his alley."

"Yeah." Livy and her mother shared a smile. "It would have."

"Mom!" A whirlwind hit her legs and wrapped itself around her waist. Dark happy eyes stared into her own. "You were the greatest!"

"I was, wasn't I."

"I always thought so." She met the equally dark, nearly as happy, eyes of Max's father. She wanted to touch him right there in front of everyone, kiss him in celebration and tell the entire world the truth. But first they had to tell Max.

"Just who might you be?" Rosie asked.

"Livy," Kim purred. "You've been hoarding the baby-sitter."

Klein cleared his throat, and Livy glanced his way, but he scowled at the approaching sisters.

"I remember you now," Miss Violet chirped.

Max still hung on tight to Livy's waist, a warm solid presence, as Livy went cold inside.

Both Miss Violet and Miss Viola stared at Garrett. "You're that young man Livy spent the summer of...of... Ach, what was it, Sister?"

Miss Viola's head swung back and forth between Max and Garrett. "The summer of 1992."

"Yes. We only saw you those few times, walking hand in hand. It was so sweet how much in love you were. That's why we were so sad when you—" She broke off as the light dawned and her gaze met Livy's. "But you're—" An eyebrow went up; her lips turned down. "I see."

The coldness inside Livy spread, making her feel distant, a watcher, as her world imploded.

Rosie and Kim stared at Garrett, then Max, then Livy. The hurt in their eyes made it hard for her to breathe. Garrett appeared as frozen as she was, uncertain, alarmed. Klein stepped forward as if to help, but there was nothing that could be done to stop Livy's house of cards from tumbling, tumbling down.

She'd thought the worst pain of her life had been standing in J.J.'s empty room, but she'd been wrong. The worst pain of all was the sensation of small hands releasing her waist, the sight of dark eyes filling with understanding and the sound of a whisper dripping with accusation. "Mom?"

"Max, we need to talk."

And she discovered she was wrong again, because the worst agony of all was watching Max run away and knowing that was justice.

CHAPTER SEVENTEEN

GARRETT CAUGHT MAX before he reached the door. Livy remained frozen, the sound of her son crying—sobbing, really—rendering her unable to move or to think.

Max fought Garrett for a minute, then threw himself into his father's arms, hiding his face against Garrett's stomach. Garrett picked him up, and Max wrapped himself around his father with complete trust.

Something Livy had just lost. She'd been so afraid that Max would be betrayed by the person he loved the most. She hadn't expected that person to be her.

"Livy?" She blinked at Garrett. "We need to go somewhere private and talk."

"I—uh, there's…" She wrinkled her brow. Why couldn't she focus?

Garrett turned to Klein. "The three of us need a private room."

"You admit you're his father?"

"I never denied that. I never will."

Klein gave Garrett his piercing cop's glare, then with a sharp nod accepted his words and him. "Follow me." He strode toward the door.

Garrett followed with Max. Livy couldn't seem to move.

"Livy?" Garrett beckoned. Max still hid his face, as if he couldn't bear to look at anyone. Livy knew how he felt. The accusing glares of her mother and her partner were beginning to make her skin crawl.

"Maybe you should talk to him alone," she said. "I don't think he wants me right now."

"I *hate* you!" Max shouted, though he still refused to look at her. "You lied and you told me he was dead!"

The wail ricocheted off the ceiling and seemed to slither down Livy's spine. She hugged herself against the chills.

"He hates me," she whispered.

Rosie's arm came around Livy's waist, giving her support when she needed it the most. "All children dislike their mothers now and again, sugar. You know that. But I seem to remember someone telling me that we all have our reasons for the things that we do. Max needs to hear yours."

Livy shook her head, but her mother shoved her forward and in a no-nonsense tone that had everyone, including Livy, staring, she snapped, "Olivia, get your butt in that room and talk to your son. Do not make the mistake I did and let things fester too long."

When Rosie spoke like that, the appropriate response was "Yes, Mama." Livy haltingly followed Garrett, Max and Klein to a conference room. She had been there several times before with clients. She wished she were with clients now. Coward that she was, Livy hung outside in the hallway with Klein.

"You going to be okay?" he asked.

"Probably not."

He put a finger beneath her chin. "Chin up. Face the music."

"I take it that's your version of 'I told you so.'"

His answer was to pat her awkwardly on the shoulder. "I've got to get back to work. If you need anything, all you have to do is call me."

Then he urged her through the door and shut her in to face that music.

"Are you really my daddy?"

Max's tear-clogged voice wavered, and Livy leaned her head against the closed door. She deserved this, but that didn't make it any easier to bear. With a deep breath, she turned. Max still clung to Garrett's waist like a koala cub to its mother. At Garrett's questioning glance, she nodded.

"Yeah, I'm your dad."

"But I thought your name was James."

"It is. James Garrett, Jr. But I changed it for the books."

Max thought about that a minute, then shrugged. "'Kay. I'm glad you aren't dead."

Garrett grinned. "Me, too."

"And I'm glad you're my dad."

"You couldn't be more glad than I am."

Max's face, puffy and wet, lightened. He rubbed his eyes with the back of his uncasted arm. "Really?"

"Of course. What guy wouldn't be thrilled to have a great kid like you for a son?"

"I'm not that great. I'm little, and geeky, and scared of a lot."

"You're perfect and I..." Garrett's voice trailed off; he glanced at Livy again, and she smiled, even though she wanted to cry. "I—I—" He cleared his throat, seemed to struggle a bit, then blurted, "I love you, Max."

Livy caught her breath. Now that he'd broken the "I love you" barrier for his son, was there hope he'd break it someday for her? And if he did, should she believe him? Or would she always wonder if he loved her merely for Max.

Max, oblivious to the undercurrents, led with his heart. "I love you, too. I loved you when you were Garrett, but now that you're Dad, I love you even better."

The wonder on Garrett's face was priceless, the love in his eyes true. Livy wanted to join them, but at that moment Max glanced her way and proved that she was an outsider still, at least where love was concerned.

"I want to live with you now, Dad."

Livy closed her eyes as the heart that had mended through Max's love shattered on his distrust.

"Why would you want to do that? Your mother needs you. She loves you."

"She lied and said you were dead. I haven't had a daddy because of her."

Livy opened her eyes. "Max, I—"

"No, Livy." Garrett gave her a warning look. "Let me."

Even if the truth pulled Max further away from her than ever, Garrett deserved to say his piece. Livy lowered her head in acquiescence.

Garrett sat Max on the table and took a chair, then he gazed into his son's eyes. "That's not true, Max. What happened was my fault, not your mother's."

Livy had expected to be the bad guy, maybe because she was. *She'd* lied; *she'd* tried to keep them apart; *she* was wrong, not him. She must have made a movement or a noise of denial, because Garrett glanced at her again.

"*My* fault," he repeated. "I ran away and I didn't come back for a long, long time."

Max's face scrunched up. "Like I was gonna do but you caught me?"

"Kind of. Except I left Savannah, and your mom had no idea where I'd gone."

"She couldn't have found you if she really, really tried?"

"No. I don't think she could have. I went from place to place. I was not a responsible guy. I was scared of a lot, just like you." He smiled a gentle smile that tugged at Livy low and deep. "Your mom trusted me, and I broke that trust. So she thought it was better if you believed I was dead. Then you wouldn't miss me so much because you'd never had me. Do you understand?"

"No." Max's bottom lip jutted out in a belligerent pout that usually made Livy want to shriek. Now she just wanted to...shriek. "Mom lied."

"Yeah. She did, and that was a mistake. But we all make them. Don't you?"

Max hung his head. "All the time."

"And your mom loves you always, right?"

"Forever and ever, no matter what."

Livy smiled even though it hurt.

"She did what she thought was best because she loved you so much. And though she lied, I'd cut her some slack if I were you, because she's your mom."

He peered at Garrett from between his bangs. "Do you cut your mom slack?"

"My mom ran off and never came back for real."

"Hmm." Max considered, face bunched tight. "That would be a whole lot of slack. I didn't think moms were allowed to run off."

"They aren't, but some do it anyway."

"Do you hate her?"

"I try not to hate. There's too much of that going around."

"Yeah. That's too bad about your mom, 'cause I like grammas. Rosie's the best, and I wouldn't mind another. But you got a dad, right?"

Garrett's face closed and he went stiff all over. "I do. But he's not the grampa type."

"How do you know?"

"He wasn't the dad type."

"Well, neither were you until you got me. So maybe your dad will be the best grampa. If you cut him some slack."

"I'll think about it."

Garrett looked at Livy. In his eyes she saw the shadows that had been there when he was J.J. and remained even when he'd become Garrett—the shadows of insecurity that his father had put there long ago. She wanted to erase those shadows, though she wasn't sure how, or even if she could. Perhaps that was a task for Max.

"Mom?" Livy met her son's eyes. "I'm sorry I said I hated you. That was mean."

"Right now, *I* hate me."

He smiled a little at that. "I was mad. I'm *still* mad, but I don't hate you."

"Gee, thanks."

"Because even when you're mad at me, when I'm the baddest I can be, you still love me, right?"

Livy nodded. "That's love." Garrett gave her an unreadable glance. "You going to forgive me, Max?"

"Maybe." His shrug had the attitude of a born heartbreaker. "Tonight I wanna stay with Dad."

That hurt.

"Sure. Fine." Her voice, too loud and hearty, revealed it wasn't fine at all.

The two of them stood. Max took Garrett's hand and tugged him toward the door. Garrett held back and fixed his gaze on Livy's face in the way he had that made her feel as if he could see everything that went on behind her eyes.

"You okay?"

"Sure," she said again. He raised his eyebrows. "Really. Thanks for this." She moved her hands helplessly. He'd done a wonderful job of calming their son while she'd been struck dumb by her own stupidity.

"Thanks for Max." He leaned over and kissed her cheek. "Really."

Max pulled on his arm. "Come *on,* Dad."

Her son left her with a smile and no goodbye. *Maybe* he'd forgive her? As quickly as she'd forgiven her own father for dying? Or J.J. for leaving?

Livy collapsed into the chair Garrett had just vacated. Well, wouldn't that be justice?

What happened in childhood was so hard to outgrow. The things parents did, however well meaning or accidental, affected their children for years, sometimes for always.

What would be Max's cross to bear, courtesy of her? Lack of trust? Dislike of women? Compulsive dishonesty?

She rubbed her forehead. *Mother guilt forever.* Put that on a T-shirt, she could sell a million.

FIFTEEN MINUTES LATER, Livy felt steady enough to leave the room. Unfortunately, what was waiting for her in the hall made her want to run right back inside and lock the door behind her.

"Sugar, I don't know why you felt the need to lie to *me* of all people."

"Or me." Kim was not giggling now. "I thought we were best friends. I told you everything."

Which wasn't exactly true. Kim refused to discuss how she'd ended up in Savannah, where she was from in the first place or why she insisted upon dating brainless bimbo boys.

But this wasn't about Kim.

"I'm sorry." Livy leaned against the wall for support, since her usual sources were mad at her. "He left. I panicked. Then the lie just grew."

"Grew big enough to blow up on you, didn't it," Kim snapped.

"I never thought he'd come back. He wasn't the type."

"Livy, I'm just so angry right now I think I'd better leave." Kim clipped off toward the exit.

"Will you be in on Monday?" Livy called.

"I'll let you know." Kim didn't even turn around.

Livy winced. "Ouch."

"If she's any kind of friend, she'll get over it."

"I lied to her for years. What kind of friend does that make me?"

"A frightened one. But, sugar, you had to have known I'd understand. That I'd never judge you."

"I was angry at you. A lie seemed the easiest way to make the questions go away. Then the lie had been around so long, it was the truth—or near enough."

"Well, I can't say as I agree with what you did, but it's done now. The question is, how are you going to clean up this mess?"

"I have no idea," Livy answered.

GARRETT HAD WANTED Max to know the truth. He just hadn't wanted him to find out the way he had. But the shock didn't seem to be having any lasting effects on the boy. He appeared completely normal as he skipped up Garrett's walk, tripped on the stairs and sprawled across the porch.

Garret began to hurry forward to pick him up. But then he remembered how embarrassed he'd always been if anyone fussed after he fell. So he hovered on the walk, held his breath until Max's head went up, revealing no signs of major injury; then Garrett could breathe freely again.

"Hey, Dad?" The boy had taken to calling him

dad with the greatest of ease. "There's a package for you. From…A. Lawton, New York City."

Oh-oh. Andrew had resorted to Federal Express. Must be serious. Of course, Garrett knew things had been serious for quite a while now. Andrew hadn't.

Max scrambled to his feet and handed Garrett the envelope. "What is it?"

"Trouble."

"You know that just from the package?"

"I know that from who sent the package. You remember the coffin in the dining room?" Max nodded. "That came from A. Lawton, too."

"Oh." Max shrugged, unconcerned with trouble that didn't include him for a change.

As Garrett let them into the house and turned on the lights, he considered what might be in the envelope. Nothing good. It was his turn to send a practical joke to his agent. By their unstated rules neither could send a joke unless it was his turn. Otherwise things might get out of hand.

The fact that Garrett had not answered the delivery of the coffin with something hilarious only proved how dead his Muse was. In the past, he wouldn't have rested until he'd come up with the perfect reprisal.

"Aren't you going to open it?" Max asked.

Funny how jokes, reprisals, contracts and careers meant little in the face of Max's smile.

"Nope," he said, and tossed the package on the table. "Let's have some fun."

An hour later, Garrett carried his sleeping son upstairs. Despite Max's chatter about all they were going to do together on their sleepover, he'd been snoring halfway through the first scary movie, the bowl of popcorn in his lap tilted in the opposite direction from his head.

When Garrett laid him on the couch in one of the bedrooms, then took off his socks and his jeans, Max mumbled, "Mom," and pulled the pillow over his head.

Tired himself, Garrett nevertheless watched Max sleep awhile. How could he have created something so perfect?

A sound downstairs drew Garrett into the hall. Was that a knock? After glancing at a motionless Max, he went to find out.

From the table in the hall, Andrew's package beckoned. Garrett stuck out his tongue at it and moved closer to the front door.

Light and dark danced on the porch. The weak *thud* sounded again. Who could be here at this time of night? Garrett opened the door to Livy.

They stared at each other. Garrett wasn't sure what to say. Why was she here?

"Is Max…?"

"Sleeping," he answered.

She stepped inside, closed the door, then leaned against it as if afraid to be near him. Had she come to end what was between them? Garrett had never been sure exactly what it was, but since there was something, he hadn't pressed to put words to it. Livy could easily have cut him out of her life and out of Max's.

But as the weeks had gone on and she'd let him stay, let him get closer and closer to their son and to her, Garrett had begun to hope they might forge a family. Still, she'd never mentioned love, not this time around, and he wasn't sure if he should, if he could, or even how.

Her face filled with confusion. "I can't think straight, Garrett. I can't sleep too well, either. You're both the boy who left me and the man who made my son smile through his tears. When you laugh, I hear him. When he smiles, I see you."

Garrett held his breath. What was she trying to tell him?

"Every time I kiss you I feel new things, then I remember old times. It used to be that whenever I smelled a summer rain, I'd have to fight not to cry, because in the space of an instant I'd see your face and then it would be gone." She snapped her fingers. "Just like you were. Every single time, I hurt so bad. I thought the memory would fade, but it didn't. Because when I see Max, I see you."

He had to touch her. He couldn't stay away. Garrett took one step, and she met him halfway. He held her gently, uncertain what she wanted but needing to give her whatever it was because she'd given him everything.

"You touch me and I forget it all. Touch me now, Garrett. Make me remember only you."

Then she was kissing him, not a kiss that said thank-you, or hello, and certainly not goodbye, but a true kiss, full of such passion that his mind went fuzzy with desire and crazy with need.

He should tell her right now that he loved her, always had, always would. But what was between them consumed, as physical as it was intangible, and as she touched his skin, murmured his name, drew him into her spell as completely as she always had, he could think of nothing but showing her with his body all he felt within his heart.

As he'd imagined countless times before, he ran his hand along her panty hose, up beneath her skirt. The satin of her skin beneath the silk of the stockings enticed him. He had to put his mouth to her neck, surround himself with the scent of her hair. So he tugged loose the rubber band and buried his face in the strands, walked his lips to the first button of her jacket, then followed his fingers down. Above the camisole beneath the suit, her breasts appeared even fuller than before, nearly spilling out of the scooped neck. Her nipple peeked just below the lilac lace.

"I want to see you in only this—" He looped his finger in the neckline. "These—" His palm stroked the stockings. "Maybe the heels, too."

Her eyes heated, and the smile she gave him was pure seduction, very little like Livy at all. "I can do that."

Even her voice was different, hoarse, as if she'd been moaning his name all night long. Garrett lifted her into his arms and headed for the steps.

She struggled. "You'll hurt yourself and be no good to me at all. Have you got a Rhett Butler complex?"

"Doesn't every man?"

"Every Yankee, anyway. I can walk."

"I'll only put you down if you run."

The smile appeared again. "I can do that."

And she did.

By the time he'd locked the door behind them, she'd shrugged off her suit jacket. The skirt slid to the floor, and she stepped out of it to stand in front of him in lilac lace and nude panty hose. But it was the sensible black pumps that drove him wild.

Crossing the floor, he unbuttoned his shirt. She shoved the material aside, pressed an open mouth to his skin. There would be no leisurely lovemaking tonight, because he wasn't going to last much longer.

He tipped her onto the bed, shucked his pants in a hurry and followed her down. With muted thuds her shoes hit the floor, then she rubbed his calf with her silk-stockinged toe. He bit his lip.

When had that become arousing? The instant Livy did it.

He got rid of her stockings, left the camisole on, loving how it felt against his hand, his chest, his mouth.

"Garrett." She'd never used his name in bed. He was overjoyed that she'd used it now, proving they'd moved onward. If they were to have a future, they had to let go of the past. Both of them.

But when she pushed against him in an erotic bump and shift, she could have called him Napoleon for all he cared. He sucked in air between his teeth. He was far too close to the edge for that sort of thing.

"Shh," he murmured against her brow, her chin, the underside of her satin-shrouded breast. He ran his tongue along the slope, blew upon the wetness until she shivered, then discovered the satin tasted as good as it felt when he drew Livy and the material into his mouth and suckled.

She cried out, and he stopped, lifted his head. "Did I hurt you?"

"No." Her cheeks were flushed; her breath came as fast as his. "I'm all right. I just need you. Now."

Since he needed her, too, always, he covered her hip with his hand and entered her with a single full stroke. Her eyes fluttered shut, and he kissed her closed lids. Then he said, "Look at me, Livy. Let me see all of you."

Once, she'd held his gaze whenever they came together. The sharing of their souls had been as intimate as the sharing of their bodies. Now that they shared a son, he wanted that intimacy back. He needed it as badly as he needed her.

He held his breath, afraid she'd refuse him the emotional bond. But as he joined them together, again and again, she opened her eyes and stared into his. When she gasped and trembled beneath him, clutched him and made him tremble, too, he cradled her face between his palms, and he kissed her gently, reverently. Then he said those words that had always been beyond him, until today.

"I love you, Livy."

Her eyes fluttered closed again, and she continued to tremble beneath him. At first he felt cold and alone, but the pull of her body, the warmth of her, drew him in, and for a while he thought only of this act of love and not the lack of words.

When the last tremors faded, she sought his hand, kissed the center of his palm, just like the old days,

and he hoped she might tell him again, as she had
once before, that she loved him. Instead, she smiled
softly and curled herself along his body, keeping his
hand in hers. Her breath brushed his chest as she fell
asleep. Curiously at peace, Garrett followed her with
dreams of the past and the present merging into one
future.

He awoke all tangled up in her. In the depths of
the night she'd turned to him again. Silent and sure
they'd shared their bodies, shared love without a single word.

He lay with her warm at his side as dawn grayed
the windows. This was the first time they'd ever slept
the night through together, and the beauty of it, the
perfect rightness in such a small thing, humbled him.

She'd lost her camisole. Actually, he'd lost it for
her, and she lay nestled against him, skin to skin. Her
breasts appeared heavier, the veins blue against the
pale satin smoothness. He longed to love her in the
light, to run his tongue along those veins, over the
auburn peaks and down into the alabaster valleys.
Garrett rubbed his eyes. With words like those someone might mistake him for a writer.

God, he missed it all of a sudden—picking one
word over another, putting this sentence before that,
the characters who became so real he heard them talking sometimes, their lives not a fable but his mission,
and most strangely, but wonderfully, the way everything sucked until, miraculously, it didn't.

That was writing. What was he going to do without
it?

Livy stirred, and he glanced at her again. Livy and

Max just might make up for the loss of all he'd held dear until now, because he couldn't think of anything more dear than his son and the woman who had given birth to him.

Garrett inched away from her. If he continued to touch her and think pretty thoughts, he'd want her again, and she looked so tired. She'd had a rough day yesterday. As rough as Max's day.

After throwing on shorts, a shirt and some shoes, Garrett trotted down the hall to check on his son. The boy still snored like a trooper.

Garrett hurried downstairs to start the coffee. As he passed the table in the hall, the package from Andrew shouted his name. He hesitated, tempted to throw the thing away, but curiosity won out and he yanked open the envelope.

A letter and a legal document spilled out. Maybe Andrew was suing him.

Dear Garrett,
Since you've decided to turn off your phone so I won't bother you, I've had to resort to courier.

Garrett hadn't turned off the phone; he just hadn't charged the battery in weeks. *Oops.*

I've been waiting patiently for your next gag gift, but it hasn't come. I'm beginning to think the joke is on me. No book. Ha-ha. Is that the joke, Garrett? If so I'm not laughing.
I know you. If you had something, I'd have it by now. So I've included a contract for a new

house. Get there, get the book done, or you're
done. You signed a contract. We gave our word.
Whatever's gotten into you, get it out. This is
your big chance. Do not blow it. Andrew.

Garrett glanced at the contract, which was for a
house in Alaska. Talk about getting away. He stuffed
the letter into his pocket, then tossed the envelope and
contract back on the table before he wandered out to
the porch.

Andrew was right. He had agreed to write a book,
and if he reneged now he'd better be dead for real
because he would be dead in publishing. The inertia
that had plagued him since he'd discovered Max was
fast dissolving and the familiar panic was taking its
place. He might *want* to write the book, but the book
did not want to be written, at least not by him.

He had a son now. If he played things right, he
might have a family. Did he dare reach for the magic
when his own magic was gone? What else did he
know but writing?

Not one damn thing. Without it he was just J.J.
again, the wandering loser Livy would rather say was
dead than claim as the father of her son.

What had happened between them last night had
touched him deeply. He'd thought it had touched
Livy, too. Yet despite his ability to break through the
barrier and tell her how he felt, she hadn't said a word
about love or the future.

Once, she'd been the only person who saw him as
special. Then he'd walked out on her and proven her
belief in him a lie. Would she always see him as that

worthless boy? Most likely, since he was very close to losing his standing as a worthwhile man.

Confused, uncertain, Garrett did what he always did.

CHAPTER EIGHTEEN

LIVY AWOKE ALONE. That wasn't so new. But considering she awoke in Garrett's bed, in Garrett's house, she didn't like it.

Sitting up, she shoved her tangled hair from her face. The room resembled the set of an x-rated movie—or what she imagined one to be: clothes tossed everywhere, her camisole hanging from the lamp, sheets crumpled, the quilt peeking from under the bed.

Last night she'd needed Garrett and he'd been there. His touch had soothed her sadness. She'd been at home, feeling lost and alone, so she'd called Kim and ended up listening to her machine. Rosie had gone out. And as good a friend as Klein had proved to be, she didn't want to talk to him. She'd wanted to be near her son. She'd wanted—no, she'd needed—Garrett.

Last night had been spectacular. In bed they always had everything. So why did she feel so unsettled?

Because he'd told her he loved her, and she hadn't been able to say the words back. To be honest, he'd blindsided her when she'd least expected it. She had not been thinking of love; she'd been living the lust.

And once her mind cleared, the thought of saying

"I love you" had brought a superstitious fear that if she uttered those words again, he'd run just as he had the last time. But this wasn't last time, and she had to stop comparing then and now.

The house was too quiet. Livy sighed and got up. She found her underwear on the floor, then a robe in the closet. Though she really could use some coffee, she took a jaunt down the hall first and peeked into every room. Garrett's belongings were all still there. Max slept in a tangle of covers on a pullout couch. She resisted the urge to kiss him. With her luck, he'd wake up and start in on her like his gramma and Kim, and she could really use a few more moments of peace.

But peace was not to be found. Nor was Garrett Stark. As Livy meandered through the place, she discovered that she and Max were the only living beings in the house.

"Like the last living cells in a dead body," she murmured, and gave an evil-sounding laugh.

Her joke did not seem funny. Nothing did when she entered the foyer and saw an orange, white and purple envelope on the table along with some legal-size documents. Though she knew she shouldn't, she picked them up anyway.

"Alaska?" Her voice trembled, and she bit down on her lip to stop that right away.

Insane as it was, Livy ran outside. He wasn't on the porch. She ran down the walk, onto the street and straight into the sisters.

"Olivia!" Miss Violet let her gaze wander from

Livy's tousled head, down the man's robe, to Livy's bare feet. "How incredibly tacky."

"Thank you," Livy said absently, looking up, then down, the street. The sisters were the only people out and about at this hour of a Saturday morning. Lucky her.

"We were on our way to speak with Rosie," Miss Viola said. "But since you're here, you may as well tell her."

"What now?" She did not need her mother arrested again, at least not today.

"We just wanted her to know that we don't want the goose back. She's no doubt shipped it to some farm and it's ruined now anyway." Miss Viola leaned over and whispered, "Consorting with common geese will do that."

"Rosie doesn't have it."

"You keep on believing that, dear." Miss Violet patted Livy's arm.

They began to walk toward home, but paused after only a few steps and turned back. Livy stifled a groan.

"Were you looking for someone, Olivia?" Miss Violet asked.

"Garrett."

"The boy's father?"

"Yes." It felt good to say that, almost liberating. So she said it again. "Max's father, Garrett Stark."

"He drove off in his car." Miss Violet pointed down the street. "That way."

All of Livy's good feelings evaporated. "Drove off?"

"He was in an awful hurry." She sniffed. "Yankees always are."

Livy didn't notice when the sisters left for good this time. *Drove off? Hurry?* Alaska? He couldn't have. Not again. Not when Max loved him so. Not when she loved him.

Why in hell hadn't she told him? Pride? Superstition? Both seemed stupid and silly in the face of all she felt now.

Livy sat on the porch steps as the sun spread over the street, over her. She was numb, confused. She didn't know what to believe. When the door opened and Max sat down next to her, she didn't know what to say.

This was why she hadn't wanted to tell Max the truth. She did not want to see the echo of abandonment in her son's eyes. She didn't know if she could bear it.

"Hey, Mom."

She cleared her throat. "Hey, baby."

"Mo-om."

"Sorry. Max."

"Did you sleep here, too?"

She glanced at him, but he stared at her innocently, without accusation. Answer only one question at a time, she'd learned. Don't tell him more than he wanted to know. "Uh-huh."

"Cool. Too bad you missed the popcorn and the movie."

He seemed to have completely forgiven her for any transgressions. Unfortunately, there might be a few more on the way.

"Yeah, too bad," she agreed.

"Where's Dad?"

"I'm not sure." True enough.

"Why did he rent a house in Alaska?"

Damn! She'd left the contract on the table where she'd found it. Good one.

"He doesn't live here, Max. He's only visiting."

"But now that he's got me, he'll have to stay." His dark eyes were full of hope. "We'll all live together and you'll marry him."

"Sometimes things don't work out the way we want them to."

"Sure they do. I've been wantin' this so bad it can't *not* come true."

Livy touched his hair. He pulled away. So much for total forgiveness.

"Believing in yourself is great, Max. And if you believe you can do something hard enough, I believe you can. But changing what is, making people do things they don't want to do... You can't make that happen just by wishing it."

Max shook his head, spilling hair into his eyes. "But he *is* my real dad. I believed it and it came true."

"It was always true. Your believing it didn't make it that way."

"I don't get it."

Livy sighed. "Neither do I."

"You think Dad left us again?"

"I don't know."

"He didn't!" Max jumped to his feet. She had to

crane her neck about to see him on the porch. "He wouldn't. He loves me."

"He does. That's a fact."

"He wouldn't run off like he did before. I believe in Dad. Can't you?"

"It's not that simple."

"Why can't you forgive him? I forgive you."

"Thank you. But—"

"There is no 'but,' Mom. I love you. You love me. Even when you lied, I still loved you. Even when I mess up, you love me. Because that's what love is, right?"

"Sure."

"Didn't you love Dad?"

"Of course."

"So when he messed up, you stopped? That's not love, Mom."

Cars passed on the street. Doors slammed on the block. The world was waking up. Maybe it was time Livy did, too.

Max was right. He so often was. In the simple faith of a child so much wisdom could be found.

"I never stopped loving him," she admitted.

"Thank you."

The deep voice from behind her made Livy gasp and jump to her feet. Garrett stood on the walk in torn running shorts and a sweaty white T-shirt. He'd never looked so good.

Her first thought was—*he's back.* Then she understood that he'd never left.

And from the expression in his eyes, he never would.

Livy jumped down the steps and into his arms.

IN SHOCK from hearing Livy say she'd never stopped loving him, Garrett still managed to catch her when she landed in his arms. He even managed to kiss her, quite thoroughly, even though he really wanted to talk.

He'd been scared, thinking about the worst thing that could happen—that Livy no longer loved him and she never would. He'd tried to figure out how he'd handle that. How on earth could he face that fear and turn it around? And he'd lit on the truth. He couldn't. If Livy didn't love him, there was no help for it, no matter how much that hurt.

Garrett lifted his mouth from hers, looked about for Max, only to discover his son had disappeared. Smart kid. He stared into Livy's eyes, saw everything he'd always wanted right there in her.

"I love you," she said.

His heart stuttered with hope. He wanted to believe, but he still had to ask. "For Max? Or yourself?"

"Both. We need you. Stay with us. Alaska sucks."

He groaned. "You saw the contract?"

"Kind of hard to miss."

"Let me explain—"

"You don't have to. We were both kids once and we both made mistakes. But now we have a child, and we'll still make mistakes. But we should make them together."

Garrett sighed and removed himself from her embrace. Her face reflected the uncertainty in his heart.

"Last night you told me you loved me," she mur-

mured. "Was *that* only for Max? Because I'm not
going to keep him from you. You don't have to say
something you don't mean just so you can see your
son."

"Livy." He spread his hands, helpless to say what
he felt. He'd never been good at talking, only writing,
once upon a time. But he tried now, for her. "I never
told another woman that I loved her because there's
never been another woman for me but you. Once, you
said you loved me and I ran. I didn't know if I could
love you the way you needed me to."

"Just loving me is enough. Why do you think you
have to be something other than what you are?"

"What am I?" He threw up his hands. "A writer
who can't write. A man who has no other profession
but make-believe."

"I've told you before—you're Max's father.
You're the man I love. To me, to us, you're everything. I love you, Garrett. That hasn't changed in nine
years without you—it isn't going to change now."

Torn, he put his hands on her shoulders. "Even if
I have to go away for a while?"

Confusion flickered over her face. "To Alaska?"

"That was my agent's idea of a joke. I'm not going
to Alaska. But I'm thinking that maybe I should go
somewhere, alone, for a little while. Try one more
time to find this Muse of mine I seem to have lost."

"Go." The speed of her answer made him blink.
"Do what you have to do. We'll be right here."

He tilted his head, searching for annoyance, anger,
distrust. All he saw was love. And that tickle of an

idea he'd had while jogging through Bonaventure Cemetery began to itch like a new case of poison ivy.

"You're sure?" he asked.

"I am!" Garrett glanced up to find Max in the doorway. "We believe in you, Dad."

"Yeah." Livy cupped his cheek, guided his face back to hers. "We believe in you."

Standing in the Savannah sun, with love shining on him from both blue eyes and brown, Garrett started to believe in himself, too.

CHAPTER NINETEEN

"COME ON, MOM." Max ran ahead, the cape of his vampire costume trailing in the night breeze.

The streets were filled with ghouls, ghosts and goblins. Halloween had come to Savannah.

Though the nights were cool, they rarely got cold; still, the passing of time whispered on the wind. Flowers fading past prime, a few leaves tumbling down and loneliness descending with the early sleeping sun.

"You think he'll be there?" Rosie asked.

"Max thinks so. And I've learned that what Max believes seems to happen. It's downright creepy."

Rosie smiled. "He believes with all his heart and soul, sugar. There's power in that."

Livy hoped her mother was right. Garrett had called, though not as often as she would have liked, but he'd always sounded distracted, busy, and he wouldn't tell her where he was.

Oh, he always said the appropriate things, that he loved her and he would see her soon, but "soon" seemed to have a different meaning to Garrett than it did to her. As the days stretched into weeks, and the weeks to a month, Livy had to admit she was getting nervous.

Because things had come full circle in more ways than one.

In Savannah, the excitement over Max's parentage had died down quicker than Livy had thought it would. Probably because lying wasn't as big a crime as it used to be.

People whispered about her for a week and then they were done. She'd gone to school and talked to Max's teacher and the principal. To her relief, the teasing for Max had been nonexistent, mainly because his dead father had turned out to be someone famous.

Klein checked in often, even asked if he should hunt Garrett down. But if she believed in the man she still loved with all her heart, she had to trust him, or they'd never get past their past.

Kim had forgiven her. As Rosie said, she was a good friend. But she'd also taken a leave and gone back home on a secret emergency. All this cloak-and-dagger stuff was getting on Livy's nerves.

Rosie had been on her best behavior. Not an arrest in weeks. She was even civil to the sisters when she saw them, though Livy didn't think that could last much longer. Livy wouldn't care when the peace ended, either. Rosie was Rosie. Everyone had his or her own opinion of her, and each one held a little bit of truth.

Eccentric? Maybe. Special? Definitely. The two of them spent time together just being mother and daughter, and Livy had to admit she'd been missing quite a bit in her mother.

''Mom, look!'' Max stood on the sidewalk to Garrett's house. The place appeared dark, abandoned, haunted. What was so great about that?

Then she saw where Max was pointing. The dining room coffin now sat in the middle of the lawn. The lid crept open, except no one appeared.

"Uh, Mom." Max appeared uneasy. "Can you...?" He waved his hand at the coffin.

Livy let out an exasperated sigh, *cloak-and-dagger, mystery-schmystery.* But she stomped over to the coffin and peered inside.

"Boo!" Garrett said.

She merely raised her brow. He was dressed just like his son—white face, red lips, black cape. She couldn't help but laugh out loud. They were so alike it *was* scary.

He climbed out of the coffin. "Did I scare you?"

"Oh, yeah. Terrified me."

He opened his cape, gathered her inside and kissed her. At least the kiss was the same as it always had been, but when he pulled back, his eyes shimmered with an emotion she'd never seen there before and wasn't able to place.

"Everything all right?" she asked.

"Why don't you tell me." He reached into the coffin and handed her several hundred pieces of paper.

"The book?"

"Most of it."

"What's it about?"

"A little boy with angel eyes."

Livy had no idea what that meant, but Garrett seemed thrilled. Though she was happy for him, disappointment tickled deep down inside. "So you did need to get away, be alone, move along."

He shook his head. "No. Read the dedication."

Livy moved closer to the street where the lights shone on passing tiny tigers, Pooh-bears and ballerinas.

For my Muse, Livy. And Max, my greatest work of art. It's not what people do that gives them worth, but who loves them. Which makes me the richest man in the world.

Her eyes burned. He'd heard her at last and seemed to believe it, too.

"It's beautiful, Garrett. But I thought you went searching for the Muse."

"My mistake. She was right here all the time. Love, Livy. It opened my heart, brought back all the magic."

"You've still lost me."

"I thought new places, fresh vistas, adventure gave me the words. But the words were in me."

"I could have told you that, Dad."

Garrett glanced down at his son, then opened the cape so Max could cuddle inside. They must look like the strangest family in Savannah, and that was saying quite a bit.

Family. Livy gave a long sigh of contentment. That sounded very good.

"Since you went to a new place and found that illusive book, I don't understand how you came to this conclusion."

"Because I went to that new place and got nothing, but when I came back here, I discovered all I needed had been there all along."

"You've been *here*."

"For the past three weeks."

Livy wondered if she should be mad, decided it wasn't worth it and kissed him again. What she'd seen in his eyes had been confidence in himself.

"Ugh!" Max escaped the cape. "If you're going to do that, I'm going to the next house with Rosie."

Livy glanced at her mother, who was smiling at them fondly with tears in her eyes. "I'll take him a few places and we'll be right back."

"Thanks." She snuggled deeper into the cape, into Garrett. "I could get used to this vampire getup. Dangerously sexy."

"You think so?"

"Always have."

He hugged her tighter. "I've got a surprise for you."

Livy smiled to herself "I've got a bigger one for you."

She hoped he was happy with the surprise. She wanted everything to be perfect this time around for them both.

He ignored her words, releasing her to pull legal-size documents out of a hidden pocket in the cape. "Here."

Livy frowned. Were they moving to Alaska after all? And it would be "they," because she wasn't going to let him get away twice. No matter how much Savannah felt like home.

But a glance at the papers revealed he'd bought the Alexander house. "Is that okay with you?" he asked, sounding anxious, as she continued to stare at the deed. "I wanted us to have a place, and I didn't think it fair to kick your mother out of the ancestral home."

"As if," she murmured.

"Will you live with me here, raise our son, be my wife?"

"Under one condition."

"Anything."

She raised a brow. "Anything? You haven't heard what it is yet."

"Doesn't matter. Anything is worth a lifetime with you. Name your price."

"A nursery."

He frowned. "You want more kids? Great. I'm game."

"You're gamer than you think." She took his hand, placed it on her still-flat stomach. "We'll need that nursery in less than eight months."

His mouth dropped open. "How did that happen?"

"The usual way. We seem to have a knack for it."

"But we…I… Uh."

"That's what I said. But sometimes life just happens, no matter how we try to control things. At least, I've learned that much. What's meant to be will always find a way. Like us."

"Why didn't you call me and tell me as soon as you found out?"

"I wanted you to come back for love, not duty."

"But I was here all the time."

"Well, I didn't know that!"

He picked her up and spun her around. "I love you. I love Max." He set her down carefully, then bent and put his mouth to her stomach. "Love you, too."

Livy laughed and mussed his hair. "For a guy who couldn't say the words, you've become awfully chatty."

"Once you know love just is, it's all over the place."

"Dad!"

Max ran up the walk. For a change he didn't trip. Come to think of it, he hadn't since his cast had come off. And she hadn't found an open drawer or door for even longer than that. Maybe all sorts of good things were in store for them. Couldn't hurt to believe.

"I got a whole bag of candy. You want to count it with me?"

"I can't think of anything I'd rather do," Garrett answered. Then his gaze hit on Rosie. "As soon as I take care of one thing."

He walked up to her. "Ma'am, may I have your daughter's hand?"

"Garrett..." Livy began.

"No. I'm going to do this right from the beginning. I might not be a gentleman by birth, but I can learn. Ma'am?"

"You want my daughter's hand, hmm? Does she want yours?"

"Yes," he said, with such complete confidence that Livy smiled.

"Well, in lieu of a bride price I'm going to ask a favor."

"Anything."

"Really? I was hoping you'd say that." Rosie smiled at Garrett and looped her arm through his. "Come on inside, sugar, and let me explain."

Her mother and Garrett walked off, heads together. Livy had known they would love each other. Later she'd pry out of Garrett just what it was her mother wanted. Favors for Rosie often meant trouble.

She gazed up at the stately gothic house that would soon become her home. She'd miss her old place, but it would always be right where she'd left it. Besides, home wasn't where you laid your head; it was where your loved ones did.

"Hey, Mom!" Max stood silhouetted in the open doorway. "Coming?"

"Sure, baby."

And for once, Max didn't correct her. Livy passed her palm over her stomach, then headed for the door.

Maybe magic did happen every single day.

EPILOGUE

DAWN SPREAD over Savannah like the wings of sleepy red-tailed hawk. Misty morning dew touched the ancient city streets. Night would not descend on the city for hours upon hours.

Max should not be up so early. His mom would have a hissy fit. But he wanted this day to last forever. Because today his mom and his dad were getting married in a family-only celebration.

So he went to his dad's office and finished the story he'd written for their present:

And so the lonely vampire and the even lonelier princess, who had a great little boy named Max, discovered that by some weird twist in time they were a family. So they lived happily forever. No one had to worry about bad stuff, because being lonely and unloved was the worst. But together there was no more lonely at all, and in their family love just was.

Max looked at what he'd written. He'd figured out that there was no such thing as vampires, even though there were a few princesses. But the happily-forever part was true enough, and so was that bit about love.

Might sound mushy, but his mom would like it and that was what counted.

The phone rang, making him jump. Max wasn't sure if he should answer, but the new machine his mom had bought, even though his dad had grumbled, clicked on and saved him the trouble of wonderin' for long.

"Garrett, I fail to see the humor in this gift."

Max recognized his dad's agent, Andrew. The guy often left messages on the machine, and he talked so funny and fast Max loved to listen to them. He put his chin on his arms and stared at the machine.

"Now, a coffin was funny. You have to admit that—" Andrew's sigh was almost completely drowned out by a loud *honk-honk*.

Max started to laugh.

"But what in Hades am I supposed to do with a goose?"

Harlequin truly does make any time special. . . . This year we are celebrating weddings in style!

To help us celebrate, we want you to tell us how wearing the Harlequin wedding gown will make your wedding day special. As the grand prize, Harlequin will offer one lucky bride the chance to **"Walk Down the Aisle"** in the Harlequin wedding gown!

There's more...

For her honeymoon, she and her groom will spend five nights at the **Hyatt Regency Maui.** As part of this five-night honeymoon at the hotel renowned for its romantic attractions, the couple will enjoy a candlelit dinner for two in Swan Court, a sunset sail on the hotel's catamaran, and duet spa treatments.

Maui • Molokai • Lanai

To enter, please write, in, 250 words or less, how wearing the Harlequin wedding gown will make your wedding day special. The entry will be judged based on its emotionally compelling nature, its originality and creativity, and its sincerity. This contest is open to Canadian and U.S. residents only and to those who are 18 years of age and older. There is no purchase necessary to enter. Void where prohibited. See further contest rules attached. Please send your entry to:

Walk Down the Aisle Contest

In Canada
P.O. Box 637
Fort Erie, Ontario
L2A 5X3

In U.S.A.
P.O. Box 9076
3010 Walden Ave.
Buffalo, NY 14269-9076

You can also enter by visiting www.eHarlequin.com
Win the Harlequin wedding gown and the vacation of a lifetime!
The deadline for entries is October 1, 2001.

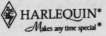

PHWDACONT1

HARLEQUIN WALK DOWN THE AISLE TO MAUI CONTEST 1197
OFFICIAL RULES
NO PURCHASE NECESSARY TO ENTER

1. To enter, follow directions published in the offer to which you are responding. Contest begins April 2, 2001, and ends on October 1, 2001. Method of entry may vary. Mailed entries must be postmarked by October 1, 2001, and received by October 8, 2001.

2. Contest entry may be, at times, presented via the Internet, but will be restricted solely to residents of certain geographic areas that are disclosed on the Web site. To enter via the Internet, if permissible, access the Harlequin Web site (www.eHarlequin.com) and follow the directions displayed online. Online entries must be received by 11:59 p.m. E.S.T. on October 1, 2001.

   In lieu of submitting an entry online, enter by mail by hand-printing (or typing) on an 8½" x 11" plain piece of paper, your name, address (including zip code), Contest number/name and in 250 words or fewer, why winning a Harlequin wedding dress would make your wedding day special. Mail via first-class mail to: Harlequin Walk Down the Aisle Contest 1197, (in the U.S.) P.O. Box 9076, 3010 Walden Avenue, Buffalo, NY 14269-9076, (in Canada) P.O. Box 637, Fort Erie, Ontario L2A 5X3, Canada. Limit one entry per person, household address and e-mail address. Online and/or mailed entries received from persons residing in geographic areas in which Internet entry is not permissible will be disqualified.

3. Contests will be judged by a panel of members of the Harlequin editorial, marketing and public relations staff based on the following criteria:

   - Originality and Creativity—50%
   - Emotionally Compelling—25%
   - Sincerity—25%

   In the event of a tie, duplicate prizes will be awarded. Decisions of the judges are final.

4. All entries become the property of Torstar Corp. and will not be returned. No responsibility is assumed for lost, late, illegible, incomplete, inaccurate, nondelivered or misdirected mail or misdirected e-mail, for technical, hardware or software failures of any kind, lost or unavailable network connections, or failed, incomplete, garbled or delayed computer transmission or any human error which may occur in the receipt or processing of the entries in this Contest.

5. Contest open only to residents of the U.S. (except Puerto Rico) and Canada, who are 18 years of age or older, and is void wherever prohibited by law; all applicable laws and regulations apply. Any litigation within the Province of Quebec respecting the conduct or organization of a publicity contest may be submitted to the Régie des alcools, des courses et des jeux for a ruling. Any litigation respecting the awarding of a prize may be submitted to the Régie des alcools, des courses et des jeux only for the purpose of helping the parties reach a settlement. Employees and immediate family members of Torstar Corp. and D. L. Blair, Inc., their affiliates, subsidiaries and all other agencies, entities and persons connected with the use, marketing or conduct of this Contest are not eligible to enter. Taxes on prizes are the sole responsibility of winners. Acceptance of any prize offered constitutes permission to use winner's name, photograph or other likeness for the purposes of advertising, trade and promotion on behalf of Torstar Corp., its affiliates and subsidiaries without further compensation to the winner, unless prohibited by law.

6. Winners will be determined no later than November 15, 2001, and will be notified by mail. Winners will be required to sign and return an Affidavit of Eligibility form within 15 days after winner notification. Noncompliance within that time period may result in disqualification and an alternative winner may be selected. Winners of trip must execute a Release of Liability prior to ticketing and must possess required travel documents (e.g. passport, photo ID) where applicable. Trip must be completed by November 2002. No substitution of prize permitted by winner. Torstar Corp. and D. L. Blair, Inc., their parents, affiliates, and subsidiaries are not responsible for errors in printing or electronic presentation of Contest, entries and/or game pieces. In the event of printing or other errors which may result in unintended prize values or duplication of prizes, all affected game pieces or entries shall be null and void. If for any reason the Internet portion of the Contest is not capable of running as planned, including infection by computer virus, bugs, tampering, unauthorized intervention, fraud, technical failures, or any other causes beyond the control of Torstar Corp. which corrupt or affect the administration, secrecy, fairness, integrity or proper conduct of the Contest, Torstar Corp. reserves the right, at its sole discretion, to disqualify any individual who tampers with the entry process and to cancel, terminate, modify or suspend the Contest or the Internet portion thereof. In the event of a dispute regarding an online entry, the entry will be deemed submitted by the authorized holder of the e-mail account submitted at the time of entry. Authorized account holder is defined as the natural person who is assigned to an e-mail address by an Internet access provider, online service provider or other organization that is responsible for arranging e-mail address for the domain associated with the submitted e-mail address. **Purchase or acceptance of a product offer does not improve your chances of winning.**

7. Prizes: (1) Grand Prize—A Harlequin wedding dress (approximate retail value: $3,500) and a 5-night/6-day honeymoon trip to Maui, HI, including round-trip air transportation provided by Maui Visitors Bureau from Los Angeles International Airport (winner is responsible for transportation to and from Los Angeles International Airport) and a Harlequin Romance Package, including hotel accomodations (double occupancy) at the Hyatt Regency Maui Resort and Spa, dinner for (2) two at Swan Court, a sunset sail on Kiele V and a spa treatment for the winner (approximate retail value: $4,000); (5) Five runner-up prizes of a $1000 gift certificate to selected retail outlets to be determined by Sponsor (retail value $1000 ea.). Prizes consist of only those items listed as part of the prize. Limit one prize per person. All prizes are valued in U.S. currency.

8. For a list of winners (available after December 17, 2001) send a self-addressed, stamped envelope to: Harlequin Walk Down the Aisle Contest 1197 Winners, P.O. Box 4200 Blair, NE 68009-4200 or you may access the www.eHarlequin.com Web site through January 15, 2002.

Contest sponsored by Torstar Corp., P.O. Box 9042, Buffalo, NY 14269-9042, U.S.A.

PHWDACONT2

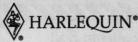

Brimming with passion and sensuality,
this collection offers two full-length
Harlequin Temptation novels.

Full Bloom

by *New York Times* bestselling author

JAYNE
—— ANN ——
KRENTZ

Emily Ravenscroft has had enough! It's time she took her life back,
out of the hands of her domineering family and Jacob Stone, the
troubleshooter they've always employed to get her out of hot water.
The new Emily—vibrant and willful—doesn't need Jacob to rescue
her. She needs him to love her, against all odds.

And

Compromising Positions

a brand-new story from bestselling author

VICKY LEWIS
THOMPSON

Look for it on sale September 2001.

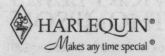